SETH BAUMGARTNER'S LOVE MANIFESTO

By Eric Luper

Balzer + Bray
An Imprint of HarperCollins*Publishers*

16.99

Balzer + Bray is an imprint of HarperCollins Publishers.

Seth Baumgartner's Love Manifesto
Copyright © 2010 by Eric Luper

www.harperteen.com

Library of Congress Cataloging-in-Publication Data
Luper, Eric.
  Seth Baumgartner's Love Manifesto / by Eric Luper — 1st ed.
    p.   cm.
  Summary: After his girlfriend breaks up with him and he sees his father
out with another woman, high school senior Seth Baumgartner, who has
a summer job at the country club and is preparing for a father-son golf
tournament, launches a podcast in which he explores the mysteries of love.
  ISBN 978-0-06-182753-2
  [1. Love—Fiction. 2. Dating (Social customs)—Fiction. 3. Interpersonal
relations—Fiction. 4. Fathers and sons—Fiction. 5. Podcasts—Fiction.
6. Golf—Fiction. 7. Country clubs—Fiction.
PZ7.L979135Se 2010   2009029706
[Fic]—dc22   CIP
                                                                      AC

Typography by Carla Weise
10 11 12 13 14   CG/RRDB   10 9 8 7 6 5 4 3 2 1
❖
First Edition

*To Mom and Dad, who (as far as I know)
never had to endure anything similar
to what happens in this book*

CHAPTER ONE

"Come on, Seth. Say something." Veronica stares at me like I'm the one who should be doing the explaining—like I'm the one who just turned everything upside down. I stare right back and keep sliding the ketchup bottle back and forth across the table like it's a hockey puck. The weight of the bottle, the cold angled glass, feels good in my hands.

"Don't be this way," she says.

"I didn't know there was a code of conduct that goes along with getting dumped at Applebee's."

"Se-e-e-eth . . ." She drags out my name like saying it really long will get me to see things her way.

Veronica sinks lower into the booth. Her black uniform shirt matches the Applebee's upholstery perfectly. I guess that makes sense, considering she works here.

Her lunch break.

A half hour.

She gave herself a half hour to drop the news and kick me to the curb.

"It's just not working out." Veronica takes the saltshaker and sprinkles it on the Formica. "Would you take off that ridiculous hat already?"

I want to smile, but I don't. We've shared this joke for weeks—ever since I got my summer job. The black, yellow, and red striped hat from Belgian Fries Express sticks up and makes my head look like the end of a hot dog. Veronica thinks it looks like the end of something else. I swipe the hat from my head and shove it between my apron and my chest.

"You're sucker punching me," I say. "Just last night we—"

"I know all about last night," she says. "I was there, remember?" She drags her finger through the dusting of salt. She writes her initials. "I just think . . . I don't know. I'm just not feeling it anymore."

I want to reach out to her, to touch her arm, to take her hand in mine. I want to cry. But I force myself to suck in a breath.

"I think that's when I realized things," she says. "Last night." Her pale skin pinkens like it does whenever she gets upset.

"Maybe if we took a week off . . . a month . . ."

"I like you, Seth. You're a really nice guy. Someday I'll probably be kicking myself for letting you go, but right now . . ."

"Right now what?"

Veronica's eyes drop, and she shakes her head. "I'm too comfortable with you."

"Too comfortable? What the hell does that even mean?" That last part comes out louder than I intended, and the man and woman in the booth across from us turn their heads. The woman is pregnant and about to pop. She glares at me as though my words have corrupted her unborn child in the womb. I bring my voice back down. "I thought couples were *supposed* to feel comfortable with each other. I thought comfortable was good."

"They are—it is, I guess—but not comfortable like my mom and dad are comfortable. You know what I mean?" She looks at me with pleading eyes, like she's the one in pain.

"No."

"Well, I can't explain it any better." She blows the wisps of hair that have escaped her ponytail out of her eyes. The waiter brings our lunch. Like always, I ordered a Club House Grill, but Veronica wanted a Grilled Chicken Caesar Salad instead of the Quesadilla Burger she usually gets. Her uniform is identical to the waiter's, with the exception of their name tags. His reads ANDERS.

What kind of stupid name is Anders?

I feel as though I recognize him—his name or his big square head—from somewhere, but I can't place the face. He's bigger than me and has one of those wide jaws that looks like the front of a Thruway plow. I want to ask Veronica about him, to share some joke about his name— what does Anders rhyme with?—but I can't change the subject. And I can't make a joke. Not now.

Then I realize that starting today Anders will be spending more time with Veronica than I will.

And I hate him for it.

"Refill?" Anders asks. His voice doesn't hint that he knows what's going on between Veronica and me, but I'm sure he does. How could he not? I'm sitting here with my hands shaking, practically crying, pleading with my girlfriend not to dump me. I'm a total spectacle. I'm the joke of Applebee's.

"No, thanks," I say.

Veronica smiles at Anders like she and I have been talking about nothing more than the weather. "I'll have another iced tea, thanks. Make sure it's—"

"Unsweetened, right?" Anders cuts in.

He disappears with her glass.

Neither of us touches the food.

I push aside my plate and go back to sliding the ketchup bottle from hand to hand. I focus on the music piping into the restaurant. It's a peppy saxophony jazz tune. I had never given much thought to Kenny G, but now I hate him.

Not a word passes between us, and it feels like a century goes by before Anders returns with Veronica's drink.

As soon as he disappears again, I say, "Maybe we could—"

"No, Seth. We can't do anything. I don't feel it anymore, and we can't be together." She draws a heart in the salt on the table and scribbles it out. "You're a great guy, but there's nothing you can say to change how I feel.

4

It doesn't work that way."

But I want it to work that way. I want to change how she feels. I mean, somehow, since yesterday, somehow since we were pressed against each other and sweaty on my parents' pool table, something changed in her brain.

"Vee, how could you come over my house last night—"

"Seth, that's not fair."

"It's fair as hell."

"Excuse me," the pregnant woman says. The man with her begins to say something, but he stops when he sees the glare on my face.

Veronica draws in a deep breath and lets it out slowly. Her bangs dance in front of her eyes. "I suppose some part of me has known for a while."

A while.

I repeat the words in my mind to see if it helps. All it does is make me feel more hollow, more alone. Tears well up behind my eyes. I stare at the ceiling speaker above our booth to fight them off. *Stupid Kenny G!*

Veronica pokes at her salad with her fork. "I'm not hungry," she says.

Somehow I'm not, either.

She glances at her cell phone. "Look, my boss is going to kill me. You're late, too."

"This is more important than Belgian Fries Express."

"I'm sure your manager wouldn't agree."

"I'm covering someone's shift because she's hungover. What's Mr. Burks going to do, fire me?"

"You've been late back from lunch three times this week."

She's right. I pull my napkin from my lap. "I'll call you tonight," I say.

Her head cocks to the side, then shakes back and forth. "I don't think that's such a good idea."

"Come on, Veronica, just because we're not dating anymore doesn't mean we can't talk." I make it sound innocent, like we can both be mature enough to put the romance part of our relationship behind us, as though we could both forget the last eight months and go back to being study buddies. But I know the truth. I want to hold on to any part of "us" that I can.

"I need time apart," she says. "That means no calls."

No calls. There's nothing I can say to that. It's like Veronica just slammed the door in my face.

Then something changes.

Veronica looks past me. Her eyes narrow, then go wide. She sinks farther into the booth. "Seth," she whispers. "Isn't that your dad?"

I turn to look, but her hand shoots across the table and grabs my forearm. Now that she's dumped me, her touch feels uncomfortable. I start to pull away.

"Don't look," she whispers. "He's with someone."

"So what? My father goes out for lunch with clients all the time."

I try to turn again, but her nails dig into my skin. "I don't think that's a business associate."

I sink into my own seat and peer around the backrest.

It's my father, all right. The hostess is leading him and some woman to another booth. As usual, my father is wearing a business suit. The tie I gave him on his last birthday—the purple and black Jerry Garcia one I thought he'd never wear—hangs loose around his neck.

When the hostess steps aside, I see the woman. Veronica was right. She is *definitely* not a business associate. That is, unless my father's accounting firm recently picked up the Bunny Ranch as a client. She is a slightly weather-beaten Eva Longoria wannabe, with black hair that tumbles over her bronzed shoulders in thick, loose curls. Her breasts threaten to leap out of her sequined camisole, and her miniskirt, which is some kind of snakeskin print, does less to conceal her lower parts than a few well-placed napkins might.

"Do you know her?" Veronica asks.

I shake my head.

"Doesn't your dad know I work here?"

"I'm not sure I ever mentioned it," I say.

"Doesn't he at least know you work in the mall?"

"I'm supposed to be off today. Anyhow, I'm not sure if he's up to date on where I'm working. It's my fourth job this year."

My father leans forward, says something to the woman, and smiles. She says something back. Then, as if they are trying their damnedest to make today, without question, the worst day of my life, my father reaches across the table and strokes the woman's forearm with the backs of his fingertips.

7

My face gets hot, and a rushing sound fills my head.

I want to melt into the booth.

I want to disappear.

But instead, all I do is stand up and walk out. I leave my now ex-girlfriend behind. I leave my cheating father behind. I leave my cheating father's mistress, too.

The mall passes under my feet like I'm in a dream—really slow and really fast at the same time. It might be Veronica's voice I hear filtering in through the static in my brain, but I can't be sure because I don't turn around.

Since I'm late back to work, Mr. Burks puts me on fryer duty rather than at the register where I usually work. A line has formed. Mr. Burks hates lines.

I lower the first wire basket into the fryer. The sizzling seems to fill a newly vacant part of me. The heavy heat of the oil reaches up and touches my face.

"Baumgartner!" Mr. Burks barks. "Get your goddamn hat on!"

I pull the hat from the folds of my apron and position it on my head.

I gaze at the roiling bubbles in the fryer until it beeps.

I heave the basket out of the oil and secure it on its hook.

After it drains, I dump the fries into the stainless steel tray.

Gil, the new kid, scoops up the fries and jiggles them into a cardboard cone, ready for one of our twenty original Belgian Fries Express sauces. "Douche," he mutters as he turns back to the counter.

When I got my job here, my friend Dimitri told me that French is one of the national languages of Belgium (along with Dutch and German), so I suppose Gil calling me a douche is appropriate. And it's true. I feel like a major-league douche.

I load up the empty basket with another package of frozen fries and lower it—crackling, sizzling, and popping—into the hot oil. Fryer duty is fine by me. I'd be useless anywhere else.

At least fries are easy.

At least fries make sense.

"Oh, and Baumgartner." Mr. Burks pokes his head around the white tiled divider that separates me from everyone else. "After your shift, be sure to leave the apron and hat. You're fired."

I know I should feel stunned or upset, but after everything that happened in the past twenty minutes, it doesn't surprise me. I have no idea what to say, and all that comes out is "What about my name tag?"

Mr. Burks doesn't think on that more than a second. "I couldn't care less about your name tag; just don't bring the rest of yourself around here anymore."

CHAPTER TWO ▶▶▎

My father bolts up straight in his seat at the head of the breakfast table. The business section lies open in front of him. "Motherf—"

"Michael!" my mother says, cutting him short.

"Did you see this?" He rattles his *Times Union*. "The CFO of Ludwig Financial got nailed raiding the company pension accounts to fund his coke-and-stripper habit."

My mother chokes back her coffee. I'm not sure if she's startled, amused, or both. She's a DJ with a local radio program called *Gayle's Romantic Rendezvous*. It's a show all about love and romance, but she never talks about anything like this on the air. Instead, she usually just plays sappy romantic dedications for couples from seven to ten every weeknight. You know, the whole "I love my husband, so could you please play some song for him, blah, blah, blah. . . ."

My father slaps the paper with the back of his hand. "It says here he blew over sixty thousand in one night at some strip club in New York City—more than a million over the past year. The stock plummeted six points just before yesterday's closing. It's bound to tank even worse this morning."

I shovel more Lucky Charms into my mouth. After five hours of staring at the ceiling and two hours of terrible sleep, raising the spoon and actually navigating it into my mouth is no easy task.

"We own two thousand shares of Ludwig!" My father pounds the table. Silverware leaps into the air and clatters back to the tabletop.

"It's all right," my mom says, folding the Life and Leisure section she had been reading. She lays it carefully beside her plate.

"It's *not* all right. I stood behind that company—I invested in them—and one horny bastard just cost me twelve grand overnight! A million bucks in a year on lap dances? How does someone do that?"

My mother sips her coffee. "It's a miracle those dancers didn't wear him down to a nub."

The laugh busts out of me before I can reel it back in, and it takes everything I have to not spew my mouthful of cereal across the table.

"Oh, I'm sorry, Seth," Mom says, her face flushing pinker than the marshmallow hearts floating in my bowl.

"Maybe you should talk about that on your radio program tonight," I say. I'm always suggesting ways my mother could make her show less girly to appeal to a demographic wider than postmenopausal women with short, sensible haircuts.

"This isn't a joke, Seth," my father says. "Where do you think we were planning to get the money to send you to college?"

I stare at my orange stars, yellow moons, and green clovers until Mom and Dad both disappear behind their newspaper sections again. My father is worried about some guy losing him twelve thousand dollars because of strippers. How much is he spending on his own distraction? Having a mistress can't be cheap.

"I wish they *had* worn him down to a nub," my father mutters. "It'd serve him right."

Sitting at the kitchen table, knowing that my father is cheating on my mother, ranks without a doubt as the most gut-shredding breakfast ever. Every cell in my body tells me to scream, to cry out to my mother that her beloved husband—the one who claims he goes to work every day, who claims to be earning a living for our family—is really out boning some middle-aged Paris Hilton who doesn't have the sense to wear something other than a lizard-print skirt and hooker heels to a place where people eat food.

This morning started like just about every other, my father hopping out of bed early to beat the nonexistent rush. He showered, sprayed on that cologne of his that fills the bathroom for three hours afterward, and got dressed before anyone else gave a thought about stirring. Then he "rattled my cage," as he calls it.

Our conversation:

> **Dad:** [shaking my leg] Rise and shine, Seth.
> The early bird catches the worm.
>
> **Me:** [groaning] Could you possibly come up
> with something more lame?
>
> **Dad:** Lame or not, you've got to get up early if
> you want to accomplish anything in life.
>
> **Me:** Didn't turn out so well for the worm.
>
> **Dad:** [shaking my leg more firmly this time]
> Stop breaking my balls and get out of bed. You
> need to get to work. You *do* have a job, right?

"So, I was thinking about getting a companion dog," my mother says. "Janet McSweeney at the club told me about this Maltese—"

"Honey, we've already discussed this," my father says.

"But I have no one to keep me company. I don't have to be at the studio until five, and I read this article—"

"No dogs," he says again, this time more firmly. "You'll be excited about the thing for three weeks. You'll buy it sparkly collars and strollers and all that. Then who will be the one walking him, feeding him, and taking him to the groomer? Me. And guess what? I don't want a dog."

"But Mike—"

"Gayle, you can't even keep plants alive."

"I did okay with our son." Mom looks over at me. She smiles and winks. We'll have a dog within a week. When it comes to my dad, Mom knows how to get things done.

"Ready for this?" my father says. "It's estimated that between the strip clubs; trips to Thailand, Costa Rica, and Cuba; and the mountains of cocaine he's snorted, that guy's blown close to seven million bucks over three years. How could they not have noticed this sooner? Jesus!" He slams the paper down, right onto his untouched plate of eggs.

"Mike!" Mom scolds.

"Sorry, honey." He reaches out and strokes my mother's forearm with the backs of his fingers. It's the same way he stroked that other lady's arm. Exactly the same way. *What a phony!* I stuff my face full of more Lucky Charms.

"What's wrong, baby?" my mom says to me. I look up at her and go back to chewing. She's remarkably well preserved for a mother. She doesn't look much different than she does in the dusty wedding photo hanging in the living room. Behind the giant shoulder pads and the huge satin bow on her ass (God, the eighties must have sucked), she was a pretty good-looking girl. Dimitri says that my mom's a major-league MILF, but I tune him out when he starts talking like that.

"Nothing's wrong," I say through purple horseshoes and blue diamonds.

"Nothing?" she says. "I haven't seen you look so glum since—"

"Glum?"

"You know, down in the dumps."

"I know what *glum* means," I say. "I just thought that word got retired from the English language around sixty years ago."

"Sorry," my mom says. "What's the term I should use?"

I shrug. "Lugubrious?"

"Kids use the word *lugubrious* these days?"

"They do if they're studying for the SATs."

"Okay," she says. "Well you haven't looked so *lugubrious* since you lost that science derby back in seventh grade."

"It was a science fair," I say.

She had to bring it up. She always brings it up. After having to put my mouth on the same nasty recorder flutes that everyone else used, I invented the Seth Baumgartner Recorder Sterilizer. It bathed the recorders in ultraviolet rays to kill off bacteria and even sprayed them with a minty-fresh flavor courtesy of a well-placed can of Binaca. Brilliant. I lost to Joe Coticchio because his mom is an engineer. Not only did he build a working model of a medieval trebuchet, but it was adjustable so that he could show how arm length affects projectile distance. I argued that public health is more important than warfare, but there was no competing with Joe's mom's CAD program, perfect bell curves, and Nerf balls flying all over the gym.

"I'm fine," I say. "Veronica and I broke up is all."

"Oh, baby!" My mother reaches out and strokes my forearm. Exactly the response I was hoping to avoid.

My father's eyes rise above his newspaper and then disappear again.

"What happened between you two?" she asks.

"Just whatever. I guess things weren't working out."

"Why didn't you tell me?" she asks. "I'm practically a relationship expert."

"Exactly," I say. "I didn't want to be tonight's on-air topic of conversation. I didn't want you playing some sappy song in my honor."

"I wouldn't—"

I shoot her a look that says we both know she would.

"Okay, I promise not to say anything on the air if you tell me what happened." She leans toward me, her eyes hungry for the nitty-gritty details. "What did she say?"

I shrug. "She said she needed some space."

"Death sentence," my father mutters.

"Mike!" My mother slaps my father's shoulder with her newspaper and turns back to me. "Veronica will come around. Just give her some time."

"And when you get a new girlfriend," my father adds, "make sure she has the same cellular company as you. All that texting is driving me to the poorhouse."

My mother and I both ignore that one.

"And I lost my job." I slip it in, hoping that news of my big breakup might soften the blow.

No such luck.

My father lowers the newspaper again. "How many is this, Seth? How many jobs have you lost this year alone?" His voice isn't so much angry as it is frustrated.

"Four," I say. "The Gap, the library—"

"You don't need to list them for me." He pushes his plate away. "Come on, Seth. Why can't you hold down a job? This is important stuff."

"And my girlfriend isn't?"

"Girlfriends come and go."

You should know. The words want to fly out, but I hold them back and mumble, "Jobs come and go, too."

"Don't bust my nuts, Seth. Come on. I want you to find another job and hold it for the whole summer. None of this jumping-around business."

"Michael," Mom says, "Seth is obviously distraught over his breakup. I'm sure whatever happened at that French fry place happened because he was so upset. Isn't that right?" My mom looks to me for confirmation.

This is my opportunity. My mother has set the ball and I just need to spike it, but the words don't come nearly as easily as I would like. "We broke up at lunch, and, well, I was covering for this other girl, and Mr. Burks—"

My father raises his hand to silence me. "Look, Seth, just find a job and keep it. You're a smart kid. Find an employer who trusts you—one who values you for your skill set."

"Maybe that's the problem," I say. "What is my skill set? Folding oxfords? Shelving books? Making French fries? Come on, it's all boring."

"Honey," my mother says, "think of something you like and get a job doing it. If you don't enjoy your job, you won't value it and you'll never do well."

I sink into my chair and slurp the milk from my bowl. "I'll get another job and I'll keep it," I say. "Promise."

But I say it to empty space because my mother is already clearing the plates and my father is halfway out the door. I watch out the window as my dad's Beemer makes its way down the driveway.

I wonder if the stress from his tumbling stock will make him run to his mistress or cause him to avoid her. Will he take her back to Applebee's again? Will he just go to her place? Maybe a seedy motel somewhere with a vibrating bed and a slimy hot tub? Just thinking about it makes me want to puke.

CHAPTER THREE ▶▶❘

"You sure you're all right about this breakup thing?" Dimitri asks me for what feels like the hundredth time.

I shift the phone to my other ear and prop my feet on the wall, one on each side of the *Army of Darkness* movie poster that hangs above my bed. "I'm good," I say.

"Seriously?"

"Seriously."

"'Cause you don't sound good."

I take a deep breath and let it out. "I'm fine."

"Okay," Dimitri says. "But I don't want you bailing out on golf tomorrow because of this. We're still playing, right?"

I try to think of a non-Veronica, non-my-dad-is-sleeping-with-some-ho excuse to cancel. I need to figure out what my father is up to. But canceling my weekly round with Dimitri would be a grave error. Dimitri takes his golf seriously. He's practicing his ass off so he'll play well in the father-son golf tournament at the end of July. The winning team takes home a ten-thousand-dollar college scholarship. Anyhow, if I bail, Dimitri will bitch about it longer than it takes to play a full eighteen holes. Maybe twenty-seven.

Besides, what would I do, tail my father? He'd spot my bright red, beat-up Camry—I call it the Red Scare—from a mile away. Would I sit in his firm's parking lot eating bag after bag of fried pork rinds like a television cop on a stakeout? No, I need to find a better way to follow him. If only I had one of those tracking devices that James Bond is always sticking onto bad guys' cars. I'd just clip that sucker to the back of his sports jacket and track him wherever he went.

"Say it," Dimitri urges me. "Say you won't cancel."

"I won't cancel."

"Say, 'If I cancel, I'm the biggest wuss in the history of the multiverse.'"

I say that, too.

"All right," Dimitri says. "I'll catch you in the morning."

I click off the phone and turn on my radio. It's nearly an hour into my mother's program. Some commercial boasts "the biggest burritos in the Capital District."

So not a date place.

I grab a tennis ball and start bouncing it against the wall. I try to hit Bruce Campbell on my poster and catch it. I'm on my eighty-fourth face strike when my mother's voice comes on:

"*Welcome back to* Gayle's Romantic Rendezvous. *I'm your host, Gayle, and I want to send out a special dedication . . .*"

Some kind of soft groove starts playing, and my mom starts talking in her low, comforting voice. My stomach tightens. She's going to do exactly what she promised she wouldn't. I can feel it.

"*My son is going through some hard times with his girlfriend right now, and I just want to let him know that he is a special young man. He means the world to his mom and dad, and it's only a matter of time before she or some other girl out there feels the same way we do. Here's a song from us to our baby boy called 'You Are So Beautiful' by the talented Joe Cocker. . . .*"

The soft groove transitions into the beginning of some song that I do not want to hear. I hurl the ball at my clock radio, but it glances off the side and bounces into the hallway. The best I can hope for is that no one who knows me heard that, but her show is the number one rated evening program in the Capital District. Before I have a chance to shut off the radio properly, my cell phone chimes.

I glance at the text.

Dimitri.

It says: *You are soooo beautiful, baby boy!*

CHAPTER FOUR

*W*hump!

Dimitri's driver scoops into the tee box and sends a divot flopping through the air like a giant end-over-end loogie. His ball sizzles across the ground, skitters over the women's tee box, and trickles down into the deep grass.

"Muffed it again!"

"Keep your head down," I say. "I'll watch where the ball goes."

Dimitri shovels seed from the plastic bin and sprinkles it over the foot-long trench he carved with his club. "At least it's not a D.O."

D.O. stands for "Dick Out." It's an unwritten rule that if you don't hit your ball past the ladies' tee, you have to unzip your shorts and hit your next shot with your wanger swinging in the breeze. Even though I've seen plenty of shots go short, I've never known anyone who's actually unzipped.

"Stinks about your job," Dimitri says, stroking his lame attempt at a goatee. He's been experimenting with his facial hair for months. Every time I see him, he's sporting something different. "You should work here at the club with me. Audrey got a job here this spring, and she loves it."

Audrey is Dimitri's sister. She's two years younger than us, just going into sophomore year. She's bony, all angles, like someone drew her with a protractor and a sharp pencil. And annoying as anything. Constantly butting in.

"Employees play free on Mondays," Dimitri adds. "And Audrey works in catering. That means free grub, too."

"I already *do* play for nothing," I say. "My parents are members here. Anyhow, I used to get all the free Belgian fries I wanted. After two days, I was sick of every sauce on the menu."

"Come on. How many freakin' fries can you eat? I'm talking burgers, dogs, wings—the whole enchilada."

"Enchiladas? I hate Mexican."

"You know what I mean."

Dimitri is not what I'd call fat, but he's definitely carrying around some spare pounds. Let's just say that if there were a sudden famine, he wouldn't be the first to go—that is, unless all the skinny people got together and ate him.

I tee up my ball. "There's no way I'm working at the club."

"Why? Too good for it or something?"

"It's not that. Shut up while I hit." I waggle my club head a few times, draw it back, and swing.

Ping!

There are few sounds more satisfying than the *ping* of a golf ball as it rockets off the face of a steel-headed driver. Although the sound is perfect, my shot sucks nuts. My ball goes hard right and punches through the leaves of some low-hanging branches. "Did you see where it went?" I ask.

"It ain't on the fairway. I can tell you that."

We grab our bags and make our way to Dimitri's ball. "So what's the deal?" he asks. "What's wrong with working at the club?"

"First of all, I need to start my college apps."

"How much time could you possibly spend on that? Crank out an essay about how you've overcome some tragedy. Make up something about how you were in a bad car accident and learned that life is precious. No biggie. What's the second reason?"

"I want to work on my podcasting this summer."

"Podcasting?" Dimitri says.

"Yeah. If I want to have any shot at getting on the radio in college, I've got to work out all my kinks. I got a new soundboard last week. That same guy at my mom's station—the sound engineer I told you about—gave me his old one. Once I learn to use it, I'll be able to put together a decent-quality show."

"Come on, Seth. Podcasting is for geeks, wannabes, and never-haves. Podcasting isn't going to get you gas money."

"What's a never-have?"

"I don't know. I just made it up. But I can tell you that it's not good. Anyway, I've listened to your lame attempts at podcasting. You suck."

"All the more reason to focus on it."

"All the more reason to quit," Dimitri says. "Some things are beyond help."

"If I'm going to be a communications major, I've got to get a handle on all this stuff." I refasten the Velcro on my golf glove. "Anyhow, I guess the big reason I don't want to work here at the club is that I don't want to be scraping and polishing my dad's spikes all summer."

"Look, I hate my parents as much as the next guy, but it's no reason to wuss out when it comes to a sweet job. Anyway, your dad's pretty cool. At least he doesn't fly all over the country playing in geekwad bridge tournaments like mine. How lame is that?"

"No, my father is just a geekwad accountant."

"Touché."

More than anything, I want to tell Dimitri what I saw at Applebee's. But even though he's my best friend, the idea of letting him in on such a big family secret . . . I'm not sure I want to do that. It would make everything feel more real.

"The third reason—" I say.

"The third reason is that you're a pussy. You're a plain no-holds-barred pussy."

"I'm not—"

"Shut up," Dimitri says. "All your whining is getting into my head. I've got a hole to win here. I'm going to spank you today, next week, and every week this summer. Then my dad and I are going to spank you and every other team at the tournament. Now that Kyle Sanders is away at

25

Cornell, it's a soft field. I'm going to kick your ass."

Thinking about the father/son golf tournament twists up my guts like I've swallowed an oscillating fan. I'd rather wrap my three-iron around my dad's neck than play with him.

Dimitri addresses his ball with his three-iron, waggles it a few times, and swings. His club slices through the cabbage and connects with a sharp *tick*. The shot flies straight and low. It's one of those slow risers I love to watch. The ball turns to the left with the curve of the fairway, lands softly, and rolls next to one of the sprinkler heads. It's about a hundred yards short of the pin.

"Nice poke," I say, trying to figure out how I'm going to recover. Hitting out of the bushes with Dimitri's ball a wedge away from the hole puts me in a tough position. I've got to play the next shot aggressively or get damn lucky with my putter.

We spread apart and head off in the direction my ball went. Past the trees I punched through, the ground is mostly dirt and roots and rocks. I head over there.

"So, that sucks about Veronica," Dimitri says.

My insides clench up even more. I've been so focused on my father that the whole Veronica mess sort of took a backseat.

"Now you're trying to get in my head," I say.

"I figure you can't screw up worse than that first shot." Dimitri points to a cluster of trees. My golf ball gleams from a rats' nest of roots next to the fattest tree. "There it is."

I drop my bag and check my lie. The best I can hope for is to punch it under the low branches—roll it out onto the fairway—and pray for a miracle on my third swing.

"You really loved her, huh?" Dimitri says.

Tears rise to my eyes, but I take a deep breath to settle myself. "She sucker punched me. One minute she's all hot and heavy, and the next day she dumps me. How does that happen?"

"You're so melodramatic. It's like I'm playing golf with Walt freakin' Whitman over here."

"Seriously," I say. I pull out my five-iron and choke down on the grip. "If Veronica can just turn off her feelings like they're a lawn sprinkler, how real could our relationship have been?"

I take a half swing and give the ball a swat. It pops off the root and makes a good line up the fairway. It bounces a few times and comes to a halt around forty yards short of Dimitri's. It's still only a stroke to the dance floor. Not bad.

"You're better off without her," Dimitri says.

"Easy for you to say. Aside from that mysterious Cassandra girl you claim to have met freshman year, you've never even had a girlfriend."

"Her name is Clarisse, and she's from Oregon. She had to go back west and—"

"Yeah, I've heard it all. You'll tell me two or three things about her and then get to the part about how she liked hooking up in the Starbucks bathroom."

"It's true," Dimitri says. We come out from under the

trees, and the sun blinds me. I pull down the brim of my cap and put on my sunglasses. Dimitri seems unfazed by the light, which is just further evidence that he's some sort of unnatural creature. "Veronica's a ditz," he says. "She's a space cadet."

"No, she's not," I say. "She's brilliant in math, pretty good in science, too."

"Okay, maybe she's not a space cadet, but she's no high-ranking space official. She's like a space private first class. A space corporal at best."

"Is 'space idiot' a rank? You'd qualify for that—probably get some kind of medal for exemplary service."

Dimitri ignores me and goes on. "I've said it since day one. You need someone who's into the same things as you." He begins counting on his fingers. "Veronica couldn't care less about golf. You guys always argue about movies. . . ."

"Guys and girls are supposed to argue about movies."

"Not like you guys. I mean, what kind of girl hates *Army of Darkness*? It's a total classic. That's why you've got to work here with me at the club."

"The girls here love Sam Raimi movies?"

"I'm just saying, you'll meet one of the members' daughters—maybe over by the pool, at the tennis courts—and you'll just hit it off. I'm telling you. There are some grade-A hotties down here, and they like golf. They like golfers."

I hike my bag higher on my shoulder. "I'm not a golfer. I'm just good at golf. There's a difference. Anyway, I've got a lot of things to sort out first."

"What's to freakin' sort out? You and Veronica only dated for a few months."

"It was eight months, which isn't so short," I say. "Right now, I just need some downtime."

"You might think you need downtime, but what you really need, my friend, is to get back in the saddle. Not only will it let you forget about Veronica, but if you really want her back, it'll make her jealous as hell."

"And you're an expert on this subject because . . . ?"

"Have you been living in a cave? There are, like, a million movies about this crap. Now shut up and swing."

We both hit up. Miraculously, my ball lands around eight feet to the right of the hole. Dimitri's shot goes long and rolls off the back edge of the green. There's hope for me yet. We're both sitting three, and I'm in better shape. I pull out my putter as we make our way up.

I hear the crackle of tires on gravel. A golf cart with an awning and several coolers mounted to the back rolls down the path from the next hole. The concession truck. A girl with long tanned legs and flip-flops sits behind the wheel. Her hair is pulled back under a baseball cap, and oversized sunglasses hide her face.

"Unless you're bringing us free food, get the hell out of here," Dimitri calls over to her.

"Bite me, you fat bastard," the girl fires back.

I nudge Dimitri's shoulder. "You're always wondering why girls don't consider you good boyfriend material. Maybe you should start by changing your opening line."

"Dude, that's Audrey."

It's been a while since I've seen her. I take a closer look at the girl behind the wheel, the girl behind the giant sunglasses and baseball cap. "Jeez, I didn't even recognize her—"

"Don't even think about it."

"Hey there, Seth," Audrey calls to me.

"Hey," I call back.

"I'm guessing you two cheap bastards aren't buying anything."

"Two bucks for a can of soda is a total rip-off," Dimitri says. "Why don't you take your gougemobile somewhere else?"

"See you losers later." Audrey shifts the concession cart into reverse and loops around the green. She drives down the fairway toward the golfers waiting at the tee box behind us. When she's gone, I check out the situation with my next shot.

"You're up," I say.

"King of the freakin' obvious." Dimitri brushes the grass with his wedge a few times and then gives a crisp stroke. His ball pops into the air. It lands on the short stuff and rolls in an arc toward the hole. It misses by a few inches and curls around to within three feet. Pretty good considering where he was sitting.

I mark my ball, polish it on the bottom of my shirt, and replace it on the grass. I kneel and dangle my putter out in front of me to try to figure out my line.

"Okay," Dimitri says. "This isn't the U.S. freakin' Open. Take your shot."

I stand over my ball, putter in hand. I rock my shoulders until my club face finds an easy swing that lightly brushes the ground. I draw the putter back and tell my brain to let my stroke happen.

Three short beeps chirp from my pocket—a photo message on my cell phone. I jerk up midswing, and the ball hops off the face of my putter blade. It takes a wider arc to the left than I planned and rolls past the hole. A foot and a half away.

"Gimme?" I say.

"Hell no," Dimitri says. "This is high-stakes golf wagering here. We've got a buck riding on this hole."

I pull my cell from my pocket and switch it to vibrate.

"If your phone starts buzzing during my swing," he says, "I reserve the right to a do-over."

"Can I take a do-over on that last one?"

"Fat chance."

Dimitri sets down his ball so the Nike swoosh points straight at the hole, and he gives a gentle stroke. His ball rolls to the edge and drops in. "That's a bogey. Sink yours and it's a push."

I make my way around the hole to my ball. As I do, I glance at the message. It's from Veronica. The photo is tough to see in the sunlight, but I can make out most of a face and the plunging neckline of a woman's sequined shirt. It's the woman from Applebee's—at least, it's part of her. Her eyes are looking upward as though she's talking to someone above the level of the camera. The text beneath the photo says: *This is her. I'll call you later.*

"What is it?" Dimitri asks.

"Nothing important."

I power off my cell and line up what should be a tap-in, but that woman's face keeps flashing through my mind. My hands are shaking, but I swing anyway. The ball makes its way to the hole and lips out, rolling farther away than when I started.

"Tough break," Dimitri says. "Concede?"

"Sure."

"At the tournament, a putt like that could cost you ten grand." Dimitri fishes his ball from the cup with the head of his putter and kicks mine toward me. "Want to go double or nothing on the next hole?"

"No way." I scoop up my ball and tuck it into the side pocket of my cargo shorts. "I've got a feeling I won't be swinging all that well this afternoon."

CHAPTER FIVE ▶▶❘

I've been hanging out at my desk in the basement all night. My cell phone sits silent next to me. It's not like I haven't been doing anything. It's not like I'm twiddling my thumbs like a total loser, hemming and hawing over whether to call Veronica. What I'm doing is setting up my podcasting studio.

Again.

Okay, and maybe I've been doing a little hemming. But hawing? I don't even know what hawing is.

With my final paycheck from Belgian Fries Express, I went out and bought a used large-diaphragm condenser microphone. It's miles better than the old, hunk-o-crap microphone I was using. That one crackled, gave tons of *p-pop*s, and pretty much blew chunks. Not to mention that this place looks more like a real studio than ever.

Now if only I could figure out a good hook for my podcast. It's one thing to play a bunch of music, but it's another to tie it all together, to keep people listening. That's the job of a good radio personality. Otherwise, people would just listen to their own tunes. I tried podcasting about golf a few times, but it was boring and was tough to tie the topic into different songs. I tried talking about B movies, but I ran out of things to talk about. Anyhow, I'm more of a Sam Raimi fanatic than a B-movie lover.

I hem a little more and glance at my cell phone.

I flip it open and scroll through the photos.

After I look at about a dozen old images of Veronica and one Dimitri took of his bare ass that I keep meaning to delete, I get to the mystery lady. The lines on her face tell me she has some miles on her. I figure she's anywhere from a rough thirty-five to a great fifty. Her teeth are white like Tic Tacs, and her skin glows in the overhead lights. The tiny beads of a green-and-yellow single-strand necklace follow the curve of her chest and disappear into her cleavage. It's not as painful to look at the woman as it was a few days ago, but it still stings.

"Seth, honey," my mother calls from the top of the basement stairs.

I snap my phone shut. "Yeah?"

"Are you still upset about me mentioning you on the show last night?"

"No." I say it too soon to be believable. After fielding a half dozen phone calls and deleting twice as many unread emails titled *baby boy*, I had burrowed under my blanket and gone to sleep.

"Come on, honey, you know as well as I do that the whole reason my show is so popular is because I stay honest with my audience. Anyhow, I left everything in general terms."

"How many baby boys do you think people figure Gayle Baumgartner has?"

"Will it help if I apologize again?"

"Couldn't hurt," I say.

She takes one step down the stairs. "Okay, sorry."

"I'll get over it," I say.

"I'm going to bed now. I've got a busy day tomorrow."

"Sure thing."

"I need to be out early," she says. "I've got a conference call with the Broadcasters' Council at nine. After that, I have a meeting at the club about the upcoming benefit for the Global Association for Diabetes."

"Shouldn't it be the Global Association for the *Prevention* of Diabetes?" I say.

"What?"

"Never mind."

"You'll have to fend for yourself for breakfast."

"No problem," I say.

I hear her come down a few more steps. *"Psst!"*

I roll my desk chair to the base of the stairs so I can see her. "I'm taking a look at dogs tomorrow, too," she whispers. "Do you have any suggestions?"

I consider her poor taste in men. "How about a girl dog?"

"A bitch?" She smiles.

The word sounds funny coming from my mother's mouth, and I get a charge out of saying it back. "Yeah, a bitch."

I want to call my mother the rest of the way down the stairs and tell her what I saw at Applebee's, but that would be the worst thing I could do. Everything would explode. Accusations would fly. They'd file for divorce. There'd be all sorts of legal battles—custody and all that. Hate, anger, fights, you name it. They'd argue over every last detail. My mom would probably get the house, and my father would have to move to some apartment with mismatched furniture and a refrigerator filled with frozen dinners and takeout containers.

I can't be the one to ruin everything. I have to figure it out.

My father's slippers make their way across the kitchen above me. The ice machine hums. Cubes drop into a glass.

"Dad's coming up, too," my mother says.

"Okay."

I hear the cabinet door open as my father works at pouring himself a single-barrel bourbon. It's his drink of choice. I tried a sip of that stuff once when my folks were out; it tastes like rocket fuel strained through dirty socks.

"I love that you're working on your podcasting," my mother says. "Just don't stay up too late. I don't want you sleeping all day tomorrow."

"All right." I tighten the knob on the microphone stand again, but I can't seem to get the mike to settle at the right height. It's either too low or too high.

"Get to bed soon," my father calls down to me. "You need to be out first thing tomorrow. Job hunting."

"Okay!" It's the first time I let any irritation slip into my voice. When I do get my next job, I'm going to buy an ON AIR sign from eBay that I can install on the basement door. Then I'll buy a crate of lightbulbs and leave the thing glowing 24/7.

I listen to my mother tread down the upstairs hallway. My father follows soon after.

I boot up my PC and start doing sound checks for a while. I learned a lot of this stuff going to the studio with my mom. Before I was old enough to stay home on my own, my mother would bring me to work during tax season so that my dad could crunch numbers. I'd sit on one of the tall swivel chairs and look at all the lights, buttons, and sliders on the soundboard. Ken, the sound guy, taught me a lot.

I'm still not used to hearing my own voice through the headphones—I doubt I ever will be—but this new microphone kicks ass. It makes my voice sound deeper, richer. I bump up the bass on the soundboard and exercise the baritone in my voice by reciting James Earl Jones lines:

"Join me, and we can rule the galaxy as father and son."

"Simba, you must take your place in the Circle of Life."

The whole father-son theme of *Star Wars* and *The Lion King* gets the veins in my neck pulsing, so I Google "James Earl Jones" and "famous lines" and find some that seem more appropriate. I like the one from *Coming to America*:

"So you see, my son, there is a very fine line between love and nausea."

Love and nausea . . . I repeat the line a few times until I'm satisfied with my rendition and scribble the two words on my pad.

My cell phone buzzes in my hand, and I jump. I glance at the clock: 12:34. Veronica says you're supposed to touch something blue and make a wish when the numbers on the clock are in order like that, but with all the crap that's happened these past few days, I have no idea what I'd wish for.

I flip open my phone. Veronica's number flashes across the screen.

"Hello?" I say.

"Hey." Her voice sounds distant. "Look, I've been thinking about what happened the other day. God, I feel awful."

The idea that she might be calling to get back with me sparks in my mind, but I push that thought back down. No sense in letting my hopes get trampled again.

"Which part?" I say.

"All of it. You know, the whole thing."

"Yeah, well, they say bad things happen in threes, so life's got to get better now."

"Threes? What was the third thing?"

"Mr. Burks canned me after I got back from lunch."

"Oh, jeez. I'm sorry. How many jobs is that this year?"

"You sound like my dad."

"Sorry." Veronica coughs with her mouth away from the phone. "So, did you figure out who that lady with your father was?"

"No."

"Your dad paid cash for lunch," she tells me. "I was hoping to get her name off a credit card or something. She ordered Onion Peels and a Pinot Grigio. You got the picture I sent, right?"

"Yeah."

"You're sure you've never seen her before?"

"Positive."

"I had Anders snap that picture when he brought over their food."

The thought of Anders with his sideburns, plowlike jaw, and popped collar sends acid rushing through my veins.

"Don't worry," she says. "I didn't tell him why."

"Praise the Lord."

"Look, Seth, you don't have to be a dick."

"How should I be? The past few days have sucked."

"Yeah . . . well, I'm sorry about that."

"Can't I just see you?" I ask. "Just to talk. Maybe we can figure something out." I feel pathetic begging, but I don't care. I need to feel like something is going right in my life. I underline the word *nausea* on my pad a bunch of times and draw a double-headed arrow between it and the word *love*. "What do you say? Just ice cream or a coffee or something."

"I don't think so, Seth." Her voice sounds wobbly. I can

tell this call is hard for her.

"Come on, Vee. Just a week ago we were attached at the hip, and now it's like I'm a tumor you had removed."

"You're not like a tumor."

"Well, you're making me feel like one."

The silence gets long and uncomfortable, and just before I'm about to ask if she's still there, she says, "I just don't think seeing each other is a good idea. Maybe it'll be fine after a while, but not right now."

"Why not?"

"It's just not."

"Is it because you still love me? Is it because you're afraid that if you see me, all those feelings will come back?"

"Of course I still have feelings for you, Seth. I'm not some kind of monster. I just don't feel *that way* anymore."

I underline the word *love* on my pad. I underline it again. Then I write the words *that way*.

"Helloooo?" she says. "Anyone there?"

"I'm thinking."

"That's part of the problem," she says. "You're always thinking, you're always brooding, but I never know what's going on in that head of yours. Sure, you joke around and all, but you never tell me what you're really feeling."

"But I love you."

"Oh, yeah?" she says. I hear her shift in her chair. "What is it you love about me, Seth? Name ten things you love about me."

A thousand things rush to mind—the way her forehead wrinkles when she gets confused, that little squeak at the end of her laugh, how she loves to spoon peanut butter on a banana before each bite, how she props her bare feet on my windshield when we're driving so that after a week or so the prints of hundreds of tiny toes light up when oncoming headlights shine through them. I want to say something, but all the words get jammed up. I can't possibly say them all at once, but each individual one sounds corny and lame and just not enough on its own.

I lean back in my desk chair and look at the bumps on the stucco ceiling. The light makes the ceiling seem like the surface of the moon.

"How about five?" she says. "Name *five* reasons you love me."

Now the pressure is really on, and I'll feel doubly stupid—quadruply stupid—if I say something short of profound.

Still, nothing comes out.

I clench my jaw and fight down all the emotion welling up.

"I thought so," she says.

I fight against the logjam in my brain, but the logjam wins. "I need some time."

Veronica sighs. "Just forget it."

The line goes dead. I scroll to the photo of the mystery woman again. What's wrong with me? Even my boring, pathetic, balding accountant father can get a girlfriend. I try to analyze each pixel on that tiny screen to figure out something—anything—about that woman. When I'm certain I'm not going to get any clues from it, I start toying with the other features on my phone: the tip calculator, the time-zone thing, the lame Texas hold 'em game I downloaded for $4.99 the week I thought I might quit school and make a go as a professional gambler.

My phone is a piece of crap. The thing is almost four years old. It's the same one my folks got for me when I was thirteen—back when my mother was paranoid about me being abducted. She got me the one with the GPS in it so she could track where I was every moment of every day. It was weird carrying that thing around, like someone was breathing down my neck all the time. But I knew better than to turn down the offer. A phone is a phone.

Thinking about the GPS tracker brings James Bond's tracking device to mind again, and I can practically hear the gears whirring in my brain. Before I have a chance to stop myself, I bound up the stairs and head out into the garage. I forward my calls to my mom's cell, mute all the functions on my own phone, and tuck it between the seats of my father's Beemer. I head back inside to the kitchen. I flip the battery around in my mother's phone so it goes dead and tug the charger halfway out of the outlet. When she picks up her cell in the morning, she'll figure she left it off the charger. She'll figure she didn't plug it in well enough and leave it here when she heads out. That'll leave her phone—and her GPS tracker—for me until at least midafternoon—until she's done with her lunch with the Junior League alumni.

My dad loves to talk about how you can't accomplish anything unless you're up and out early. He says the way

42

to get ahead in life is to make your move before anyone else. He's always saying the early bird catches the worm. I wonder how hard it would be for the worm to catch the early bird. For me, Seth Baumgartner, to catch my father.

I head back downstairs, slide my microphone in front of me, and get started on my first podcast.

EXCERPT FROM THE LOVE MANIFESTO ▶▶❙

Intro Music: "It's Not Over" by Daughtry

Hey there. You don't know me, but I'm going to tell you a story.

Once upon a time, there was this guy. Let's call him Steve. Steve knew this girl from school. We'll call her Valerie. Steve and Valerie had known each other for a long time—since first grade, in fact. They were in a lot of the same classes but were never buddy-buddy. Friendly but not friends. Know what I mean?

Anyhow, Steve and Valerie found themselves partners in chemistry class. That meant they had to work together. At first they both hated it, wanted to be with their own friends. But after a while, they grew to tolerate each other. They were in the lab doing experiments before school. In the afternoons they were in the library or at one of their houses doing homework. Before long, Steve and Valerie started talking on the phone. And conversation shifted from just chemistry to chemistry and a few other things. Friends. Parties. A little gossip. Whatever.

Pretty soon, their conversations were less about schoolwork and more about those other things. Then one afternoon at Steve's house—while they were plotting points to make a graph that showed the temperature of water as it was heated in relation to time—Steve and Valerie kissed.

They kissed and did a pretty good job of wrinkling up their half-done graph. After that, Steve and Valerie were a couple.

I know you've heard stories like this before. Of course, the people probably had different names. Maybe they worked at the grocery store together or met at the mall. But what do all of these stories have in common?

<Sound effect: crickets chirping>

No guesses?

Well, I'll tell you. They all fail. At least, the huge majority of them do. Virtually every high-school relationship fails. Virtually every college relationship fails. Those that succeed to the point where the two actually walk down the aisle and exchange rings . . . depending on the research you believe, somewhere between forty and sixty percent of those relationships fail. You can do the math, but those odds are pretty crappy.

So why are there so many radio shows that celebrate love when really we should be consoling all the people recovering from failed relationships? That's where the *money is. The money is in the misery.*

Why do people put up with it all? Two people could be as happy as two monkeys in a banana tree—better than two monkeys in a banana tree because banana tree monkeys probably fight over the bananas, and that's when the poop-flinging starts.

<Sound effect: chimps screaming>

Two people could be getting along great and then all of a sudden one of them will drop the bomb. Break up. Cheat. Whatever.

That is exactly what happened to me, and I'm here to tell you all about it.

All I can say is that love sucks and I've got some pretty good stories in between songs to prove my point. And if anyone out there can tell me what it means when a girl says she's "too comfortable" with you, I'd appreciate it if you filled me in.

Be sure to leave a comment if you have any questions or ideas or opinions. And remember to tell all your friends about the show. Sure, the audio quality sucks and I haven't quite figured out how to use my soundboard yet, but when you start at the bottom, the only way to go is up, up, up.

So, this is The Love Manifesto, *where I'll be spinning all the tunes that remind us how much love hurts.*

Outro Music: "Love Hurts" by Joan Jett & the Blackhearts

CHAPTER SIX ▶▶|

"**W**hat do you mean you want to figure out what love is?" Dimitri asks through his fist as he stuffs a handful of French fries into his mouth. "That might be the lamest thing I've ever heard."

"What's so lame about it? My mom talks about love on her radio program, and she's the number one rated slot in the Capital District."

"But your mom has a show that caters to love-starved housewives who hang out at craft fairs and garage sales all day. What do you have?"

I boost myself onto the trunk of the Red Scare. The backs of my thighs practically sizzle on the metal, and I hop off the car. "Son of a bitch!"

The guy emptying the garbage cans at Poindexter's

Snack Shack, the greasy burger and ice-cream stand we hang out at, glares at me. "Watch it," he says. "This is a family establishment."

"Sorry," Dimitri says. "My friend here's got Tourette syndrome. He can't control himself. Swears like a freakin' truck driver."

The Poindexter's guy looks me up and down like he's not sure whether or not to believe Dimitri. "Yeah, well, maybe you two should sit at the picnic table at the end so the kids around here don't hear you."

"What kids?" Dimitri says. "It's a Thursday afternoon. There's no one here but us. Anyhow, Tourette syndrome is a disability. You wouldn't ask someone in a wheelchair to go to the last table, would you?"

"I'm not saying you *have* to go to the end. I'm just asking if you wouldn't mind. Anyway, if his tics are that bad, he should be on Clonidine." He pulls the trash bag from the can and replaces it with a new one, tying it tight around the lip of the can. He pushes past Dimitri, bumping his shoulder hard on his way to the Dumpster. "I'm a fourth-year med student, dickwad."

Dimitri and I head to the picnic table at the end. On the way, I flip open my mother's cell phone as discreetly as I can and hit the button to track my father's car. The phone thinks on it for a few seconds, beeps, and shows that he's still downtown at his office, exactly where he's been all day.

At least, that's where his car is. I jammed the cell phone between the seats. Who knows? Maybe that woman picked him up. Maybe my father walked somewhere. Maybe she came for a visit to his office for a quickie on his desk. The GPS will only pick up the location of the car. Next time I should hide the cell in his briefcase. No, not there. He wouldn't take his briefcase to lunch. Maybe I could put it in the lining of his sport jacket? My ancient phone is too bulky for that. Between the seats of the Beemer is the best I'm going to get.

Dimitri and I sit on the last picnic table and face Delaware Avenue. Across the road and beyond a fence, the ground drops away to a deep forested gorge.

I take a bite of my cheeseburger and gesture toward Poindexter's. "You remember when this place almost slid into the river a few years back?"

Dimitri shakes his head.

"There were all kinds of mud slides over there." I point to the river winding quietly behind brown thickets and clumps of trees. At one spot far below us, a retaining wall rises from the banks. "We were, like, six. I remember being afraid that Albany wouldn't have any soft-serve ice cream anymore. I was big into chocolate-vanilla twist back then. The Army Corps of Engineers came and fixed everything."

"Thanks for the history lesson," Dimitri says. "Who're you, Lord freakin' Acton?"

"Who?"

"Lord John Emerich Edward Dalberg-Acton. He was a historian—the guy who said, 'Power corrupts, and absolute power corrupts absolutely.'"

"How stupid of me," I say.

"Seriously, Seth." Dimitri takes a huge bite of his hot dog. A glob of ketchup drips down his shirt. "Son of a bitch!" he says through his mouthful. He grabs a napkin from my stack. "My mom's gonna freak."

"I'm sure you'll survive," I say. "Your mom is used to your slobbish ways."

"Yeah, but she's still going to freak. Moms are programmed like that."

"Didn't Van Gogh cut off his ear for love?" I say. "What drives a guy to do something like that?"

"He was a lunatic. It had nothing to do with love and everything to do with dementia. Psychosis. The guy probably needed Klonopin or Klondike bar or whatever that guy called it." Dimitri dabs at his Izod with the napkin but only manages to spread the ketchup around. "This is a brand-new shirt. My mom's going to have my head."

I take a sip of my water. "I started a podcast about it, you know."

"You started a podcast about my shirt?"

"No, you pinhead. I started a podcast about love. Really, it's sort of antilove. I stayed up last night to do it. It's mostly music, sort of like my mom's show, but I'll talk between the songs, answer listener questions, all that. I'm going to do it all summer."

"This is going to be classic," Dimitri says. "You whining all summer about how your love life sucks. What's the show called?"

"No way am I telling you. It'll just screw me up. I'll start filtering what I say because I'll know you're listening."

"Come on, Seth. I'll find it anyway."

"No you won't. I'm using a pseudonym."

"I'll just Google 'love' and 'podcast.' I'll find it."

"You'll find porn and that's as far as you'll get."

"Only until my hand gets tired," Dimitri says.

I cringe. "Remind me never to touch your mouse."

"There's never cross contact," he says. "I'm ambidextrous. Right hand for the mouse; left hand for—"

"No details necessary."

A dark blue Scion pulls into the parking lot, and a bunch of girls pile out. Looks like a good chunk of the volleyball team. One of them is Audrey. This time, her baseball hat and oversized sunglasses don't fool me. The girls head toward the window of Poindexter's.

"Hang out here a second." Dimitri walks over and starts talking to them. He gestures to me, and the girls look over. I lift a hand and wave. A few of them wave back. One of the girls shakes her head and says something to Dimitri. Dimitri starts talking some more. Audrey looks at me and waves.

My mom's cell phone buzzes. It's Veronica.

Does she want to apologize? Does she want me back? Does she want to pledge her eternal love?

I suck in a breath and let it out slowly, hoping to chase away the legion of butterflies Riverdancing in my gut. I flip open my phone. "Hey," I say.

"Hey," she says. Then she's the one who takes the deep breath and lets it out slowly. "We sort of got off track when we were talking yesterday. I know you probably don't want to hear from me, but I forgot something."

To secure the lid of my coffin with three-inch decking screws? almost comes out of my mouth, but I hold it back.

"What'd you forget?" I say.

"I followed that woman out to the parking lot when she left Applebee's."

"You what?" I heard her perfectly well, but the words come anyway.

"Don't worry," Veronica says. "I hung back until your dad got into his car. The two of them, your dad and that woman, they gave each other a long hug, a kiss, the whole bit."

A week ago I would have run to Veronica for advice and support, but now I hate that she knows about this. I hate that she feels as though she's part of everything.

"Is there a point to your call, or are you just trying to make me feel worse than before?"

"No, there's a point," she says. "After your dad took off, I followed the woman to her car. How do women walk in heels that high, anyway?"

I assume she's not waiting for a response from me. How would I know? I let the silence grow between us as I watch Dimitri chat it up with the girls. Now he's gesturing to the stain on his shirt. One of the girls points to it and says something. Audrey adds something, probably about how their mom is going to go nuclear.

"The lady drives an old Acura Integra," Veronica

says. "It's a two thousand one. Moon roof, leather seats, the whole bit. It's dark green with that wing thingy on the back. What're those things called?"

"A spoiler?"

"Yeah, a spoiler."

I don't see how this could be important. "Who cares what she drives?" I say. "Who cares that her car has a spoiler?"

"That's not all. She had a FOR SALE sign in the window. How'd you think I knew it was a 2001 Acura? I can't tell the difference between a Cadillac and a Corvette."

"And . . . ?"

"And the FOR SALE sign had a phone number written on it."

"You're kidding."

"No, right there in the window. A phone number. It's got to be hers." Veronica gives me the number. I key the digits into my mom's cell phone and save it. "I know you're probably still really pissed at me, so I'll hang up now," she says.

"Hey, Vee, maybe we could . . . you know—"

"No, Seth. It's not a good idea. I called to give you that phone number. That's all. I need some time apart."

Time apart? *Time apart?* What does she mean by that? Would she consider getting back together down the road? That maybe we could hang out sometime? That maybe we have a chance? How much time is "time apart"?

"Hellooooo?" Veronica says. "Anyone there?"

"I'm here."

"I've got to get going," she says. "My mom is taking me dress-shopping. I just thought you'd want that number."

I don't want to say thanks, but I do and hit the End key. Dimitri is still busy talking to the girls, so I check to make sure my father's car is still in the firm's parking lot. After the phone thinks and beeps, I discover the little red dot is on the move. The Beemer is on Washington Avenue, almost as far as Lake Street. Could he be headed back to the mall? If he were, he'd have probably hopped right on the highway. It's the quickest way to get there from downtown. I shield the screen and squint against the sun so that I can see the map a little better. He turns left on South Lake.

Dimitri heads toward me. "One of the girls over there told me club soda would help get the ketchup out," he says. "I hope Sprite works the same."

I snap the phone shut and stuff it in my pocket.

Dimitri boosts himself onto the edge of the picnic table, pours some of his soda on a napkin, and starts dabbing at his shirt. "God, Audrey is such a pain. She totally ran interference on me chatting up Rebecca Malley."

"Who's Rebecca Malley?"

"Some girl on the volleyball team with her." Dimitri motions to the girls. "She's the one with the cutoff tee and the ponytail. The tall one." He points to my phone. "Hey, who was that?"

"Just jerking around with my ringtones."

"Bullshit. You were just talking with someone. I saw you."

Crap.

54

"Oh, that?" I say. "That was Oprah. She wants to do a show on me. I told her to have her people call my people."

"You don't belong on *Oprah*," Dimitri says. "You belong on *Jerry* freakin' *Springer*."

Dimitri has no idea how right he really is. I want to whip open my phone to see where my father is headed. I want to see every turn, to see what lights he gets hung up at, what back roads he winds through. And of course where he ends up. But I'm stuck. There's no way I can ditch Dimitri at Poindexter's Snack Shack. And if I bring him, I'll have to tell him everything.

"What was that all about?" I say, pointing to the girls who by now are sitting several tables away eating ice cream. "I mean, aside from getting stain-removal tips, trying to talk to Rebecca Malley, and getting annoyed by your sister?"

"Grade-A hotties, huh? You can have the brunette, Seth. I know you're a sucker for a miniskirt."

"How shallow do you think I am? What were you guys talking about?"

"I told them about your podcast."

"You didn't. . . ."

"I did. I asked them if they'd listen to something like that. You know, to get a sad-sack guy's perspective on love."

I don't want to ask, but of course I have to. "What'd they say?"

Dimitri tucks the rest of his hot dog neatly into his mouth. He picks up his soda and takes a sip. "I'd tell you, but I'm too good a friend."

"No, really. What'd they think?"

"They thought it was pathetic, like a baby crying for its mommy. . . ." Dimitri makes a pouty face and gurgles and whines a few times. The girls look over. I shrug with one of those everything-is-okay-over-here expressions on my face.

"You know," I say, "that hot dog you're eating probably has pig uterus in it or something."

"If eating pig uterus is wrong"—Dimitri swallows the last chunk of his hot dog—"I don't want to be right."

"So, how did you do that?" I ask him.

"How did I do what?"

I jerk my chin at the girls. "How did you just go up and talk to those girls? You act like it's nothing."

"You act like it's *something*," he says. "It's just my sister and her geeky volleyball friends."

I pick at a splinter on the edge of the table. Someone carved two sets of initials, E. W. and A. K., into the surface of the wood with the word *4EVR* just beneath it. I wonder how long that's been there. The table looks about a hundred years old. I wonder if E. W. and A. K. are still together. Somehow I doubt it.

Dimitri crumples up his plate and napkin and tosses the paper over his head like he's doing some kind of Harlem Globetrotters hook shot. The wadded-up trash bounces off the edge of the garbage can and lands on the pavement. He trudges over, picks up his litter, and slam-dunks it into the can. "Look, I eavesdrop on Audrey's phone calls all the time. Girls are just as nervous about talking to guys as we are talking to them."

"Then what's your excuse?" I say.

"Excuse for what?"

"Why don't you have a girlfriend? Why haven't you *ever* had a girlfriend?"

"I did," Dimitri says. "Two summers ago. Clarisse. The one from—"

"Yeah, the one from Oregon. Starbucks Special."

"It's true."

I lie back on the scorching wood of the picnic table and close my eyes to the sun. It definitely doesn't suck to be unemployed in the summertime. Okay, it's true I could use some gas money and some dough to buy a few choice items. But there is something to be said for chilling at Poindexter's and tanning all afternoon.

But gas money wins out.

"Do you know if there are still positions open at the golf club?" I say. "The thought of going back to the mall makes me want to hurl."

"Go down and talk to Mr. Haversham," Dimitri says. "There are always openings for the crap jobs. The trick is to try and pick something where you'll meet tons of girls."

"I told you. I'm not interested in hooking up with members' daughters."

"Why not?"

"Rich girls?" I say. "Forget it. Too high maintenance."

"But you're a rich *guy*. It's a perfect fit."

"We're not rich. My father does the books for the club. We get a major break on membership."

"Have you ever seen my house?" Dimitri says. "Compared to me, you're rich."

I can't say anything to that. Dimitri's family isn't what I'd call poor, but his house is small. It's in one of those old blue-collar neighborhoods near the highway, which I guess fits, being that his father is a welder and his mother works in the lingerie department at Macy's.

My dad is just about as white-collar as you can get—too-tight knee-high black socks that leave pressure rings around his calves and everything. As for my mom, she's as corporate as you can get: a rising star in broadcasting, number one source of advertising dollars at the station, and on the board of three different local charities.

The sun bakes my face like my head is under the heat lamps at Belgian Fries Express. I put on my sunglasses, and my retinas thank me. My hand traces the outline of the cell phone in my pocket.

"Are you serious those girls hated the idea of the podcast?" I ask Dimitri.

"Well, no, actually. A few of them just shrugged. Audrey and some other girl said it was cute."

"Cute?"

"Cute and interesting."

I sit up. "Cute and interesting is good."

"And the brunette with the braids said you sounded deep."

"Deep." I glance at the girls. They're most of the way through their soft-serve cones. The brunette's hand

58

is covered with melted ice cream and rainbow sprinkles. "Deep is good."

"Deep is real good, but you need your downtime, remember?"

I can't take it anymore. I pull out my phone, flip it open, and check on my father. His car is at the intersection of New Scotland. He's turning right. I need to get my mom's phone back before she gets home from the club. I'm risking getting snagged, but this is too important.

"You doing anything right now?" I ask.

"What'd you have in mind?"

I pull out my keys and jingle them. "Just a cruise around town. No big whoop."

CHAPTER SEVEN

"I can't really tell." Dimitri squints at my mom's phone some more. "It looks like he's stopped on New Scotland Avenue—somewhere near the elementary school."

I run through all the businesses I remember in that neighborhood and all the reasons he couldn't possibly be going to them:

Optician: He doesn't wear glasses.

Italian deli: Prosciutto gives him indigestion.

Gas station: He only fills the tank at that place where it's a nickel cheaper.

Hair salon: He's not the highlights-and-perm type.

Wine shop: Mom usually takes care of that.

Anyhow, there's nothing in that part of town he couldn't get right where he works. Nothing he'd need to run all the way over here for during lunch hour. I hang a left onto Ten Eyck and step on the gas to try to beat the light on

Matilda, but the car in front of me slows down when it turns yellow.

I stomp on the brakes. The shoulder strap tugs at my shoulder. The antilocks vibrate under my foot. Dimitri braces himself against the dashboard with his hand. My car comes to a stop inches from the car in front of us.

"What the f—?" he says.

I pound the steering wheel. I pound it again.

"Who cares what your father does on his lunch hour, Seth? What's with all the espionage?"

"I need some tunes."

Dimitri connects my mp3 player and, as usual, "Dueling Banjos" cranks out of my speakers. For some reason that song is stuck on my iPod. Whenever I turn the thing on, it plays full blast. It doesn't come on at the beginning, either, when the banjos are quiet and slow; it comes on right in the middle when the instruments are going apeshit, when those banjos are really dueling.

"Jeez, Seth!" Dimitri says. "Haven't you figured out how to get this freakin' song off here yet?" He forwards to the next tune.

"Still working on it."

"Isn't that song from that movie? What's it called? *Deliveryman* or something?"

"*Deliverance*," I say. "Never seen it."

"My dad told me never to watch that one. He said it would scar me for life."

"How bad could it be?" I say.

Old movies are the last thing I want to talk about right

now, but Dimitri has no idea how close I am to throwing up, screaming, or doing something completely insane, and I want to leave it that way.

"*Deliverance*," he says. "It actually sounds sort of uplifting."

The light changes. I head up to Marwill and take a right. "Any movement on the GPS?"

Dimitri studies the screen. "Nope."

"There's a convenience store down that way and a pizza place," I offer.

"Those are farther up," Dimitri says. "He's closer to the firehouse. Maybe he's volunteering."

I don't even bother responding to that one. We head down Academy Road, and I hang a left onto New Scotland. My hands are starting to shake, so I grip the wheel tighter.

"You haven't answered my question, Seth." Dimitri wiggles my mom's cell phone in the air. "What's with all the *Bourne Identity* crap?"

I hate lying to Dimitri, but what choice do I have? This is stuff I definitely don't want anyone else to know. I can just see us sitting at a restaurant when we're thirty, both of us with our jobs and our lives. Maybe we'll still be best buds, maybe not. Maybe we'll both be married, maybe not. But none of it will matter. Regardless of what happens between now and then—what schools I've gone to, what degrees I've gotten, or how many millions of dollars I've made—all that Dimitri will think about is how I'm that guy whose father cheated on his mother.

So I tell him the first lie that pops into my head.

"Anniversary," I say. "My folks' anniversary. It's next month."

"So what?"

"So my mom thinks my dad is going to forget again. He's forgotten three of the past five or something." I snatch my player from Dimitri and skip to a better song, then drop it into the cup holder. "My mom asked me to keep on my dad's back about it so he won't forget."

Dimitri's stare practically burns twin holes into the side of my face. "Are you serious?" he says. "You made me leave that carload of grade-A hotties at Poindexter's and drive across town in your four-hundred-degree car to see whether or not your dad is buying your mom an anniversary gift? Couldn't you have just asked him?"

I get a heavy feeling in my stomach because I have to drag out the lie some more. "It's their twentieth anniversary coming up," I say. "It's important to her."

"Is that cotton? Jade? Sapphire?"

"Huh?"

"You know. That list of traditional and modern anniversary gifts? It's on the back of every Hallmark calendar. What's twentieth?"

"I don't even know what you're talking about."

"Then how are you supposed to help your father get your mom a gift?"

"I'm not supposed to help him pick a gift," I say. "I just have to make sure he gets one. I think she'd be happy with a ream of printer paper."

"Paper?" Dimitri puffs out a laugh. "That's *first*

anniversary, traditional."

"This is important to my mom," I say. "You know, that he remembers."

"If it's so important, why is she on your back to dog him about it? It should only matter if he remembers on his own."

I'm out of lies, so I fiddle with my sun visor and ignore his question. The light at New Scotland turns red, and I give my brakes another workout.

"Easy on the pedal there," Dimitri says. "I just never took you for a Stormtrooper is all. I had you pegged as Chewbacca."

"Chewbacca?"

"What's wrong with Chewbacca? He's cool."

"As if," I say. "I'm Boba Fett all the way."

"You ain't no Boba Fett, Seth. If anyone is Boba, it's me." Dimitri turns the air-conditioning to full blast, plants his arms on the dashboard, and airs out his armpits.

I make a left onto New Scotland.

"Are we coming up on the dot?" I gesture to my mom's phone. "Are we getting close?"

Dimitri peers at the screen. "Damn close. He should be right ahead of us, a few hundred yards."

I slow the car and roll up New Scotland Avenue. Before long, I make out my father's Beemer. It's facing us from the opposite side of the street, parked in front of the flower shop. I had forgotten all about the flower shop. It's the one my parents used when my grandfather died back when I was seven or eight.

I remember listening to my grandfather talk to my dad at the hospital. He said that when he croaked he wanted a simple funeral—no fancy stuff. Plain pine box. Graveside service. In fact, he told my father, "Jam a hambone in my ass, let a dog drag me around, and bury me wherever that dog lets go." Nonetheless, when the funeral came, my mom insisted we do a few nice arrangements—something tasteful and cheery.

I hang a right and hook around the block so I can nose out of one of the side streets. A wall of shrubs and a fence provide perfect cover.

"There are, like, a million spots over there," Dimitri says, pointing toward the flower shop. "You don't want me walking in this heat, do you? I'll have a stroke."

"I'd rather park here."

"Okay, Jason Bourne." Dimitri unbuckles his seat belt and reaches for the door handle. "Off we go."

I grab his arm, maybe a bit more urgently than I should. "Hang on," I say. "Let's just see what he comes out with."

"Who cares?" Dimitri says. "Either he's getting her flowers or he's ordering her flowers. Your dad doesn't strike me as a Beanie Baby sort of guy."

"It's like you said. I want to see what he does on his own. You know, without my help."

Dimitri slouches in his seat. "You're acting freakin' weird."

I let the car idle. Dimitri fiddles with the music until he finds a song that suits him. While we're waiting, I scan the area. There's no sign of a green Integra with a FOR SALE sign in the window, which takes a load off my shoulders. But it also makes me wonder why I'm sitting here. Even if he's in there buying flowers for his girlfriend, he could always tell me they're for Mom. And what would I do if I did snag him in the act? Would I just run up and clothesline him? Would I curse him out? Or would catching him just make him sneakier the next time around?

I clutch the steering wheel until my fingers go numb. The truth is, it won't matter what he's holding when he comes out of that store. He could come out with a giant heart-shaped Mylar balloon with the words *For My Beloved Concubine* printed across it and tell me he bought it for Mom as a joke. The man obviously has no trouble lying.

"We have movement," Dimitri says, his hands curled in front of his face as though he's holding a pair of binoculars. "Suspect is on the move. And . . . holy crap, who's that?"

My eyes swivel to the flower shop just in time to see my father start down the porch stairs with one arm around the mystery lady. She walks snug against his body like he's sheltering her from the sun.

Dimitri taps my leg a few times. "Who the hell is—?"
"Shhhh!"

My father leads the woman to his car and opens the passenger door for her. There's no doubt it's the lady from Applebee's. She lifts a red rose to her nose. Her shoulders rise and fall as if she's taking a deep breath. My father helps her into his car, shuts the door carefully, and walks around to his side.

I know I should go over there. I know I should confront

66

him. Throw myself onto the hood of his car or something. What better time to do it than when she's with him? Yet something glues me to my seat. All I can do is stare.

"What the hell?"

"Shhhhh!" I say again.

Within seconds, my father's taillights go on and he pulls away. He disappears around the next corner into the maze of Albany's side streets.

Some free download-of-the-week from some nobody band starts to pump from my speakers. I tell myself to delete it as soon as I get home. I'm glad it's not a song I'm likely to hear again—on the radio or anyplace else—because my mind will always associate it with seeing my father walk out of a flower shop with some woman who is not my mother.

When my father's car is long gone, when the song is over and I'm just staring at an empty parking space, Dimitri taps me on the shoulder. "Who was that woman, Seth?"

My head barely shakes from side to side. "Probably just his secretary or something."

"Why would he be buying his secretary a rose in the middle of the summer?" Dimitri asks. "Administrative Assistants' Day is in the spring."

"Drop it, all right?"

"Today is Canada Day," he says. "I heard it on the radio. But I don't even think Canadians buy flowers for Canada Day. That's more of a picnics-and-parades sort of holiday."

"Just drop it."

"Hot secretary, though."

I glare at Dimitri and he shuts up. He turns off the music as if he knows how much I can't stand to hear it.

I pull out onto New Scotland Avenue and hang a right, away from where my father drove.

Dimitri raises his hand like he's asking my permission to speak.

"Yeah?"

"Maybe she's helping your father pick out an anniversary gift for your mom and the lady in the shop just gave her that flower. You know, a day-old rose or something."

My brain scrambles to fill in the blanks—to make Dimitri's explanation work. And it might have worked if I hadn't seen the two of them at Applebee's or if Veronica hadn't seen them all over each other in the mall parking lot. Or if my anniversary story wasn't utter bullshit. My parents' anniversary isn't until February.

"Yeah," I manage to say.

The truth is that my father has no good reason to be here. And he especially has no good reason to be here with that woman.

I grab my mother's cell phone from Dimitri and scroll through the saved numbers. I get to the one Veronica gave me—the one she got from the FOR SALE sign in the mall parking lot.

"What are you doing?" Dimitri asks.

My thumb hovers over the Send button. "I was thinking of taking a look at a used car."

CHAPTER EIGHT ▶▶|

My hands are still shaking. The phone call to set up the test drive was tougher than I thought it would be. The woman caught me off guard, picked up on the first ring, just when I realized she might still be with my father. He could have been sitting right there next to her. We talked a little about her car and set up a time to meet at her apartment complex tomorrow. With all the thoughts racing through my mind, it was a miracle I was able to do that much. Now, it's all I can do to press the button on Dimitri's remote and flip through the television channels.

"Check out this one." Dimitri tosses a lingerie catalog to me. It spins across the couch and lands on my lap. I toss it to the side.

When I get tired of scanning channels, I glance at the catalog. It's for women with large bust sizes—anything from DD through L. *What the hell would an L look like?*

Since Dimitri's mother is the manager of the lingerie department at Macy's, their house is always littered with catalogs like this. Dimitri peruses the new arrivals and hoards the ones he likes best. It's interesting to see which ones he keeps, because the women in this catalog, aside from having mammoth-sized boobs, are not particularly attractive. Most of them have plastic-looking hair, plastic-looking smiles, and enough makeup to kill a few dozen laboratory rabbits. I can't imagine any woman with breasts that large being able to smile, let alone stand upright.

I go back to channel surfing.

"Dude," Dimitri says. "I share goddesses wrapped in silk, ribbons, and lace with you and you'd rather click through home-improvement shows and old episodes of *Judge Judy*? What's wrong with you?"

"What am I supposed to do, start beating my chest and jumping up and down like an ape?"

"I don't know," he says, "but I can tell you that watching the second half of a *Flavor of Love* rerun is not the right thing to do."

I drop the remote and flip through one of the catalogs. It's divided into sections. One part is just panties and shows panty-clad pelvises. Another is just bras and shows bra-clad torsos. Another section is two-piece matching sets. Another section shows different kinds of hosiery, and yet another shows robes and sleepwear. It's all very clinical, bordering on scientific. Every model looks exactly the same, with the same expression and the same posture. Then I come across another catalog. This one shows models wearing all kinds of bizarre outfits with straps and buckles and latches.

"Do they sell this at Macy's?" I flash Dimitri the catalog spread. "These things look more like something you'd use on Houdini before you toss him in a trunk and pitch him into the Hudson River."

Dimitri glances over. "Not sure," he says. "My mom gets all kinds of freaky catalogs. A while back there was one that had all kinds of whips and handcuffs in it. I was younger—like in fifth grade or something."

"What'd your mom say?"

"She told me it was a Halloween catalog. I knew she was full of it—especially since the catalog disappeared from my book bag that night. She's long since stopped trying to keep the bedsheets of my mind fluffy and spring fresh."

"Way too late for that," I say.

"That's the truth." Dimitri pushes his fingers through his hair and leans back against the arm of the couch. It's the first time all day I notice he's shaved. He's given up on the goatee and opted for an oval patch of fur under his chin. "So, what attracted you to Veronica in the first place?" he asks me. "I mean, what set her apart from other girls—aside from the fact that she was the only one in town who would give you the time of day?"

I chuck a catalog at him and he swats it down.

"Seriously?" I say.

"Yeah."

I lean back and stare at the chandelier. It looks completely out of place hanging in the middle of the living room, but I like the crystals spinning in the sunlight.

"It was how she challenged me. I remember we were in social studies freshman year and we broke into groups to discuss capital punishment. It was one of those debate projects where each group was supposed to take a different stance and we would argue issues in front of the rest of the class."

Dimitri lifts his finger to stop me.

"Yeah?"

"Is this going to get less boring any time this century?"

I fling another catalog at him. He swats it down again.

"Kidding!" he says.

"I guess my point is that it was a lot of little things, all the details. They all added up to something bigger."

A girl's voice comes from the kitchen. "Did you ever tell her that?"

It's Audrey. She leans against the door frame, a glass of soda in her hand.

My face flushes, and I wonder how much she's overheard. All of it, I'm guessing.

"Get out of here, snoop," Dimitri says.

"I'm not a snoop. The living room is a common area. I can't help what I hear in a common area."

She comes fully into the room and lies sideways across the La-Z-Boy. Without her giant sunglasses and baseball cap, I can get a better look at her. She was blessed with a face that looks nothing like Dimitri's. Not that Dimitri is ugly per se, but it creeps me out when brothers and sisters look alike, as though they both fell out of the same mold and were fitted for different plumbing. With Dimitri

72

and Audrey, Dimitri looks more like their father; Audrey, more like their mother.

"Did you ever tell Veronica what you liked about her?" she asks me.

I shrug.

"Guys are stoic," Dimitri says. "We're like cavemen. Mars and Venus. Whatever you want to call it."

I square up the catalogs and put them on the coffee table as far away from myself as I can. It's weird having them around when Audrey is in the room.

Audrey picks one up and absently flips through it. "Do you want her back?" she asks me.

"Get out of here." Dimitri flings a pillow at her.

She smacks it aside and turns to me. "Do you want her back?" she says, this time more intently. "If Veronica came begging for forgiveness, would you take her back?"

I'm not sure what to say. I want to say yes, but I also want to say no, and it all comes out at once. "Yeah, I guess. Maybe. It doesn't matter. She doesn't want anything to do with me."

"Forget about that," Audrey says. "Figure out if you want to get back with her. The important question is whether it's the right thing for you. If it is, make her a list."

"A list?"

"Sure." Audrey crosses her legs. A blue flip-flop dangles from her toes. "Make a list of all the reasons you love her."

"Yeah," Dimitri adds. "You can call it 'Seth Baumgartner's Lame-Ass List of Reasons He Loves Veronica.'"

I ignore Dimitri and think on Audrey's suggestion. It's

not the worst idea I've ever heard—Veronica *did* challenge me to list ten things I loved about her. Under pressure, I couldn't put together five. Given a week, I probably could think of a few hundred. Plus, if she read all the reasons at once, maybe she'd understand why I couldn't list just a few. It'd be like looking at a mosaic instead of at all the individual tiles. It would add up to something bigger.

Audrey grabs another catalog and flips through the pages. "Hey, Dimitri, are you the one who folded the corner of this page down?" She spins the catalog to face him. The page is covered with girdles that have built-in padding to make a woman's backside look bigger.

Dimitri studies the catalog. "I thought you could use some help in that area," he says.

"Yeah, I think I'm all set."

"Are there really women who want their asses to look bigger?" I say.

"Big booties are all the rage," Audrey says, gazing at the pages.

"I guess. . . ."

"You guess what?"

"I don't know," I say. "Wouldn't it be weird to hook up with a girl and discover she's wearing a giant pair of elastic underwear with fake ass-cheek implants in them?"

"No different than a guy who stuffs his underwear," Audrey says.

"Guys don't really stuff their underwear, do they?" I say.

"I wouldn't know about that," Audrey says.

"Women are a wily bunch," Dimitri says. "The ass girdle helps them create an illusion. Like makeup and high heels help them create an illusion. Guys, on the other hand, we're much more straightforward. What you see is what you get." He grabs his belly and jiggles it. "Chub and all."

"Charming," Audrey says.

Dimitri clears his lap of catalogs. "Let's go grab a Rosie O'Donnell burger at Poindexter's. This caveman is freakin' hungry." Dimitri turns to Audrey. "You want to tag along?"

"It's only been an hour since you ate lunch over there," she says.

"What's your point?"

"I'll never figure you out, big brother. Anyhow, thanks but no thanks. Kevin is picking me up in a few minutes."

"Who's Kevin?" I ask.

Just then a horn honks in the driveway. I glance out the window to see a bright yellow Wrangler idling in front. The top is down, and a blue-and-green surfboard sticks out of the backseat. A skinny guy gets out and pushes a mop of brown hair from his face. He's holding a bouquet of dandelions.

Audrey springs up.

Dimitri looks out over my shoulder. "Kevin is some guy Audrey is dating to piss off my dad."

"Any guy I date would piss Dad off. Anyhow, Kevin is a good guy."

"Where you going?" Dimitri asks her.

Audrey snaps a pale green rubber wristband that's

around her wrist. "Some protest down at the capitol building. Something about preserving the area's pine bush."

Dimitri laughs. "You said *bush*."

I look out the window again. Kevin sees me and tentatively lifts a hand to wave. "What's with the surfboard?" I ask Audrey.

"Kevin says you never know when you might want to catch a wave."

"Has anyone told him we're a hundred and fifty miles from the nearest ocean?" Dimitri says.

"I think it's cute," Audrey says.

Dimitri turns to me. "Let's go, Seth. My treat."

I glance at the time on my cell. Correction: my mom's cell. Shoot. I've got to get this thing back on the charger before she notices it's missing or she'll tear apart the kitchen tile by tile.

"No can do," I say. "My mom needs me to help her with something."

"What's your mom need help with in the middle of a weekday afternoon?" Dimitri asks.

"You have no idea."

CHAPTER NINE

The instant I walk in the front door, my mother calls to me. "Have I got a surprise for you!"

I bound into the kitchen to see her holding what looks like a deformed potato with bulging eyes and big, hairy ears.

"Isn't he precious?" she practically squeals.

The tiny thing wiggles its legs and grunts.

"You got a bald hamster?"

"It's a dog! Isn't he the cutest little guy?"

I jiggle the jewel-encrusted collar that falls over one of his tiny shoulders. "I didn't realize dogs came this small. Or that you'd be getting one so soon."

"Well, Donna down at the club—you know, Donna Teal, the woman in the business office? She told me she knew a reputable breeder, and it just so happened that he had a litter ready to go. Chihuahuas." She holds the dog to her nose and breathes deep. "He's even got that new puppy smell."

Mom holds the dog out, but I politely decline. I'm not putting my nose near something that probably just licked its own butt. The puppy narrows its bugged-out eyes at me and growls.

"Does he have a name?" I ask.

"I'm going to let your father do the honors," she says. "It'll help him warm up to the little rascal." She tucks the puppy under one arm as though he's a football and starts searching around the counter.

"Have you seen my cell phone?" she asks.

I pretend not to hear her to buy myself a few seconds. I feel for her phone in the front pocket of my shorts and realize I can't give it back. Not yet, anyway. My own phone is still wedged between my father's car seats and forwarding calls to hers.

"I said, do you know where my phone is?" she asks again. "It was on the charger when I went out this morning."

"I haven't seen it."

Mom starts digging through the basket where she keeps her old magazines and catalogs.

"Did you look in your purse?" I ask her.

"Already checked." She snatches the cordless phone off the wall cradle. "If it's anyplace within earshot, I'll find it." She begins keying in her own number. "Is my number nine-three-four-five or nine-three-five-four? I always forget."

"No idea," I say. "I've got you on speed dial. Umm . . ."

If I don't shut her phone down in time, I'm totally busted. I plunge my hand into my pocket and scramble to find the power button with my thumb.

"I think it's nine-three-five-four," she says.

Thank God for baggy pockets in cargo shorts. I flip open her cell. My fingers play across the buttons. Her key pad is a little different than mine, so I'm not really familiar with it. It's a larger button off to the right. I depress the largest bump I can find and hold it in. The phone plays a little tune as it powers down.

Mom perks up. "Did you hear that?"

I ignore her and make my way to the refrigerator. "You want an Arnold Palmer?"

"That'd be great." She goes back to digging through the junk baskets lined up on the counter near her charger.

Crisis averted.

I grab the lemonade and iced tea pitchers from the fridge and place them on the counter. I get two tall glasses and fill them with ice. The four secrets to a perfect Arnold Palmer are to (1) mix it fresh, (2) add a little more iced tea than lemonade, (3) shake it into oblivion, and (4) pour it over tons of ice. I take the stainless steel shaker from the liquor cabinet and press it into the ice maker. The refrigerator hums and lets a few cubes drop.

My mother lowers the dog to the floor. He begins sniffing around the cereal cabinet. He must like Lucky Charms as much as I do. Maybe we'll get along after all. Mom slides into one of the barstools at the center island. She stares out the sliding glass door. "Hot one out there today, huh?"

"Sure is."

I pour the iced tea and lemonade and jam the cap onto the shaker. When I begin to shake, the steel gets chilly and begins to sweat. I pop off the top and pour the two drinks.

"Dimitri and I were down at Poindexter's," I say, "but it's too hot. I figured I'd come home and work on my podcasting."

"How's that shaping up?"

"Going okay, I guess."

"You mind if I take a listen one of these days?"

I sip my drink. "I'm still working out the kinks," I say. "Soon, though. I promise."

"Whenever you're ready. I do have the—"

"Number one rated show in the Capital District," I say. "I know."

My mother slouches in her stool. "Any thoughts on a job? It'll be the first thing your dad asks when he gets home."

"You mean the first thing he asks after he calms down about you getting a dog?"

"Oh, come on, Seth. How can you not love that little snookums? Within a week, your dad will be head over heels for him." She watches the puppy stumble around near the sliding glass door. "I asked at the studio—you know, about a summer job—but they only have unpaid internships left."

"I'm thinking about working at the club," I say.

Mom smiles. "I always thought you should work down

there. You love golf. It's a perfect match." She slides her glass in front of herself. "That's all you used to talk about. Begging for this club or that. Wanting some special ball because you read an article that said it would improve your drive or give you better spin."

I take a sip of my drink. "So what's been up with Dad lately?"

She looks puzzled. "What do you mean?"

"I don't know." I slide into the barstool next to her. "He's been riding me harder than he usually does."

My mother wraps her hands around her glass like she's trying to absorb every bit of cold she can. "He's under a lot of stress lately. There's a lot going on."

More than you know is what I want to say, but all that comes out is "What kind of stuff?"

She gets a faraway look, and her lips press together like there's no way lemonade or iced tea should even think about getting past. She brushes her fingertips across the countertop. "It seems so long ago your father and I picked out these tiles. I remember it like it was yesterday." Her hand lingers over one with a crude design of a cobalt blue, yellow, and orange flower on it. "We brought home a few dozen—all the hand-painted ones—from our honeymoon. Mexico. Cabo San Lucas." She smiles, and I can tell her mind is someplace else. I've heard the story a hundred times, but I let her go on. "Your father was so proud when he talked the merchant down from six dollars a tile to four. It took so long to find other tiles that came close to matching. It's not perfect, but it's close enough."

It's a nice story, but I can't help but wonder who's going to get the hand-painted tiles in the divorce. And then I wonder what Dad's recent stress has to do with buying these tiles, something that happened twenty years ago.

"Hey, Mom," I say. "Is getting married all it's cracked up to be?"

My question jars her from her waltz down memory lane. "What?" Her eyes leave the tiles and lock onto mine. "Why do you ask?"

"I don't know. I was just wondering. Everyone is brought up to believe getting married is the goal—getting married and having kids. But all the jokes—everything you see on television, all the sitcoms—are about how being married totally sucks."

"That's just television, sweetie."

"But they wouldn't make all those jokes if something about it wasn't true. I'm sure you and Dad love each other and everything—"

"Of course we love each other."

"I shouldn't have brought it up," I say.

Mom straightens the coffeemaker so the rubber feet are perfectly aligned with the edge of the tiles. "Your father has got a lot on his plate right now." Her eyes look through me. "He's preoccupied. When he gets preoccupied, he takes it out on everyone around him. It's just the way he is."

It's not often my mother and I have a conversation like this, but somehow it feels like a door has swung open and I can say anything right now. I push again. "Do you like being married?"

"Of course I do. If I wasn't married, I'd never have had you."

"No, I mean aside from me. If I wasn't in the picture."

"But you are in the picture." She reaches across and touches my arm. "I can't separate you from it."

"Well, suppose I'd be in the picture either way."

My mother pulls her arm back as if my suggesting life without my father burned her. Her elbow knocks into her glass, and it topples over. The glass lands heavy and shatters against the countertop. The Arnold Palmer cascades over the edge to the hardwood floor. The new, unnamed dog waddles over and begins lapping at it.

I hop up. "I'll get a towel."

My mother leaps from her stool. "No, I've got it." She scoops up the dog and hands him to me. "Put him in his crate, would you? It's in the laundry room. Then go on downstairs. Get to work on your podcasting. Make your mother proud." She surveys the spill. "I've got this."

I feel the door of our conversation—the one that was wide-open just a second ago—closing. I grab the roll of paper towels sitting next to the sink. "No, let me help you."

My mom snatches the roll from me. "I've got it," she says, this time more firmly. "I'm such a butterfingers."

"You sure?"

"I'm sure. Go on downstairs, baby. Please."

Slam.

Door closed.

Conversation over.

I look at the dog curled up in my hand. His fat puppy belly is smooth and warm. I move forward again to help her but realize she doesn't want me around.

Sweat trickles in a single line down the small of my back. My mother says she can't imagine her life without my father; I wonder if she'll be saying the same thing six months from now when it's just me, her, and this grunting, stumbling, pathetic dog.

EXCERPT FROM THE LOVE MANIFESTO ▶▶▮

Intro Music: "Area Codes" by Ludacris

Hey there, I'd like to welcome you to the second episode of The Love Manifesto. *The second episode ever. Someday, when I have my own syndicated show—you know, with big advertisers and everything—you can say you were here when it all began. You watched the tiny acorn grow into a mighty oak.*

Right . . .

That last song was "Area Codes" by Ludacris. It's about the women he's got all over the country—in all different area codes. And an excellent song to open up the topic for today.

But first I want to talk about something else. Earlier today, someone asked me to list all the reasons why I loved my ex. That got me thinking. And since I like a challenge,

I'm going to share the list with you, my loyal listeners. Don't you feel lucky? Let's see . . . the first reason I love my ex is because she always leveled with me, good news or bad. Sure, it blew up in my face when she dumped me, but she'd been straight with me before that.

Reason number two is the way her face lights up when she gets her McDonald's French fries. Of course, I just got fired from a French fry place, so I'm still a little fragile. But, honestly, is there anything more perfect than that little bit of fried sunshine?

Now before I bore everyone with more stories about my girlfriend—sorry, my ex-girlfriend—I'm going to talk about another subject that is cutting me deep. And, yes, it's all tied into this topic of love. The topic is parents. You might be wondering what parents have to do with the song "Area Codes" by Ludacris. Just hang in there.

Thinking about my parents and their relationship skeeves me out. Thinking about them having sex totally skeeves me out. I mean, can anyone out there even look at their parents kissing? I think we're hardwired to be disgusted by that. But I'm getting way off topic here.

At first I wasn't going to mention this one on the air, but I've decided to keep it real here on The Love Manifesto. And there's no way I can keep it real without bringing this up.

I saw something the other day that freaked me out. No, it wasn't my parents kissing. No, it wasn't finding condoms in my father's nightstand. No, it wasn't my folks hooking up on the kitchen counter—that was when I was five. God, that was disgusting. What I saw the other day totally blows all that stuff out of the water.

It was much worse.

If you want a hint, just listen to the song I just finished playing.

But if you want to hear all the gory details, you'll have to stay tuned. . . .

<Sound effect: dramatic organ music>

All I can say is if my dad is so unhappy with my mom, why wouldn't he just tell her he wanted a divorce? Why wouldn't he suggest they go to counseling to try to work things out? I mean, he must've been head over heels for her once, otherwise they would never have gotten married, right?

Well, before I reveal too much too soon, I'll let you guys listen to another tune. And when we return I'll share some feedback I got from a listener about what "too comfortable" means and maybe list a few more reasons I love my ex. This one is called "Last Time" by Secondhand Serenade. . . .

Outro Music: "Last Time" by Secondhand Serenade

CHAPTER TEN ▶▶▮

The two-story brick buildings of the Schuyler Village condominium complex sit on the hill behind the hospital. The complex isn't far from Dimitri's house and is nothing like the high-end condos they just built down the road. The place is bordered on two sides by a chain-link fence and on another by the highway. We trawl around until we find the Acura parked next to a row of blue Dumpsters. I pull into a space and stare at my father's girlfriend's car. It seems to be in pretty good shape for an '01, with only a few small scratches on the left rear bumper and a hairline crack in the taillight on the same side. Peeling tribal decals stretch along the side from the front wheel well. The moon roof is open, and the windows are down. A colorful CD hangs from the rearview mirror. The disc turns in the breeze and catches the sun with each rotation.

"I still don't understand why you want to test-drive a

pimped-out Integra." Dimitri pats the dashboard. "The Red Scare here is running just fine."

"Camrys are granny cars," I say. "I want something that makes a statement."

"Well, that thing certainly makes a statement," Dimitri says. "Unfortunately, that statement happens to be 'Hey, everyone, look at me. I'm a guido!'"

"Racist much?"

"My mom's grandfather was off-the-boat Sicilian. I'm one-eighth Italian. That makes it self-deprecating humor, not racism." Dimitri fidgets in his seat. "So, what are you going to do with the Camry when you buy that Acura?"

"Who's saying I'm going to buy it?"

"Well, *if* you buy it."

"I guess I'd sell the Camry. Actually, I would have to sell it."

"You should cut me a wicked deal, Seth. Most of the fries between the seats are mine anyway. That gives me partial ownership. I'd just be buying out my equity." Dimitri rolls down his window and rests his elbow in the sun.

"Shut that," I say. "You're going to let out all the air-conditioning."

"There's no air in here to start with. How do you condition something that's not present? What time did you say you were going to meet this lady?"

"One o'clock."

"We're only fifteen minutes early," he says. "Let's knock on her door. The car's here. She's got to be home."

Last night I did a reverse lookup on her phone number

to find out her name. It's Luz Rivera. *What kind of name is Luz anyway? How do you pronounce it? Is it "Luhz" like* lug nut? *"Looz" like* loose?

The number 1103 is painted in faded yellow at the foot of the Acura's parking space. I look for the apartment numbers on the brick buildings and locate hers. The curtains are closed on the windows of all four units, and there is no sign of movement inside.

"Come on," Dimitri says. "Let's go."

"Nah," I say. "I'd rather wait until one. No surprises, you know?"

"Suit yourself, but I'm heading down the hill for a swim. That pool we passed on the way in looked sweet."

"Knock yourself out," I say. "Most of these condo complexes have pool memberships, though. You might get checked on your way in."

"What do you know about condo pool memberships?"

"My uncle up in Halfmoon lives in a place like this. He bitches about them raising the fees all the time. You have to show a badge and stuff."

"We'll see about that." Dimitri flings open the door and heads down the hill, his flip-flops still *thwap, thwap, thwap*ping long after he makes the turn around a row of tall bushes. I press the button and close Dimitri's window. I need something to settle me down, so I crank my tunes. As usual, "Dueling Banjos" comes on. It pumps through my speakers so loud, I'm afraid I'll awaken President Chester A. Arthur's corpse down at the Albany Rural Cemetery. I fumble with the dial to jump to the next song.

Before I have a chance, my cell phone vibrates in my pocket. I yank it out. It's Veronica. She's called a few times today but hasn't left a message. It's funny that I was the one who wanted to keep in touch, and now she's the one calling all the time. I snap the phone shut and toss it on the passenger seat. If it's important, she can leave a message.

A glint of light catches my eye. At first, I think it's the CD spinning on the Integra's rearview, but it's coming from higher up. The door to building 1103 swings open, and the Applebee's woman—Luz Rivera—walks out with a towel over her shoulder. Her hair is pulled back in a ponytail. She sticks a pink Post-it note on the window of her door and lets her tanned legs carry her down the concrete steps.

She turns away from her car.

Toward the pool.

Toward me.

I slouch lower in my seat and hope it's enough to hide me. I know it's not. I stay still and hope the woman walks by. I stare at her through the corner of my sunglasses.

She is wearing black low-heeled sandals. Her toenails are painted ruby red.

She looks at me and stops.

My breath catches somewhere between my lungs and the back of my throat.

"Is that 'Dueling Banjos'?" she says through my closed window.

I nod. My hand scrambles for the Pause button as I stare at her. The straps of a baby blue bikini peek out from under her tank. I knock the iPod to the floor and lean forward to grab it. I fumble with the buttons and finally just yank out the cord. I must look like a total idiot. I sure feel like one.

"I haven't heard that song in years," she says. "What're you, some kind of redneck or something?"

I roll down my window because it's the polite thing to do, but all I want is to hit the gas and get out of there. "Nah. It's my friend's mp3 player," I lie. "I'm just screwing around with it."

"Are you the kid coming to look at my car this afternoon?"

"Not me," I say. *Damn! I chickened out!*

"At four grand it's a steal. I'd love to keep her, but . . ."

I want to let her finish, but her pause goes on so long that it starts getting even more uncomfortable than it already is. "I'm just waiting for a friend," I say.

"The 'Dueling Banjos' friend?"

I force a smile. "That's the guy."

"Well, if you see someone poking around my car, tell him to come find me at the pool," she says. "I've got to unwind a little."

"Will do."

The woman smiles and walks on, her shoes *click, click, click*ing down the hill and around the row of hedges.

I drop the Camry into gear and hang a U-turn. I roll down the hill, past the woman, and around the bend. I pull up to the pool. It's surrounded by a chain-link fence and a dozen or so sunbathers. Dimitri is sitting on a recliner next to the lifeguard, who is perched on the edge of a wooden bench. Her blond ponytail pokes through the hole in the back of her baseball cap. Dimitri is a sucker for the whole ponytail–baseball cap thing.

I honk the horn twice.

Dimitri looks up and waves me over.

I honk again and motion him toward me.

Dimitri gives me the finger.

I honk again, this time longer. A few of the sunbathers turn their heads.

Dimitri gets up and makes a show of walking through the gate to my car. He opens the passenger door. "What the hell?" he says. "Come hang out for a few minutes. Jill over there is pretty cool."

"We've got to go." I glace in the rearview mirror. Luz Rivera is just rounding the building at the top of the hill.

"What's the matter? You look like you just saw a gorgon."

I don't have time to argue that if I just saw a gorgon I would have been turned to stone and entirely unable to drive my car. "I'm fine," I say. "We just have to get out of here."

"It's a no-go on the car?"

"Not a good fit," I say.

"Give me your pen."

I hand Dimitri the leaky felt tip I keep in my armrest. He trots back to the pool and talks to the girl some more. He jots something on her hand. Then he jots something on his own.

My eyes shift to my side-view mirror. It states clearly on the mirror, "Objects Are Closer Than They Appear," and Luz Rivera looks damn close. Too close. I slouch down again. She walks by my car without a glance and heads toward the pool. Dimitri holds the gate open for her and takes a good long look at her from behind as she struts past. He's clearly not looking at her face because he shows no sign that he recognizes Luz from the flower shop yesterday.

"I thought the pool at the golf club cornered the market on all the grade-A hotties, but that place rocks." Dimitri slides into my car. A line of sweat darkens his Polo shirt from his chest to his belly. "Did you see that lifeguard?" he says. "Smokin'. We swapped numbers. I bet she's got a hot friend for you, too. You know how it is; hotties travel in packs."

"I already told you, Dimitri; I'm off the market." My words come out sounding terse. I pull away from the curb and head to the end of the driveway. My tires chirp as we head onto the main road.

"Who gave cleats to that rhino?" Dimitri says.

"What rhino?"

"The one doing a tap dance on your nuts," he says. "What's with the attitude?"

"I wanted to leave," I say. "You mooch rides off me all the time. The least you can do is move your ass when I want to take off."

"Jesus," Dimitri says. "You got the runs or something?"

I don't answer.

"Come on," he says. "You can tell me. Was it that Rosie O'Donnell burger you had at Poindexter's yesterday? That

94

thing always gets my intestines doing the Charleston."

"Sometimes I think you're speaking another language," I say.

"The Charleston. You know. That dance from the twenties the flappers used to do." He grabs his knees and starts wiggling them back and forth.

Dimitri goes on to regale me with stories of his bowel habits and what he knows about the Charleston. I crank up my music. It's not hard to drown him out, but no matter how loud the music gets, I can still hear that woman's voice in my head:

I've got to unwind. I've got to unwind. I've got to unwind.

Applebee's. The flower shop. Who knows where else. Hasn't she been doing enough unwinding with my dad?

EXCERPT FROM THE LOVE MANIFESTO ▶▶|

Welcome back to The Love Manifesto, *a podcast where we examine what love is, why love is, and why we are stupid enough to keep going back for more. That last song was "Gold Digger" by Kanye West, and it has tons to do with what we've been talking about today. But first, GrapeApe97 tagged me in a meme. He wants me to list twenty-five things that people might not otherwise know about me. That's a tough one to do while I'm trying to hide my superspy identity, but I'll list a few.*

The first is that I love Sam Raimi movies. Most people know him for his work on the Spider-Man movies, but I think his best work was the Evil Dead trilogy. That was a really campy series of horror movies from the eighties and nineties. I have all the DVDs and have practically worn them out.

Second, when I was a kid, I wanted a pet monkey. Actually, I wanted a monkey that wore a Superman costume. Of course, he'd have to have monkey diapers under there, but there are few things cuter than a monkey in a Superman costume. And, of course, a tuxedo for formal affairs.

Another thing is that I'm good at golf, but I don't love it. I grew up with a golf club in my hands, and as a kid I played a lot. I think my father had visions of me being the next Tiger Woods. But being good at something and loving it are totally different things. And I do not love golf.

Another thing about me is that I'm still off the market. I mean, sure, I'm single, no girlfriend, all that; but if I started dating right now, I'd be a total terror. I'm just not ready. I've got a few things to sort out first.

So, sorry, GrapeApe97, that's as much as I'm going to share, at least for now.

Continuing with the ex list . . . I think we're on number nineteen, which is that no matter how hard I tried, I couldn't keep anything from her. I'm not a bad liar, but somehow she could see right through me. And number twenty: She had the cutest hum when she would do her Spanish homework. Okay, I know! I'm going to get a lot of crap from you guys out there on how girly I'm sounding right now. But it's true.

Now on to other news.

New stuff.

I saw her. I actually spoke to her. I spoke to the woman who is sleeping with my father. I was pretty sneaky about it. She doesn't suspect a thing. At least, I don't think she does. I mean, why should she, right?

Now that I know where this woman lives, I can officially begin surveillance. Does anyone have any surveillance advice? Aside from lots of high-octane coffee and glazed donuts, I'm not sure what a cop actually does on a stakeout.

All right, let's get to some music. My father roped me into a late-afternoon round of golf, so I've got to cut this show, post it, and get down there. Somebody please remind me to keep my mouth shut. The last thing I need is to drop a hint to my father that I suspect anything.

This next song is called "Dueling Banjos." Sure, it's an old one. Sure, it's a weird one. I'll explain the importance of it when we come back.

Intro Music: "Dueling Banjos" by Eric Weissberg

CHAPTER ELEVEN ▶▶▌

"Okay, I'll admit it," my father says as we walk up to the tee box on the twelfth hole. "The little bastard is growing on me."

Mr. Peepers. My father named the puppy Mr. Peepers. Supposedly, it's a character from an old *Saturday Night Live* episode, some monkey man or something. My dad freaked out when he came home and discovered a dog peeing on papers in the laundry room, but it only took a few hours for him to warm up to the fuzzy little guy. I warmed up to him too when he started humping the tennis ball I put in his crate. His paws were barely touching the ground, but when I went in there this morning, he was showing that ball who's boss.

"I just wish he'd stop scratching up the hardwood," my dad says.

"He's only eight weeks old. I'm sure he'll stop at some point."

"He'd better. Otherwise he'll be stripping, sanding, and

refinishing the floors." The thought of a Chihuahua running a rotating sander is funny, but I don't crack a smile.

My father tees up his ball.

There was no avoiding him when it came to today's round of golf. My father stalked into the basement as I was answering a few comments from the podcast. I got more than fifty downloads just today. It's a good thing he didn't have a chance to read what I was typing. With my allowance—almost a full week's worth of gas money—in his hand, how was I supposed to say no to a late-afternoon round? Anyhow, I was too panicked to do anything but pop on the screen saver and tell him I'll grab my cap.

Every time I look at him, thoughts of Luz Rivera flood into my mind. I try to keep focused, to let golf consume me. But the game never pulls me away from real life like it seems to do for most guys who play.

Swack!

My father's swing is so regular, so mechanical, that a team of MIT geniuses would have trouble building a robot nearly as consistent. He turns at the hips, keeps his elbow in and his head down. If I didn't see his face, I wouldn't be able to distinguish between him and a pro golfer. His ball rockets from the tee faster than the speed of the golf club should allow. It soars over the reeds, over the small patch of fairway, and lands lightly on the left side of the green. Although I've seen plenty of golfers stick it right next to the pin on this hole, it's a respectable shot for 170 yards—a shot I'd be stoked about.

"I yanked it." He thumps his tee into the ground with

the head of his five-iron like he's driving a railroad spike into concrete.

"It was a good shot," I say.

"It's on the upper tier, a two-putt at best."

"At least it's on the green."

I tee up my ball and take a few practice strokes. I swing. My shot flies higher than I wanted. It's a towering shot that might have been all right if the wind wasn't cutting across the tops of the trees. My ball begins to drift.

"Motherf—"

"Watch your mouth," my father warns.

It's hard to watch your mouth when you're busy watching your ball sail away and plummet into a sand trap with a distant *thump*.

There are so many variables in golf: wind, slope of the ground, length of grass, thickness of grass, height of the landing surface relative to the hitting surface, and so on. And that's just the external variables. You also have to think about the internal stuff: type of grip, where the ball sits in your stance, the width of your stance, the angle of your downswing, and all sorts of other crap.

And I always seem to forget a few dozen of them.

"Teed it up too high," my father says.

"Guess so."

"Want your mulligan?"

"Nah, I never use my do-over on a par three."

"Suit yourself," he says. "That's a deep trap. I got stuck down there once and . . ." I let him go on with his story, but I completely tune him out.

One of the things I like about golf is that there's so much to concentrate on that there's never a lot of pressure to talk about anything beyond the game. Most of the time you're thinking about your last shot or your next one. Between holes, you talk about your clubs, the weather, the time you hit an eagle at some tournament someplace. Whatever. But there's never any pressure to talk about personal stuff. At least it's been like that for the first four holes. Now it all comes to a screeching halt.

"So what's been bothering you?" my father asks.

I slide my club into my bag and take a seat behind the wheel of the golf cart. "I hit into the stupid trap."

"No, I mean over the past week or so. You've seemed real bent out of shape. Your mother and I, we're sort of concerned."

If I were a girl, I'd be able to blame it on cramps and that would shut him up. What do guys get to blame things on? "I've just been down in the dumps is all."

"Look, Seth, I had my fair share of girlfriends. I know what you're going through. This sort of thing will pass. You just have to buck up."

"Buck up? Sounds like something from a cowboy movie."

"You know, take a deep breath. Move on. You need to find another girl and get back in the game."

Just what I need, a string of clichés. "You sound like Dimitri."

"Well, maybe your friend isn't as dumb as I thought."

I'm glad Dimitri wasn't around to hear my father say

102

that. He'd gloat about that back-handed compliment for weeks.

I stomp on the pedal. The golf cart whips forward, and I steer us down the path that runs along the right side of the hole. I hook around the sand trap to the gravel walkway behind the green. "It's different nowadays, Dad. Dating is different."

"How is it different?"

"This isn't the cheeseball seventies." I step from the cart and pull my sand wedge from my bag.

"What's that supposed to mean?"

"This isn't the age of polyester shirts with wide lapels. This isn't the age of gold medallions and hairy chests. And this sure isn't the age of partner-swapping free love."

I glance at my father to see if he has any sort of reaction, but he just laughs. "I was born in nineteen sixty-nine," he says. "I wasn't a teenager until the eighties."

"Well, this isn't the age of acid-wash jeans, mullets, and Michael Jackson gloves, either." I grab my club and tramp down into the sand pit. It's a deep one. My ball is sunk so low in the sand, it looks like a fried egg.

"You watch too many movies," he says. "Anyway, brooding about it isn't going to help any."

Brooding. Isn't that what Veronica said I did?

"You need to get out and do something to distract yourself," he goes on. "Your grandfather would have put a shovel in my hand and sent me out back to dig a ditch."

"That's weird."

"He used to think sweat was the best way to work

off any kind of emotion. Told me it was cheaper than any shrink."

I point at the trap with my sand wedge, at my ball lying there buried past its equator. "Looks like I'll be digging a ditch soon enough."

My father lets me assess the situation. It's not good. The green sits about eight feet above me. To make matters worse, my ball is on the back slope of the trap, which will give my shot a lower trajectory. I should have taken my mulligan.

I know it's hopeless, but I swing.

Hard.

White powdery sand poofs into the air. It rains down on the upslope of the trap and onto the fringe of the green. I look for my ball. It's sitting in the trench I've just dug with my club.

This time, my father doesn't say a word about the string of nasty words that spews from my mouth.

"Take another stroke," he says. "Hit behind the ball."

I line up again, wiggle my feet into the sand, and swing. My club comes down and pops the ball into the air. I scramble up the hill to see where it rolls. I get there just in time to see it take a hard turn to the left, away from the hole.

Shoot, I forgot to account for the slope of the green.

I'm sitting three strokes with no less than a forty-foot putt.

"Good up," my father says. He tosses me my putter and drives the cart around to the other side of the green.

He's farther away, so it's his shot.

"I guess things are different today," he says. He lines up as I pull the flag and toss it to the side. "When I was your age, we used to date. We didn't pair off and stay with the same girl for months on end. Maybe some guys did." He draws back his putter and swings. His ball rolls toward the high side of the green, reaches the ridge, and trickles down to the lower tier. It picks up speed and veers to the right, coming to a stop within three feet of the hole. It's an amazing shot, considering where he started.

"Nice one," I say.

"Don't kids casually date anymore?" he asks.

I want to tell him kids do that all the time, but Veronica and I were different. We were a couple. I also want to point out that clearly nothing has changed with *him* since his high-school days—that he's still dating as often as ever—but I keep my mouth shut on that one, too.

"I guess I'm more monogamous," I say.

"Nice ten-dollar word."

"It's like cars," I go on. "Why keep test-driving them? If you know you like BMWs, then why would you go and try out an Acura Integra?" The words come out of my mouth before I have a chance to put them through any sort of filter. I don't know why I say it. I just do.

I glance at my father from behind my sunglasses. He makes no indication that he picked up on my dig. He walks to his ball, marks it, and steps away from the hole.

"Want me to tend the flag?" he asks.

"No, thanks." I stand over my ball and swing. My ball

starts out on a path that would take it nearly five feet to the left of the hole, but the slope of the green brings it in a gentle rightward arc. Like it's traveling on a steel track, the ball rolls to the edge of the cup and drops in without slowing. Dead center.

I just knocked in a forty-footer.

Maybe longer.

My hands shoot into the air like Rocky Balboa's. It might be the longest putt I've ever sunk, and the only person who was here to see it was my no-good cheating father.

That's when Audrey bolts from the woods. Her hands pump in the air just like mine, and she rushes onto the green like it's the final seconds of a college bowl game rather than a quiet golf twosome.

I watch Audrey spin around on the green and jump into the air. I want to celebrate with her—to spin around and jump into the air, too—but no matter how happy Audrey seems and no matter how happy I feel, I can't. All I can do is run through the conversation I just had with my father and wonder how much she overheard.

CHAPTER TWELVE ▶▶|

"You've got to keep that back elbow pinned to your side." I take a swing to show her and launch my ball straight and long.

"My elbow *is* pinned to my side," Audrey insists. It's after the round with my father, just after Audrey's shift, and she and I have decided to hit a bucket or two. I can't figure out how I got talked into it. I hate the golf range. And Audrey's swing is terrible.

I watch her hit a few more. Her elbow keeps coming up like a chicken wing, and every one of her shots slices off to the right.

"Back elbow. Back elbow."

"Shut up," she says. "Maybe I'm trying to hit to the right. You ever think of that?"

"You're full of it." I stand behind her and hold her elbow against her right side to show her how to turn at the hips. "I used to do the exact same thing," I say. "Keep your head down and that elbow tight or you'll be all over the course."

Audrey hits another. It pops straight into the air and lands about ten feet in front of us. "Maybe I like variety."

I press Audrey's elbows against her sides and bend her arms. I turn her palms up and lay her club across her forearms. It's an exercise my golf instructor showed me when I was eleven. "Turn at the hips and keep the club balanced," I say. "Twist back and forth a bunch of times. Get used to how it feels."

She does as I ask, but after a few repetitions the club slides off her arms. "The range is so boring!"

"It's only boring because you don't know the right way to do it." Did I just say that, or was it my father speaking through me?

"So what's your big secret?" she asks.

"Okay, my big secret is that I hate the range, too. I'd rather be out there playing, but if you give yourself goals, it becomes a lot more bearable. Most people just grab their driver and see if they can pound it against the back fence or hit the ball-collection truck."

"I'd love to hit that truck."

"It makes an awesome clanging sound," I say, "but the groundskeeper gets pissed off. Anyhow, if you want to get anything out of the driving range, start with your wedge or nine-iron and hit a few dozen balls, enough to get into a rhythm. Then slowly move to your longer clubs. I go in two-club increments: nine to seven to five to three."

"Then what?"

"Then I grab my wood." Before the words finish coming out, I know what's next.

Audrey chuckles. "You said 'grab my wood.'"

My cheeks heat up. "You're no different than Dimitri."

"Oh, I'm different, all right." She coils back with her iron in her hands and swings. Her ball rockets into the air and lands ninety yards straight out. It bounces another ten and curls around the back of the practice flag.

"Do that again," I say.

Audrey hands me her club. "Do what again?"

A horn honks behind us. A yellow Wrangler with a surfboard in the backseat pulls up, and Kevin hops out. He walks across the practice green to us. He's lanky, with dark floppy hair that covers most of his face. "Hey, what's up, Aud?"

"Hey, Kevin. This is Dimitri's friend Seth."

Kevin pushes his hair from his eyes with one hand and extends the other to shake. It's a limp sort of shake, like I'm squeezing a piece of uncooked chicken. "What's up, man?" he says to me. "Giving my lady a golf lesson?"

"Looks like she's the one schooling me," I say.

"I'll just wait over there," Kevin says, flipping a thumb at one of the benches. "You guys take your time."

"Nah," Audrey says. "I think I've learned everything I need to learn today."

"You sure?" Kevin says. "I don't mind waiting."

"No, it's cool," Audrey says. She starts to trot across the grass toward the Wrangler.

Kevin jerks his chin at me. "Later, dude."

"Later," I say.

As they walk away, Kevin slips his arm around Audrey and she leans into him. I bend down to grab my clubs and hear two car doors slam. Kevin starts his Jeep, and some mellow reggae starts to pulse from the speakers.

"Bye, Seth!" Audrey calls to me. She waves as Kevin pulls away. I lift Audrey's club in the air and use it to wave back. Then I watch the blue-and-green surfboard disappear down the driveway.

CHAPTER THIRTEEN ▶▶

"Aren't you going to eat?" My mother is talking to me over the sounds of the James Cattrall Orchestra. It's the same band the club gets for every big function, and the Fourth of July Dinner Dance Gala is the biggest of the biggies. "Lemon chicken over pierogi. It's your favorite."

I poke my fork at my plate. "I had a late lunch." The truth is that seeing my parents together, laughing and smiling, having a gay old time, makes my digestive system want to work in reverse.

I take a sip of water and glance around the dining room. The dance floor is packed with people strutting around like they have no idea how ridiculous they look in their brass-buttoned jackets and stuffed-beyond-capacity sequined gowns. I wish Dimitri were here. He'd have a blast ripping everyone apart.

I slouch in my seat.

"Something bothering you?" my father asks.

It's been two days since our round of golf, since my BMW/Acura comment, but after we finished on Friday my father and I have hardly spoken a word. We've hardly even crossed paths.

"I'm good," I say. "It's just this jacket. It's pulling tight across my shoulders."

My mother winks at me. "My baby boy is getting so big," she says.

My father points at my chest with his butter knife. The butter square clings to it like it's a refrigerator magnet. "I always said you should have been a halfback."

"Puh-leeze," my mother says. "Golf and tennis, those are the only sports that matter." She nudges my shoulder with her fist. "You can play them until you're ninety."

My dad tries to catch my attention, probably so he can roll his eyes about my mother's comment, but I drop my gaze to my plate. My mom goes on about how golf and tennis are the best sports, and my father goes back to buttering his bread. They smile at each other across the table.

"Hey, I'm sorry for talking about you again on the radio program." It seems like my mother has been making it a nightly feature on her show. Now she's getting calls from listeners to console her, to send me reassuring messages. "I just know how down you are about everything, and telling my listeners about it helps me get it off my chest."

I did not hear the show these past few days, only fielded

the phone calls and emails from all the kids who did. I let her apologize but don't pay attention to her words. Instead, I look out at the dance floor and wonder what it is about the Macarena that gets people to want to stand in a line and do flagless semaphore in the four cardinal directions. It reminds me of schools of fish, each fishy following the ass end of the fishy in front of it. One darts to the left, and they all dart to the left. I read once that there are caterpillars that follow the one in front of it so unconditionally that they'll keep marching until they die. If the band kept on playing, would these people Macarena themselves to death?

"You're not listening to me." My mom's hand slides across the table and squeezes my forearm. "Are you thinking about Veronica?"

"I guess."

"Don't sweat it," my father says. "It was puppy love. Mr. Peepers love. Before you know it, you'll be dating some other girl and you'll forget all about that one."

The hair on the back of my neck bristles. If I followed my dad's philosophy of relationships, I'd have been screwing someone else long before Veronica had the chance to dump me. That or I'd have been digging ditches in the backyard until my parents had a few Olympic-sized swimming pools to show off to the neighbors.

"Mike, that's not what Seth needs to hear," my mom says. "This sort of thing crops up on the radio program all the time. He's going through a difficult period right now. He needs to process his feelings."

113

My dad takes a bite of his roll and moves his attention to the band.

"Seth, my boy!" It's Mr. Haversham, the director of the club. His voice sounds more like a tuba than anything that might come out of a human being. His seersucker jacket barely stretches across his paunch, and his cheeks, part ruddy from the sun and part ruddy from the wine, make his head look like an overinflated party balloon. He extends his hand and I shake it. "So glad to have you join our team," he says. "Have you given any thought to what you want to do around here?"

"I was thinking about the pro shop," I say. "I stay current with all the new gear, and I'm pretty good on the computer." The truth is that aside from working in the restaurant, the pro shop is one of the only air-conditioned positions at the club. It's a sweet gig.

"Sounds great," Mr. Haversham says. "We could use a young gun down there. Old Al, he still thinks knickers and knee-high socks are all the rage. Maybe you can bring him up to speed." Mr. Haversham takes a long sip of wine, and I swear I can see his face turn two shades redder.

"You'll do great over there," my mom says to me. "Maybe you can help me pick out some new clubs. I've been meaning to get a new set."

Mr. Haversham points at me with the rim of his wineglass. "See, you're selling already. Come by Tuesday morning, and we'll get you started."

"Sure thing," I say.

Mr. Haversham walks off, and I can't help but stare.

He's wearing brown-and-white saddle shoes. Inside. It's one thing to wear saddle shoes on the course—it's pretty standard, even nowadays—but to wear them to an evening event? They make him look like an overgrown three-year-old.

"You'll like working here," my father says. "Everyone's really nice."

"I know," I say. But really, I'm just looking forward to working around Dimitri. Even though he'll be outside in the heat and I'll be in the pro shop, it'll kick ass to see him on breaks and after work.

The band gets louder. They must pump up the volume after the main course gets cleared. They start into that "Celebration" song, and people get up from their seats and stampede toward the dance floor.

Audrey clears our dishes. It's the first time I've noticed her.

"Took you long enough," she says. "Your head's been buried in your plate all night."

"You've been to our table already?" I say.

"Four times."

Her hair is braided into two strands that curl over each ear and trail down her back. With her hair out of her face, her eyes are lighter than I remember.

"How's business?" I ask.

"I'm in the weeds tonight," she says, reaching across me to grab the half-empty basket of bread. She smells of fryer oil and laundry detergent. "Chef Rigby recommends the cheesecake. They brought it in special from some cheesecake-making nuns who live in the hills. Apparently, aside from praying, they bake up a storm."

"We'll keep that in mind," my father says, extending his hand. "You seem to know Seth, but I'm not sure we've had the pleasure. Your name tag . . ."

I look at her name tag. In bold block letters it says ROGER.

Roger?

"Oh, this is Audrey," I say. "Dimitri's sister. Remember her?"

"Audrey!" my mother chimes in. "Ohmygod. We haven't seen you in . . . gosh, it's been years."

"Four," Audrey says. "Dimitri and Seth's eighth-grade graduation. We came to your party afterward. I threw up orange soda all over your Persian rug."

"I don't . . . I don't remember that . . ." my mother says.

"Sure you do," my dad cuts in. "You complained about that stain for weeks."

My mother goes rigid in her seat. "Michael, I did not. . . ."

"I'm just kidding." He rubs Mom's shoulder. "So, Audrey, how are things going here at the club for you?"

Audrey hoists her tray onto her shoulder. "It's a good mix of inside and out," she says. "Lots of different things to do and not enough downtime for me to get bored. Anyhow, I'm just glad I'm not in the heat all the time. Dimitri's been sweating his—"

"Head off," I cut in, afraid of what anatomical part

116

she might come out with.

"Yes, he's been sweating his *head* off." Audrey smiles at me. "So, unless you guys are low-carbing it, I'll put you in for three cheesecakes."

"Actually, we *are* low-carbing it," my mother says, "but Mike has been picking at bread all night anyway. After hearing about those nuns, I suppose I could be convinced to hop off the wagon, too."

My father nods. "And coffees all around."

"You're going to love it," Audrey says. "It's peanut butter chocolate." She heads into the kitchen through the swinging double doors, her long brown braids bouncing against the back of her tuxedo shirt.

"She seems nice," my mother says. "She looks nothing like she did three years ago."

"That's for sure," my father adds.

I think back to when I first became friends with Dimitri, when we were in fifth grade and Audrey was in third, how she and her friends used to listen at Dimitri's bedroom door while we talked about the new manga books, video games, and whatever movie was busting box-office records. How once she overheard Dimitri say that he thought Jenna Leominster was cute and that he thought she liked him back because he saw his initials on her notebook. Audrey went skipping through the house chanting about how Dimitri and Jenna were going to get married, and the next thing I knew I was pulling Dimitri off Audrey, holding his arms back so he couldn't swing at her anymore. I felt bad for Audrey back then. She looked so tiny, so thin and delicate.

Things sure have changed. Nowadays, I suspect Audrey could handle herself in a saloon full of undead barbarian pirate ogres.

My mother takes a sip of wine and stands up. She pokes me in the shoulder. "How about a quick dance?" she says. "That is, unless you're too embarrassed to be out there with your mom."

"I'll take a pass," I say.

She turns to my father. "Then why don't you spin me around a few times?" she says. "We never get to dance anymore." My father rolls his eyes—he's not a dancer, either—but he knows he's on the hook. He pulls his napkin from his lap and leads my mom to the dance floor. When they get there, he does this little side-to-side stepping thing with his hands jammed in his pockets. Dimitri danced better when he was doing his lame excuse for the Charleston in the passenger seat of my car.

Before I have a chance to devise an escape plan, my parents are back.

"Hey, Seth," my father says. His voice is ten times more cheery than it should be. "Have you ever tried cognac?"

"Cognac?"

My mother is wringing her hands like she did the time I cracked my forehead open in first grade and had to be strapped to a wooden board so the doctor could get the stitches in. I glance around to try to figure out what the trouble is.

"A couple of the guys and me are going out onto the patio for an after-dinner drink." Dad slaps me on the back and urges me to my feet. "Grandpa Chester gave me my first cognac when I was about your age. I thought it might be fun if we had a little tonight."

"Anyhow, you'll want to get a good spot for the fireworks." My mother glances at her watch. "It's after nine now."

It's weird enough that my parents spent all of five seconds on the dance floor. It's even weirder that my father is offering me booze. But when my mother shows interest in me getting a good spot for fireworks that are going off more than five miles away, I know something must be really wrong.

My eyes dart around even more, scanning for something out of place. My mother moves between me and the dance floor as my father ushers me toward the French doors that lead to the patio.

And then I see her.

Veronica.

It's hard *not* to see her. As she dances, her silver dress shimmers like mercury. She's with some blond guy whose back is to me. She's wearing a smile so wide, I'm surprised it fits on her face. She's doing this shimmy thing and bending forward and back over and over again.

And all of a sudden it feels like one of those scenes in a horror movie—the part when the good guy first sees the monster—where the view both sucks back and gets closer at the same time. Classic Sam Raimi.

My mom sees my face and knows I've seen what she and Dad were trying to protect me from. She steps closer.

"Seth, I'm so sorry."

"She shouldn't have come here," my father says.

"It's okay," I say. "I'm fine with it."

But it's not okay. I'm not fine with it. I stare at Veronica a few seconds longer until my father's tugging gets stronger than my need to run over to my ex-girlfriend—the ex-girlfriend who is dancing at *my* club with some other guy. Veronica shimmies again, and it reminds me of a mating ritual, like a red-assed baboon displaying her ripened fertility to the male baboon.

I let my father pull me toward the patio, all the while staring at Veronica and the guy she's dancing with, all the while staring at the two baboons. The guy turns around and, for a brief second, I get a glimpse of his face. It's that bastard Anders from Applebee's—the guy with the chin like a Thruway plow who was our waiter the day Veronica dumped me. Some part of me knew it all along.

My face ignites, probably redder than Mr. Haversham's.

Veronica glances up. Her gaze locks on mine, and her smile vanishes. She takes a step toward me. I hesitate, too, until I see that she's thought better of coming over. Maybe she can see something in my eyes. Maybe she's afraid of upsetting Anders or of making a scene at the club. She shakes her head, barely shakes it. Then she turns away and goes back to dancing, this time with a little less shimmy than before.

I let my father finish pulling me outside. The heavy night air and the blood pulsing through my neck make my tie feel tight. I undo my top button and yank my collar loose. Music thrums behind me. The smell of cigars washes over me. Someone puts a cognac snifter in my hand, and I take a sip. The brandy burns my lips, sears my throat.

I cough.

Someone laughs.

"That'll put some hair on your chest," one of the men says, clapping a heavy palm on my back. I drain the rest of the cognac, and a few of the sport-jacketed men—Mr. Gilbert, Mr. Tattinger, and some men I don't recognize— give feeble cheers.

"That's Louis the Thirteenth de Rémy Martin," Mr. Tattinger says. "It's the best of the best. Fifteen hundred a bottle. Chad—you know my son, Chad, don't you Seth? He got into Yale this week. Better late than never."

More men laugh.

My father pours me another. "This is it for you," he whispers. "Drink slowly."

I swirl the golden brown fluid in the glass just like the men are doing and gaze through it at the Albany skyline. The first firework of the night—a red, white, and purple burst—illuminates the horizon. It makes the cognac sparkle. The report of the firework is delayed, and it makes the show seem disjoined, incomplete. The James Cattrall Orchestra starts with some patriotic tune, and I hear my father's voice creep in around the edges of the static in my head: "Happy Independence Day," he says.

I hold up my glass but don't say anything in return. Independence isn't something I want to celebrate right now.

Throngs of people start coming outside to watch the

show. I head to the far corner of the patio, where the lights from the party have trouble reaching. I sink into a deck chair at one of the glass tables and put down my snifter.

"You old enough to be drinking that?"

The voice startles me.

It's Audrey. She's sitting at the next table under cloak of darkness. Her feet are propped on the patio railing. The glow of a handheld video game illuminates her face.

"You young enough to be playing that?" I say.

"Touché." She keeps playing whatever she's playing, not looking up once. "You won't be able to see the show from over here, you know."

"Never much liked fireworks," I say.

"Me neither."

We sit in silence, her playing and me drinking. I watch the flashes reflect off low-hanging clouds and listen to club members "Ooh" and "Aah" at the bright sparkly lights.

"So did you start your list?" Audrey asks.

I look over my shoulder to see if Veronica and Anders have come out to watch the show, too. The thought of them together repulses me, sends my stomach flipping into knots. It also makes me want her back more. But something in me doesn't want Audrey to know that.

"What list?" I say.

Audrey pauses her game. Her ROGER name tag catches the light from the patio. "Wow, she hurt you more than I thought."

I want to tell her she's wrong, but denying it would be pointless. I think back on the time Veronica and I spent together, of our first kiss over our chemistry homework, of the first rose I ever gave a girl and how she closed her eyes when she smelled it, how she plucked the petals off one by one and we made out on top of them on her bedroom floor. I think about all the clumsy fumbling around we did in the darkness of my parents' basement and how we would sift through our tangled clothes, careful I didn't put on her pink Abercrombie T-shirt and wear it upstairs by mistake. Then I think about her doing all those things with Anders, and I want to fling my fifteen-hundred-dollar-a-bottle glass of cognac off the patio in the rare chance it might hit Anders's Mercedes or whatever it is he drives.

"Yeah, I started my list." I almost tell her I've already shared thirty-seven of my reasons on *The Love Manifesto*, but, of course, I keep that part to myself.

"How's it going?"

"Okay, I guess." I take another sip of the cognac, let it burn my throat as it slides down. I place the glass on the table and push it away. "Why do you care?"

She considers my question. "I just think it's something you need to do. I don't know her personally, but from what I've heard she's a bitch."

Words rise to defend Veronica, but I let Audrey go on. "And that Anders guy. His family joined the club a month or two ago, but I can already tell they're a bunch of tools. They're always sending stuff back to the kitchen, complaining about this and that, wanting items taken off the bill. If you ask me—"

"Which I didn't."

Audrey smiles. "Which you didn't. But if you ask me, the two of them deserve each other. Him ending up as drunk as his father, staggering around, unable to sign his own bar tab. She'll drive him home and sadly laugh it off when he can't remember coming home with red wine spilled on his Armani jacket and his pants down around his ankles."

"And you know this because . . ."

"Because I'm psychic."

I grab the armrests of my chair and angle my seat toward her. "Because you're psychic?" It comes out more as a challenge than a question.

"Well, not really," she says. "It's just that Veronica is not the girl for you. You need to get her out of your system is all."

"So, what, am I like a wounded bird you scooped into a shoe box? Are you going to nurse me back to health?"

"Who says I scooped you anywhere?"

A few more fireworks go off, the little white ones that make big pops.

"So, how's your friend Kevin?"

Audrey keeps her eyes locked on the horizon. "He's good. He gave me a dozen roses today."

"Hey, you must be doing something right," I say.

"Thanks, Seth. . . ."

"For what?"

"For making me feel like a hooker, like I need to perform a certain way to procure gifts."

"I didn't mean—"

"I'm kidding." Audrey looks up at me. "Plus, I do *everything* right."

Audrey laughs as the grand finale of the fireworks begins. The "Oohs" and "Aahs" get louder. "What's with the name tag?" I manage to say.

She slides my glass in front of her and expertly swirls the liquid. She takes a sip, and her eyebrows lift as though she appreciates fine cognac, as though it doesn't taste like liquid hell. "It says in the employee handbook that we have to wear a name tag, but it doesn't specify it has to be our correct name. I like the sound of Roger. It's rugged, a little nerdy, and definitely refined."

"If there's something you're not, it's refined," I say. "You came from the same womb as Dimitri."

"Don't remind me." Audrey leans on the arm of my chair and flips open her Nintendo DS again. It's the hot pink one. "At least he came out a few years before I did," she adds. "He was eleven pounds when he was born. Probably made things easier on my soft baby skull."

"That's true," I say. "I'll bet you could have come out like this. . . ." I stretch my arms wide and start flapping them like bird wings.

Audrey laughs, her eyes still fixed on her video game. Her teeth sparkle. Whose teeth sparkle in the light of a Nintendo DS? I want to touch her arm, just as a friendly thing, but I don't want her to get the wrong idea. I mean, she's Dimitri's little sister. She's the pesky girl who stole the reflectors off my bike so she could put them on her own. I try to get a glimpse of anything Dimitri-ish about her. She is long, slender. Very *not* Dimitri.

Her eyes meet mine. "Too bad my brother's been a pain in the ass ever since."

I raise the glass of brandy. "You ain't kidding."

EXCERPT FROM THE LOVE MANIFESTO ▶▶|

Intro Music: "The Bad Touch" by Bloodhound Gang

Welcome back to The Love Manifesto, *a podcast where we examine what love is, why love is, and why we're stupid enough to keep going back for more. That last song is called "The Bad Touch" by Bloodhound Gang. You might be wondering why I played that one, and the answer is simple. Today we're going to be talking about mating rituals.*

Now, I hear you saying, "Mating rituals? Stop talking crazy." You're probably saying that going out with a girl—casual dating and all that—has nothing to do with mating rituals. But that's where you're wrong. Dating is a mating ritual. Push-up bras, high heels, and bright red toenails are mating rituals. That shimmy thing girls do with their boobs when they dance is a mating ritual. Blasting music in your car as you cruise up and down Central Avenue on twenty-four-inch chromed-out spinners is a mating ritual. We do those things to get the attention of a mate, one who is searching for something we have.

And it's no different from what Charles Darwin saw when he wrote about natural selection a hundred and fifty years ago. Darwin looked at peacocks and wondered about their beautiful feathers. He looked at elks and wondered why their antlers were so ridiculously huge. Antlers bigger than chandeliers don't lend themselves to survival; they lend themselves to getting some hot elk bootie.

But here's where this crap gets interesting. Darwin was right when he said sexual selection is more important than natural selection. Attracting a mate and having babies is more important than surviving the elements, getting food, having the longest neck to reach the highest branches, or any of that other stuff. No babies means no future for the species. Period. Bye-bye. Hasta la vista.

<Sound effect: jungle noises>

It's all about finding someone to spread your genetic code with. Sounds sexy, right? But it makes me wonder if that's why those overpowering feelings of intense love only last for a short time—weeks, maybe months at best. Is it because those feelings only last until the female and the selected male have had a chance to do the deed?

I loved my ex—heck, I still love her—but back then the love felt different. At first it was like I was floating, soaring through the clouds, a total rush. After a while, it changed. I'm not sure how or why, but it changed. It got duller, but

128

deeper. It was there like the wiring of a house is there. You don't see it, you don't think about it every day, but it's there and it works.

And then she yanked everything away. She yanked it away for some total jerk.

<Sound effect: dramatic organ music>

We're up to number forty-seven in what you, my listeners, have dubbed the "biggest display of nadlessness in the history of mankind." I don't care. Judging from the leap in downloads, at least some of you are enjoying the show and telling friends about it. Not to mention that I woke up today with an actual theme song in my inbox. How cool is that?

Anyway, number forty-seven is how she would text me when I least expected it. Early in the morning. Before she went to sleep. It was cool. Hearing that cell phone beep still makes me jump. At least it used to. . . .

So, back on topic. Are girls looking for Mr. Right, or are they looking for Mr. Right Now? And if girls aren't monogamous, why do couples stay together for the long haul, even after the heart-thumping excitement has worn off?

I guess you'll just have to stay tuned.

Outro Music: "Milkshake" by Kelis

CHAPTER FOURTEEN

My father called to say he'd be home from work late, and on impulse I hopped in my car. When I got to Schuyler Village Condominiums, I found Luz's Integra sitting in her parking space. There's a car in one of the guest spots, too, but it's a Chrysler 300, not my father's Beemer. And whoever owns it could be visiting any of the apartments.

So I wait.

After about two minutes, waiting gets boring, so I climb out of the car and make my way over to Luz's stoop. I stand at the bottom and dare myself to climb the concrete steps.

I don't.

There are four units in the building marked 1103. I can see from the doorbells that they are lettered A through D. Aside from the name Miller on Apartment A's doorbell, no names are posted.

That leaves B, C, and D.

I stare at the small glowing row of doorbell buttons, hoping some clue might come along and clobber me over the head.

Nope.

As I make my way back to my car, I consider the mailboxes sitting under the pink glow of the halogen lights. I head over there.

My cell phone beeps. Text message. I flip open my phone. Veronica's name is plastered across the screen. Who else? She's texted me around a dozen times since Saturday night.

So sorry u had 2 c me w Anders. Tried 2 call b4 but u nvr pkd up.

I shut my phone and drop it into my pocket.

She could have left a voice mail. She could have texted me. She could have done a whole load of things. How about not going to my golf club's Fourth of July party in the first place?

The halogen light buzzes above me. A bug sizzles against the hot bulb. I find a mailbox labeled *L. Rivera* in messy black handwriting. Beneath her name is printed the number 1103-D. She's in Apartment D. I'm such a genius. I tug at the small metal door in the hopes I'll see what kind of catalogs she gets—as if I might figure something out about the woman by knowing whether she gets JC Penney or J.Crew. Maybe one of Dimitri's mom's leather-and-chains catalogs. No such luck. The mailbox is locked.

I walk back to Luz's building, climb the concrete steps, and peer through the window on the front door. A broken umbrella and a few plastic-wrapped phone books litter the entryway. There's a door on the left marked with the letter A and a door on the right marked with the letter B. Both have brass knobs, deadbolts, and peepholes. A well-lit staircase leads upward.

I go back to my car and slide into the front seat. I eyeball the upper-right bay of windows, the side I figure must be Apartment D. The windows are dark, with the exception of a thin sliver of light between drawn curtains.

If only I had one of those microphone dishes and headphone getups they have on the sidelines at NFL games—the ones they use to snoop on the goings on in the huddle. That thing could probably hear every last sound in her apartment.

I consider snatching the CD swinging from Luz's rearview mirror and popping it into my player. I wonder if there are any songs on it.

I take a sip of my Slurpee. The seven alternating layers of Coca-Cola and cherry flavorings have melted into the perfect cherry Coke mix. The bottom half is syrupy liquid, while the top is all shaved ice. My stroon (straw/spoon hybrid) roams the depths of the cup for that elusive region that is the perfect Slurpee consistency—half icy slush, half syrup. I suck up too much ice too fast.

Crap! Brain freeze!

Pain stabs the deepest, most sensitive parts of my brain like thousands of ice picks. I clench my eyes and rub the roof of my mouth with my tongue in the hopes the friction might defrost my head. It doesn't help.

Finally, the peak of the pain subsides. I leave my eyes

shut until my gray matter thaws. Then I open them.

And that's when I see her.

Charging barefoot down her concrete steps.

Charging toward my car. Pointing toward me.

She's wearing an oversized pink US ARMY tee that reaches the tops of her thighs. No shorts. No shoes.

"You're that guy I saw hanging around here the other day," she says to me. "You're that 'Dueling Banjos' redneck. What are you doing out in front of my house? Are you stalking me?"

My pounding heart launches into my throat. I drop my Slurpee into my lap and shift my idling car into gear.

I'm pointing the wrong way and there's no exit at the back of the complex—only a bunch of garage bays, a shed, and a slew of Dumpsters against a retaining wall. I spin the wheel hard right and begin a frenzied three-point turn.

"Did Mr. Taggert send you down here? Are you from the workers' comp board?"

I have no idea what she's talking about, but I figure sticking around while Luz is out for blood isn't the wisest idea.

I throw the car into reverse and spin the wheel in the other direction to start the second part of my turn. My car lurches backward, and I pray I don't hit this woman. The police report flashes through my mind. I see my father's expression when he finds out I've backed the Red Scare over his mistress as though she were a speed bump.

The Slurpee seeps through my shorts and soaks my nuts with icy syrup. I'm not proud to say that I know "ball freeze"

133

is far worse than "brain freeze," but it is. Nevertheless, I don't waste the second it would take to put my cup back in the cup holder.

Luz grabs my shoulder through the open window. She smacks the roof of my car with the other. "Get out, I want to talk to you!" I shift into drive and hit the accelerator. My car surges forward, and I'm terrified I'll run over Luz's toes. Her nails bite into my shoulder. Pain lances through my arm, but I keep the car moving. Finally, her grip slackens and she lets go. I stomp on the pedal and my Camry kicks up all kinds of gravel as I fire down the driveway.

"Yeah, keep going!" I hear her voice over the revving of my engine. "Coward!"

As I round the bend past the bushes, I sneak a glance in my rearview mirror. Luz is barefoot in the middle of the road. She's still yelling something at me, but I can't hear her over the engine. I pull out onto Northern Boulevard and head off into the night.

My left shoulder, the shoulder Luz grabbed, feels like someone swabbed it with kerosene and tossed a lit match. I pull up my sleeve and see four claw marks—like bloody colonel stripes—across my arm. Luz Rivera drew blood. She drew blood and made me soak my crotch in frozen cherry Coke Slurpee syrup.

Time to get home. I've got to clean my wounds. I've got to put on my headphones and get behind the microphone. Someone's got to hear about what happened tonight, and I sure as hell can't tell anyone I actually know.

Intro Music: "Bleeding Love" by Leona Lewis

Hi there, and welcome to The Love Manifesto, *and this is a special emergency report. Holy crap is this report special. Something so bizarre happened tonight that I couldn't get home fast enough to tell you about it. Excuse me, I couldn't get to the multimillion-dollar studio fast enough. Jesus! It stings like a sonuvabitch. Hang on.*

<Sounds of fumbling around>

Okay. There. I had to take off my blood-soaked shirt. I'm sitting here bare chested and wounded, doing this podcast because that's how important The Love Manifesto *is to me.*

So anyhow, I figured out where my father's mistress lives, and she came at me. I was sitting in my car at her apartment complex, minding my own business, drinking my patented seven-layer cherry and Coke Slurpee mix, when the skank came charging out of her apartment like Wolverine and attacked me!

She clawed me right across the shoulder with her deadly talons.

<Sound effect: screeching hawk>

I swear this woman is insane.

She must hone her claws to razor-sharp points for just such an occasion. I'm bleeding like a stuck pig over here—not that I've ever seen a stuck pig bleed or anything.

<Movie sound bite: quote from *Dodgeball: A True Underdog Story*: "Nobody makes me bleed my own blood—nobody!">

So the question remains: What the heck is my father doing with this woman? Not only is she not my mother, but she is a raving lunatic.

Jeez, my shorts are soaked from the Slurpee that dumped onto my lap. Hang on while I take them off.

<Sounds of fumbling around>

Okay, I'm back. It's a good thing this isn't a vlog. Otherwise you'd be able to see me in all my glory, wearing little more than my Chuck Ts and my stained-pink-on-the-front boxer briefs.

While I clean my wounds and deal with my uncomfortable crotchular stickiness, I'll play some music for you. This one is particularly appropriate. Stay tuned to The Love Manifesto *for more exciting news as it develops. As for me, I think I might need a rabies shot and a transfusion.*

Oh, and if you're dying for another reason why I love my ex-girlfriend, here's one: She never clawed me across the shoulder or drew freakin' blood.

Outro Music: "Lyin' Ass Bitch" by Fishbone

CHAPTER FIFTEEN ▶▶|

"Just in case," Audrey says. She hands me a small object wrapped in wax paper and begins to walk alongside me as I weave my way through the employee parking lot to the clubhouse.

"What is it?" I ask, peeling back a corner.

"Haven't you ever seen a sandwich before?" She hoists her bag higher onto her shoulder and starts working on the top button of her tuxedo shirt. "It's chicken salad."

I check my watch. I'm already five minutes late. "Of course I've seen a sandwich before, but why are you giving it to me?"

"I thought you might get hungry this afternoon."

"I'm hungry now." I begin to unwrap the sandwich.

Audrey stops me and rewraps it. "Save it for later," she says. "You don't want to walk into your first day of work jamming food in your face."

138

"It's just Mr. Motta," I say. "I've known the guy since I was, like, three."

"You still have to make a good impression," she says. "Anyway, you'll need the boost later on in the day. Blood sugar levels. All that." Audrey begins working at her hair, pulling the braids back and tying them up with some kind of fastener. Before I have a chance to ask her any more sandwich questions, she heads off toward the rear entrance to the kitchen. "Toodles!" she calls over her shoulder.

I watch her disappear around the corner of the building, and I head to the pro shop. The bell jingles when I open the door. Mr. Motta is busy slicing into some cardboard boxes, pulling out stacks of straw hats. He doesn't look up, so I figure I've got a minute. Maybe I could eat just half the sandwich.

I peel back the wax paper so a corner is peeking out. The sandwich looks gorgeous. Two thick slices of wheat bread, lettuce, tomato, and a generous helping of chunky chicken salad.

I open wide and take a bite.

Words can't describe what I feel next. The sandwich is salty, sour, spicy, and bitter all at the same time. Something in it tugs at my innards, like my stomach wants to leap out through my throat. My tongue burns, and my eyes water. My gag reflex goes into overdrive and I frantically search for a garbage can. I burst back outside and hack my mouthful into the nearest planter I can find: hosta, daylilies, impatiens, and now a bite-sized chunk of chewed-up repulsiveness.

The.
Worst.
Sandwich.
Ever.

CHAPTER SIXTEEN

Mr. Motta slides a putter from the rack and hands it to me. His forearm muscles are thick and ropy from the thirty years working construction he's been telling me about all morning. "So, Seth, m'boy, I developed the system myself. There are colored stickers on the tags of every item. You know the colors of the rainbow?"

"Roy G. Biv," I say.

Mr. Motta stares at me. "Who the hell is that?"

"Roy G. Biv? It's a mnemonic device."

"The only pneumatic device I know of is a jack-hammer."

"*Mnemonic* device." I pronounce it slowly to make it clear. "It helps you remember stuff."

"What's Roy G. Biv help you remember?"

"The colors of the rainbow," I say. "Red, orange, yellow, green, blue, indigo, violet."

Mr. Motta thinks on it a second. "What the hell kind of color is indigo?"

"No idea," I say. "I'll look it up on Wikipedia and let you know."

"Son, you are speaking a different language than I am. We don't have any indigo *or* violet here in the pro shop. We have purple. We have red, orange, yellow, green, blue, and *purple*." He counts the colors off on his fingers. "The closer a sticker is to being red, the harder you push it. Red means it's a dead item—discontinued or off season and we're trying to unload it—or we have huge margins on it. I want you selling red items. I want you selling orange."

I take a few practice strokes with the putter. It has a massive head and an offset face. The weight of it feels good in my hands, and the triangular grip fits my fingers perfectly. "Don't you want me selling things people need? Things that will improve a player's game?"

"That's secondary." Mr. Motta wraps his girder of an arm around me and lowers his voice as if there might be some spy from another pro shop hiding under the clothing rack. "Seth, m'boy, first and foremost this establishment needs to turn a profit. Otherwise, when our contract runs out, the powers that be will lease this place to someone else—someone who'll hustle the bigger margin items and generate some income for the club."

"But—"

"But nothing," Mr. Motta says. "Bigger margins mean more money. Think red. Think orange."

The idea of selling something to someone just to turn

a profit makes no sense. It seems smarter to put the right equipment in a person's hand. It's what will keep them coming back. Otherwise, members will just shop at Golf Galaxy out by the mall or buy online and pay forty percent less for the same equipment. People come to a pro shop for the pro—not margins, off-season gear, and Roy G. Biv.

"Don't fill your mind with selling right now," Mr. Motta says. "Stay at the front counter for the first week or so. Haversham says you're good with the computer, so you should have no problem. The Golf-O-Matic software does just about everything you could want. It blocks out tee times in seven-minute increments, knows when all the leagues are playing, everything. Answer the phone and keep people happy. For the time being, that's your job."

"Sounds easy enough."

"It's damn easy," Mr. Motta says, "until you screw it up. That's when all hell breaks loose. If you forget to enter a tee time, it'll jam up the rest of the day. And if that inconveniences any of the board members, you'll be dethroned faster than a coke-snorting beauty queen."

I take my place on the stool behind the glass display counter. "Don't sweat it, Mr. Motta. I've got this covered."

"Make sure you do."

I start clicking around the screen. "This looks pretty simple."

Mr. Motta comes around behind me and points at the monitor. "The times highlighted in green mean—"

"League play," I say.

He claps me on the back. "Sounds like you have things under control. Just get that phone before the third ring and get those golfers scheduled in the open slots. If anyone wants to buy something, you send them my way."

"Sure thing."

"Now come on and help me get the new shipment of shirts on the table. This job ain't about sitting on your ass. The new polos with the embroidered club crest just came in, and they aren't going to sell themselves—not in those boxes, anyway."

Me helping Mr. Motta means that I open all the boxes and fold and stack every shirt in size order, while he puts his feet up in the back office and drinks his blueberry iced coffee. Six big boxes need to be unpacked, so I get started.

Sort, sort, sort.

Fold.

Sort, sort, sort.

Fold. Fold.

And on it goes.

The phone rings only once, and I schedule Mrs. Noonan and her three friends for a two o'clock round. Dr. Kaback comes in with his wife for their eleven o'clock tee time, and they decide to take a cart. I toss them the key. Then I go back to sorting and folding. I hear snoring from the office. When I glance in, Mr. Motta has his feet propped up on the desk and his blue Callaway cap pulled over his eyes. I close his door so he'll stay that way.

If it wasn't for the replay of the 2004 Masters on the Golf Channel, I'd be snoozing, too. It's the tournament where Phil Mickelson birdied five of the last seven holes to beat Ernie Els by one stroke. It ended Mickelson's reputation for being the "best player never to have won a major," and boy did he do it with style.

As Phil takes his tee shot at the seventeenth, something hard cracks against my skull. I look down to see a golf ball rolling across the carpet. It disappears under the shirt table. I stand up, and there's Dimitri. His face glistens with sweat, and his shirt is soaked except over his belly-button depression.

"What the hell was that for?" I say.

"You're such a suck-up."

I rub the growing bump on my head. "What'd I do?"

"How'd you get the number one cherry job at the freakin' club? I've been working here since I was twelve, and I'm not even in the pro shop yet."

"And that's my fault because . . . ?"

"It's not your fault, but I'm beginning to think these folks at the club are trying to keep the black man down."

"In case you haven't noticed," I say, "you're not black."

"I know I'm not black—not even one-sixty-fourth on my father's side—but with my Mediterranean complexion maybe they *think* I'm black." He holds his forearm next to mine in comparison. "It's still racist."

"Do you wake up in the morning and challenge yourself to be stupider than the day before?"

"It just happens naturally," Dimitri says. "Just do me a favor and put in a good word for me with Motta." He puts an arm around my shoulders, and I shrink back, not so much from the pain of my wound as from the stench. Dimitri smells like an incontinent skunk that fell into a crate of rotten eggs. I can feel his sweat soaking through my shirt, his smell permeating me. "I've been trying to get a job in the pro shop for, like, forever," he says. "It's the only air-conditioned position at the whole club short of—"

"Short of catering. Yeah, I know."

"And this is supposed to be one hell of a hot summer— global warming and all that. I can't take it anymore. I have to get out of the heat."

"I'll mention it." I move around the back of the counter and hoist myself onto the stool—partly to figure out all the features of the scheduling software, but mostly to get away from Dimitri's funk. I start sliding the mouse around and clicking on random buttons.

"Where'd you get the sandwich?" he asks.

I glance at the chicken salad sandwich, cut carefully from corner to corner, sitting on wax paper next to the register. A single bite from one edge. A shudder spreads through me. I slide it within Dimitri's reach. "Audrey brought it for me."

"Audrey brought you a sandwich?" He picks up the unbitten half. "She's never brought me a sandwich."

"You told me Audrey brought you food all the time."

A guilty smile breaks out on Dimitri's face. "I said no such thing."

"Sure, you did. You said it when we were playing golf a few weeks ago."

"Oh, that was just a bunch of bullshit I made up to convince you to work here. Audrey has never given me anything I haven't paid for, except a headache. But about this sandwich . . ." Dimitri pulls the wax paper toward himself. "Even if she's Rachael freakin' Ray, which she's not, a girl doesn't bring you a sandwich without an ulterior motive. I'm going to have a few words with her." He picks it up and takes a huge bite. He chews twice before his face twists up. He gags and lets the saliva-covered lump drop from his mouth into the garbage can. "That's freakin' terrible! How do you screw up chicken salad?"

"No idea," I say. "It's just chopped up chicken and mayo, right?"

"Supposedly." Dimitri takes a swig from his water bottle and rinses out his mouth. "That sandwich tastes like unwashed feet." He takes another swig of his water and shudders. Then he leans across the glass countertop to get a look at the monitor. "Hey, can you download porn on that thing?"

I push him off the counter. "You got Windex and paper towels in your pocket?"

"Why?" he says.

I point at the glass. "You left tit prints." A single belly crescent and two perfect boob circles fog the countertop like a ghostly smiley face.

Dimitri pushes out his chest. "They're man-boobs, thank you very much. And I'll have you know I'm proud of them." He points to the television. "Mickelson there, he's king of the man-boobs. He's the patron saint of man-boobs."

"Phil Mickelson does not have man-boobs," I say.

"Come on, Seth, look at the guy." We both examine Mickelson walking up to the seventeenth green. "The guy has got to be a C-cup at least. I know. I was raised around all those catalogs." He cups one hand in the air and demonstrates as he speaks: "A . . . B . . . C . . ." Then he hold two hands up like he's going to catch a basketball. "D . . . At least I'm not parading around with some mysterious podcasting persona."

"Whatever. I'm having fun with it."

"Yeah, but *The Love Manifesto*?"

My breath cuts short, and I stop clicking the mouse. "You found it?"

"No, I just guessed. But come on, dude, how lame can you get?"

"It's supposed to be ironic."

"More like pathetic."

"How long have you known?"

"I found it last night, but I stayed up until the wee hours listening to all your episodes. Jeez, when they came out of that flower shop . . . I didn't know your father—"

"Shut up, all right? My folks are members here." I look down at the monitor and go back to clicking.

Something hard cracks against my skull again, and the golf ball drops to the glass countertop with a bang. I hear Mr. Motta jar from his sleep with a loud snort. The golf ball rolls across the counter and drops to the floor.

"Jeez, what was that for?" I say.

"For not telling me about your father, dickwad. I'm

supposed to be your best friend."

I finger the spot on my head where the second ball struck. Another bump is rising next to the first.

"And now you totally have to get me a job here," he says. "I've got something to lord over you."

"You're going to blackmail me for a job in the pro shop?"

"No, but I can *threaten* to blackmail you. There's a difference."

"Blackmail?" Mr. Motta says from behind me. He staggers out of the office, still bleary-eyed from his nap, and surveys the tables stacked high with folded polo shirts. He gives a slight nod before saying anything. "What's all this I hear about blackmail?"

I fire a glance at Dimitri. "Nothing," I say. "We're just kidding around."

"Well, less kidding and more organizing. You fold a mean shirt, Seth."

"I worked a few months at the Gap," I say. "They make you unfold and refold everything each night even if it doesn't need it."

"Is that right?" Mr. Motta rubs his gray stubble. "Then why don't you get to unfolding and refolding everything around here? Spiff this place up a little."

"Sure thing," I say.

Dimitri nudges me.

"Oh, Mr. Motta," I say. "I could do a much better job of unfolding and refolding if I had Dimitri here to help out. He worked at the Gap, too."

"Dimitri did not work at any Gap." Mr. Motta runs his hand over the perfectly even rows of shirts. "He's been filling watercoolers and cleaning ball washers around here since his legs were too short to reach the pedals of the maintenance cart."

"The Gap was a winter job," Dimitri says.

"Don't yank my crank." Mr. Motta looks me up and down. "But I've known you a while, Seth. If you say Dimitri is good for the job, I'll let Haversham know. He can start tomorrow."

"Thanks, Mr. Motta," Dimitri says. "You won't regret it."

"That remains to be seen. One thing's for sure. You'd better not come to work looking like you do now, or you'll be out as quick as you came in."

Dimitri looks down at himself. "What do you mean?"

"You're sweatier than a sumo wrestler's jockstrap. I can't have your salami smell all over the merchandise. Now get the hell out of here."

"Sure thing, Mr. Motta," Dimitri says. "Tomorrow I'll be clean and dry. Neatly pressed. The whole bit. I promise."

"Now scram before I change my mind."

Dimitri scrams. In fact, I can't remember ever seeing Dimitri move so quickly in his life. He must really want this position.

Mr. Motta winks at me. "Don't forget you have seniority over that clown, Seth. That makes you the boss."

"I've only been here four hours."

"Seniority is seniority," he says. "When I'm not here, you're the boss."

"But you're always here," I say.

"*Here* is a state of mind, son." He hoists a thumb over his shoulder and points to the back office. "When I'm back there, I'm not here."

CHAPTER SEVENTEEN

"Are you sure you know what you're getting into?" Audrey asks me. I bumped into her on my way out of work, and she lured me to one of the picnic tables behind the club restaurant. It wasn't too tough with the armload of food she pinched from the snack cart. She tears a soft pretzel in half and offers me the unbitten part. "Dimitri is fine in small doses, but you'll be working with him eight hours a day. He's going to wear you down like a cheese grater on Camembert."

"I think Camembert is a soft cheese," I say.

"What's that got to do with anything?"

"You don't use a cheese grater on soft cheese. It would get all clogged up."

"Yeah, well maybe Dimitri will get *you* all clogged up."

"Come on," I say. "Don't you think I know how to tune him out by now?"

"I've lived with him longer than you've known him, Seth. When it comes to finding ways to annoy, Dimitri is a master."

"He's not that bad," I say.

"Say that again in two weeks."

Audrey stuffs a length of soft pretzel in her mouth and gazes down the hill. From where we're sitting we can see the eighteenth hole from the tee box to the green. Two carts, one of the last foursomes of the night, buzz down the path that runs along the fairway. All I want to do is ask her what she put in her chicken salad to rank it as a chemical weapon, but I'm afraid I'll hurt her feelings.

"So what's up with Kevin?" I say.

"What about him?"

"I don't know. He just seems kind of . . . mellow."

"So?" Audrey says.

One of the golfers gets out of his cart and inspects his ball, which is lying on the second cut of rough. I'd use a half swing with my wedge.

Audrey goes on, "I used to go out with Pete Zimmer."

"The guy who—"

"Yeah, the guy who got busted for stealing the street signs. Kevin is a nice change of pace."

"You mean from a very fast pace to a sloooooow one?"

Audrey beans me with a length of pretzel. It bounces off my cheek and lands in front of me. I pop it in my mouth.

"Kevin is not slow. He's just . . ." Audrey pauses. "He's nice. He's interested in things, in making a change. He's a

153

great kisser, too. I could go on if you like."

"You can stop there," I say.

"Anyhow, nice is a good thing."

"I guess."

"You guess what?" Audrey says. "What's the matter?"

"You guys just seem pretty different, but it's none of my business." I take a bite of the Butterfinger Audrey gave me. There's something about that unidentifiable stuff in the center of a Butterfinger that is just so good. It flakes apart in your mouth, but before you know it, it gets all gooey and sticky.

"You can't just leave it at that," Audrey says.

"What do you mean?"

"You can't just say something provocative like that and then stuff candy in your mouth."

"Sure I can." I stuff another piece in my mouth. "Yummy."

"Seriously," she says.

I gather the trash from the table and wad it into a tight ball. "I think sometimes it's easier to see something if you're not the one mired down in it."

"What?"

"I don't know. I guess he's just not the sort of guy I'd picture you with."

She leans forward. "So what kind of guy would you picture me with?"

I think on it for a second. "Someone who challenges you more."

Her eyes narrow. "You don't mean *you*, do you?"

"Oh, God, no. I didn't mean—"

"Because you've got a whole boatload of stuff you're mired down in. Anyhow, I'm pretty sure you wouldn't be nearly as good a kisser as Kevin."

I cram more pretzel in my mouth to give me an excuse not to say anything.

We let time go by as the other golfers hit up. Mr. Mancuso, one of the board members, gets out of his cart. He's wearing a huge straw hat and a stretched-tight pink shirt. He pulls a club out, approaches his ball, and takes a few practice swings.

"It must be tough to golf when your belly gets in the way like that," I say.

Audrey smiles and tucks her foot under herself. She takes a sip of her bottled water.

"Five bucks says he hits that ball long," I say.

"You've got yourself a bet," she says almost immediately. "Mr. Mancuso is a great player."

He takes a few more practice strokes, draws his club back, and strikes. His ball pops into the air, bounces in the center of the green, and rolls off the back edge. Long.

He slams his iron into his bag. I can hear him cursing from here.

"How'd you know he'd do that?" Audrey asks.

"Because we're sitting up here. It's easier to see something if you're not the one mired down in it."

"Touché." Audrey looks back down at the green. "Plus, I'll bet Mr. Mancuso is a crappy kisser, too."

"Nasty," I say.

"Totally nasty."

"So what else is going on in your life?" Audrey asks.

For some reason, I want to open up and tell her everything. I want to fill her in about Luz and my father, about tracking them around Albany, about the podcasts, about everything. But I don't.

"Do you work a full forty hours here?" I say to her.

"Changing the subject?"

"Until I get my five bucks."

"I just gave you *ten* bucks in free food," Audrey says.

"It was given before I won the bet. That makes it a gift."

"What if I give you free food tomorrow?"

"Then we'd be even," I say.

"Same time? Same place?"

"Sounds like a plan."

Audrey takes another bite of her pretzel. "Fair enough."

The sun dips below the tree line and a shadow reaches across the fairway to touch us. Mr. Mancuso chips back onto the green and putts in. He begins to walk off, but one of his buddies motions for him to go back and replace the flag.

Audrey takes the last bite of her pretzel. She reaches across the table and plucks mine from my hand. "You're not eating this, are you?"

But before I have a chance to tell her I want it, she stuffs it in her mouth.

CHAPTER EIGHTEEN ▶▶▍

The doorbell has already chimed four or five times before I have a chance to roll out of bed and tear down the steps. I figure it's the UPS guy. My mother ordered all sorts of stuff for Mr. Peepers from some fancy online store. As if Mr. Peepers doesn't already have enough stuff.

The trouble is that the person impatiently ringing the bell is not the UPS guy, and as soon as I fling open the door I wish I had stayed buried under my comforter.

It's Veronica.

Don't get me wrong; she looks great in her pink Hollister tee and white shorts. Her hair is pulled back into a ponytail, which makes her cheekbones seem even higher, like an elf straight out of Tolkien. Even though she's smiling, her tight lip gloss–covered lips hint that it's forced. I want to shrink behind the door and tell her to go away.

"Hey." She flicks her chin toward my free hand. "How's Benedict doing?"

I look down and realize I'm holding on to the stuffed animal I made in seventh-grade sewing class. His face, scrunched up from too many threads pulled too tight, is coiled into a grimace, and his bare, gangly limbs hang almost to the ground. He was supposed to be a fearsome troll, but he turned out to look more like a deformed Teletubby.

I toss Benedict out of sight.

"I've been trying to get in touch with you," Veronica says. "We need to talk."

I so don't want to do this while wearing nothing but sweat shorts. "Well, here I am," I say. "I'm a captive audience." Actually, I'm more than a captive audience. After spending most of last night working on my list of reasons why I love her, Veronica has been on my mind for almost twelve hours. Now I'm standing in front of her mostly naked. I remember the claw marks on my shoulder and angle my wound away from her.

"I've been calling and texting and IMing and still I have no idea what to say. I just . . ." She runs a hand up one of the pillars that flank the porch, and for a second I wonder if all my wishing and list making has paid off. "I don't know," she goes on. "I feel like I need to apologize for what happened. I should have realized you'd be at the club with your family. I shouldn't have gone."

I try to decide whether she's here to get back with me or just to apologize, but I can't quite figure it out. Clearly, she's uncomfortable, nervous, but I would be nervous too if I were knocking on my ex's door after showing up at his family's club with another date. Veronica's eyes meet mine but then shift right back to her hand, which is still moving up and down the pillar. I don't believe in such obvious symbolism so I decide to ignore it.

"You want to come in?" I ask. "My dad's at work and Mom is running errands."

"How's your mom doing?"

"She's fine," I say. "I think she's at the chiropractor or something."

"No, I mean the other thing. Your father. Applebee's. All that."

I play with the brass knob of the door lock. The deadbolt slides in and out.

"You didn't tell her?" She says it like I'm the bad person, like anyone in his right mind would march right in without all the details and destroy his parents' marriage.

That feeling rises in my chest, the same feeling I had when I found out Dimitri knew. But this time it's much worse. I shrug. "Come on in," I say. "You want something to drink?"

Veronica glances down at the driveway, empty except for my car and a new phone book wrapped in blue plastic. "Why don't we sit out here on the steps?"

"Let me get a shirt on," I say. "It'll just take a second."

"Maybe I should just get going. I've got to be in for my shift a little early this afternoon and—"

"No, don't go." I step out into the heat and squint

159

against the sun. I sit on the top step all the way to the left so Veronica, if she chooses to sit down, has to plant herself on the side opposite my claw marks. I pat the spot next to me.

Veronica sits. She places her purse between us like it's some kind of buffer and inhales deeply. "I still love that cologne you wear. That Seth smell." She says it like it's been longer than eight days since she's been near me. "My stomach was inside out going to the club with Anders the other night. I wanted to tell you beforehand, but I couldn't bring myself to do it. At first, it was just easier not to say anything, but as the party got closer it got harder and harder to tell you. I know it made everything a hundred times worse. After I saw your face at the party, well, I needed to explain, to clear the air. Whatever."

Veronica leans forward so her knees press into her chest. "Anders and I, we met at work. I didn't like him at first, but we have so much in common. I guess we just hit it off."

"Seems so." I pull my knees tight to my chest until I realize I'm mirroring her position exactly.

"One night we got to talking after work and . . ." She shakes her head and lets her sentence die off.

I don't need it spelled out for me. Veronica hooked up with Anders before she dumped me. A word we learned in Mr. Green's English class back in ninth grade flashes into my mind. It was during the Shakespeare unit and is defined as a man who is being cheated on by his woman.

Cuckold.

At seventeen, Seth Baumgartner is a cuckold.

Veronica kissed me after she was already cleaning Anders's back molars with her tongue. My fists clench into tight balls, like I have no fingers, no thumb, just a solid mass of flesh and bone at the end of each arm.

"Why are you telling me this?" I ask her.

"Like I said—"

"I heard you the first time, but none of this has to do with me: what you didn't like about me, why your feelings for me changed, why you screwed around with me after you hooked up with some other guy. These things you're telling me, it's all about you."

"I'm trying to—"

"You're trying to make yourself feel better."

"That's not true."

"It is true." Now that I've started, the words come easily. "I don't need to hear you justify what you did. I don't need the whens and wheres of you and that piece of crap, what's his name?"

Veronica leans away, props herself on stiffened arms. "Anders."

"Yeah, Anders. I don't need to know any of the details. Believe me, Veronica, I heard the important part loud and clear. No matter how much I want to be with you, you don't want to be with me." I turn away, look at the azaleas so Veronica won't see how close I am to crying. My chest tightens, but I fight back that first sob. "You hook up with me and then dump me the next day. All the while you're boning some guy in the mall parking lot. Couldn't have been clearer if you drew a diagram."

Veronica gets up and stomps down the steps. She plants her fists on her hips. "Jeez, Seth. I came down here to apologize, and all you can do is be an asshole about everything."

"I'm the asshole?" I perk up, all thoughts of crying gone. "What do you want me to do, Veronica, rush down the steps after you? Should I tell you it's okay you cheated on me?" I pause to give her a chance to jump in. She doesn't. "Look, it's been a pretty shitty week. Quite possibly the shittiest week of my life. And although you've played a part in all of it, I've got bigger issues to deal with than you and me."

Veronica's eyes train on my shoulder. "What happened to you? It looks like—"

"None of your business," I cut in. "And while we're on the topic, why don't you keep your nose out of my family situation? It stopped being your problem the minute you decided to be the daily special at Applebee's."

"Applebee's doesn't have daily specials." She's trying to be funny, to break the tension, but I don't let a smile—not even the trace of one—creep onto my face.

Veronica takes another step away. "Wow, Seth, I used to complain that you didn't talk enough, but I think it might have been better that way. I was going to tell you that I don't even like Anders that much, that—"

"That makes it worse," I say. The tears rise up in my face, threaten to spill. I let them simmer back down before I go on. "You dumped me. You threw away everything we had, and you did it for a guy you don't even care that much about. Is that supposed to make me feel better?"

She stares at me. I stare back.

Her eyes are pinpricks, the whites visible all the way around. I'm guessing mine are the same. We ignore the chirping birds. We ignore the lacy patterns the sunlight makes as it filters through the leaves of the swaying maples. We ignore everything and just stare.

Until the tinny chiming of a bicycle bell breaks the silence.

Da-ding! Da-ding!

"What's going on with you two lovebirds?" It's Dimitri feigning ignorance. If there was any question before why he can't find himself a girlfriend, it's obvious now. He's riding a sparkly pink Schwinn with a banana seat and high, curved handlebars. Pink and silver streamers flutter from the handgrips. His shoulders are hunched and his knees reach his chest with each pump of the pedals of the too-small bike. If it weren't for the orange T-shirt and bright yellow towel and flip-flops, he'd look like a trained bear at the circus.

Veronica and I turn our eyes to Dimitri as he rolls up my driveway and lightly bumps his front tire into the first concrete step. "It's my sister's old bike," he says. "Mine's got a flat."

"How's it going?" Veronica asks him coldly.

I exhale a stale breath.

"You know, hanging and banging." Dimitri leans back on the bike and pops the front tire up onto the lowest step. "Probably too much hanging and not enough banging, though. I didn't interrupt anything, did I?"

Veronica glances at me, waiting for me to answer.

"I'm not sure," I say to her. "Is he interrupting anything?"

Veronica waits a beat. "No," she says. "I was just leaving." She snatches up her purse and heads down the driveway.

"Need a lift anywhere?" Dimitri calls after her. "There's plenty of room for two on my banana seat."

Veronica flips a middle finger over her shoulder as she turns down the sidewalk. She lives only four and a half blocks away, so I don't feel too bad about not offering her a ride.

"Yeesh," Dimitri says. "Some people just don't appreciate 'old school.'"

I kick the front tire of Audrey's bike. "More like grammar school."

Dimitri flicks his wrist like he's revving a motorcycle. "She'll be sorry when I get my Harley and I don't let her ride bitch."

"You're not getting a Harley," I say. "Your mom would kill you."

Dimitri shades his eyes with his free hand and squints down the street after Veronica. "Looks like that was shaping up to be an unpleasant conversation anyway."

"You're not kidding."

"Why'd she come over?"

I tell Dimitri everything Veronica said and how I responded. As the words pour out, my mind races about all the things I should have said, all the things I should have done. Dimitri gives surprisingly few editorial comments and seems truly impressed. "Wow, you got right up in her grille, huh? Glad you're finally growing a pair."

"Yeah," I say. "A heck of a lot of good it's doing me. I pretty much just destroyed any chance of ever getting back with her."

"Do you want to?" Dimitri asks.

"Sure I do," I say without pause.

"Why?"

The question takes me off guard. Dimitri and Audrey have both asked me *if* I want to get back with Veronica, but no one has asked me *why*. I thought all the reasons on my list were answering that.

"She was a total tool to you," he says. "What kind of insensitive bitch shows up unannounced with a date at a party she knows her ex is going to be at?"

My eyes dart to Dimitri. I hadn't told him about Veronica showing up at the club, and I didn't mention it on the podcast, not yet anyway.

"Audrey told me," he says.

Instinct tells me to defend Veronica, to tell Dimitri that things are probably just as hard for her as they are for me, but I know that's not true. Even if I wasn't feeling sorry for myself, I know that couldn't possibly be true. She's the dumper; I'm the dumpee. She moved on; I didn't.

"Hey," Dimitri says. He bumps his front tire into my shin. "Why don't we go swimming before your puppy dog eyes melt out of your head?"

"I'm not going to the club until I have to be at work," I say.

"Who said anything about the club? I've been talking to Jill, the girl from the pool at the condo complex. You might not have scored a car that day, but I have a chance to score myself. Either way, we'll be in a pool."

"Go without me," I say, moving toward the house.

"Just shut up and put on your bathing suit."

CHAPTER NINETEEN

"What're you parking all the way over here for?" Dimitri says. "The pool is practically on the other side of the complex."

"If you don't like how I park, feel free to ride Audrey's bike next time." My words come out sharper than I intend them to. The truth is that I'm afraid if Luz sees my bright red Camry, she'll put a cinder block through my windshield.

Dimitri glances at his watch. "It's just that I told Jill we'd be down around twelve. It's already half past."

"Since when are you worried about being on time for anything?"

"Since I might get some nookie. In case I haven't mentioned it, Jill is hot. Smokin', actually. Come on, Seth, catch a clue."

"Clue caught."

"She says her friend Caitlyn—"

"Forget it."

"Come on, you're not still off the market, are you? It's been more than a week since Veronica and you split up. Anyhow, she's a jerk. She flipped you the bird."

"She flipped *you* the bird," I say.

Dimitri and I walk along the sidewalk, side by side, our towels over our shoulders. The heat rises from the concrete and bakes my legs. It'll be good to get over to that pool.

"So what's the deal with your father and his girlfriend?" Dimitri says. "Why would he take her to Applebee's? That might be okay for high-school students—poverty-stricken college kids, maybe—but not when you're, like, forty and successful. Doesn't he know Bongiorno's Italian Restaurant is a better aphrodisiac than jalapeño poppers? Even I know that, and I never go on dates."

Thinking about my dad with Luz makes my stomach twist up. "Nothing to tell," I say. "I'm not going to confront him about it. As far as I'm concerned, it's a dead issue."

"Dead issue, my ass. You rant and rave about it on your podcast every other night. It bothers you. It bothers you more than this business with Veronica. You won't be able to let it go, Seth. I know you."

He's right. It's the furthest thing from a dead issue. I hate dodging Dimitri's questions—especially because we're about to go swimming in Luz's condo complex—but I'm still not ready to talk about it. It's one thing to blab about it on the podcast, even with Dimitri listening. Talking into a microphone distances me from everything. It all comes more freely, looser. But I just railed into Veronica. I got right up in her face—something I have never done before. Was that me talking, or was it my podcasting personality? The words came like they do when I'm wearing the headphones and sitting behind the mike, concentrating more on my soundboard than on filtering the words coming out of my mouth.

"Do what you want," Dimitri says, "but I'd never let an opportunity like that slide."

"Opportunity?"

"Open your eyes, Seth. This is a total cash cow. I'd be right up my father's butt about it. I'd be getting all kinds of stuff out of the deal."

"You wouldn't do a thing."

"Sure I would. If it were my father, I'd take the guy out to dinner. I'd take him right to Applebee's—just me and him. Hell, I'd request the very same booth he sat in with his mistress, and I'd start laying out all the new rules: later curfew, bigger allowance, a case of beer each week, the whole bit. He'd be staring at me over his nachos—"

"Cheesy Bacon Tavern Chips," I say.

"Whatever it is they serve over there. Anyhow, he'd be sitting on the other side of the table wondering if I'd gone completely insane, and I'd stop, look him in the eyes, and say, 'I know about her.'"

"No, you wouldn't."

"It's brilliant! I'd be getting that new iPod I've been looking at and that multimedia laptop. I'd be getting cable in my room, and if I worked it right, I'd be driving a car."

"You don't even have a license," I say.

"If I had a hand on my father's freakin' purse strings, I'd sure as hell get one."

I want to ask him if he's given any thought to the effect the news would have on his mother, what it would do to his parents' marriage, how it would destroy Audrey, but Dimitri is on a roll. And one thing I've learned is not to get in the way of Dimitri when he's rolling. As he adds to his wish list of blackmail booty, we make our way across the road toward the fenced-in pool. Jill is sitting in the same chair she was sitting in the first time I saw her, the day Dimitri met her. She's wearing a tight white tank top with the word *Lifeguard* printed across it in bright red. Dimitri always goes after girls with big chests. It's like a prerequisite for him. But considering how much Windex it took to clean Dimitri's man-boob prints off the countertop at the pro shop, I suppose it's pretty equal opportunity.

A bunch of other people are sunbathing. Luz isn't one of them, and I relax a little. Now I only have to worry about her showing up between now and three thirty, when we have to leave for our shift at the club. Two kids wearing water wings are running around the pool. One leaps in and sends a splash high into the air. A girl in a pink-and-green-striped bikini who was lying on one of the recliner chairs jerks up, startled by the cold water. I can't help but stare. The girl is around our age. Her shiny dark hair is cut short in the back and gets longer toward the front. It seems to follow the line of her jaw perfectly. She's wearing huge rectangular sunglasses that make her head seem small, like a pixie's. The girl scowls at the kids, lies back down, and turns her face back to the sun.

Jill waves at us, and it breaks my gaze. We wave back.

"So you'd blackmail your own father?" I say to Dimitri.

"Sure. It's not as though I'd frame him or anything. But if he dug his own grave and jumped in, I'd have no trouble standing over it with a shovel."

"Just yesterday you were ready to blackmail me for a job. Now you're talking about blackmailing your own flesh and blood. Do I detect a trend?"

"Hey, you have to take the edge where you can find it."

"Sounds like you can toss that MBA application right in the trash."

"When I get into business school, I'll teach *them* a thing or two." Dimitri puts his hand on the gate latch and stops. "So, I've been thinking about it, and I've decided I want to be on your podcast."

"You what?"

"You heard me. I'll make up an alias—Billy Bob Poltroon or something. I'll be your occasional guest. You can interview me and get my opinions on love and all the stuff going on with me. How many downloads are you getting?"

"Around a hundred a day—give or take. Hey, someone even wrote a theme song for me!"

"Sweet." I can tell Dimitri is picturing himself with the headphones on in front of the microphone. "So when do you want me to come over for the show?"

"I'm not sure. . . ."

"Come on, I'm living the kind of life people dream about."

"Who dreams about raking traps at a golf club and hovering over lingerie catalogs until two in the morning?"

"Come on," Dimitri says. "Look at Jill over there." She waves again. Dimitri is too busy with his story to notice, but I wave back. "You're wasting valuable airtime whining, bitching, and complaining all the time. Having me on, it'll be interesting—and maybe a little uplifting. I guarantee it."

"How can you guarantee anything?"

"We'll go by number of downloads. We'll graph your growth over the previous few weeks, and if I don't make the show grow even faster—if I don't make that curve leap—I'm done."

"You want to make a graph?" I say.

"Yeah. The x-axis will be time, and the y-axis will be number of hits."

"And you call *me* a geek?"

"I'm not a geek; I'm more like a nerd."

"What's the difference?"

"You have so much to learn," Dimitri says, shaking his head. "A nerd is someone who's really into learning and studying. You know, like a bookworm. A geek is someone who is really into one particular thing—*Star Trek*, computers, *Dr. Who*, poker, whatever. Then there are dorks."

"What's a dork?"

"A dork is the worst of the three. It's someone who has trouble socially. Some people are dorks but not geeks or nerds. Most nerds are dorks to some degree but not necessarily geeks. They all seem to travel hand in hand, though. All your podcasting makes you a geek. I'm a nerd because I'm always reading things—just things in general. I'm definitely not a dork. Neither are you, but if you don't get back in the saddle soon, you'll head down that path. And once you head down the path to dorkdom . . ." Dimitri shudders. "Well, I don't even want to think about what would happen."

I'm beginning to think Dimitri would be great on the podcast. He's quick on his feet, he's funny, and he uses all kinds of colorful expressions. But that lame studio in the basement of my parents' house is my territory. *The Love Manifesto* is mine. The idea of adding a cohost feels weird, like I'd be less in control.

Dimitri rests his hand on the gate latch as though he won't open it until I give him an answer. "Come on," he says, grinning. "Give me a shot."

"I'll think about it."

"Cool." Dimitri lifts the latch and lets me walk into the pool area first. "Yo, Jill!"

"Hey, Dee-Dee!"

Dee-Dee? She calls him Dee-Dee? Dimitri lets her?

"This is my friend Seth. I told you about him."

We exchange smiles, and I lean over to shake her hand. She lifts her fist, so we bump knuckles instead. Her tank top is doing very little to conceal her cleavage, and she's not doing anything to help it succeed. I silently thank whoever invented sunglasses for helping oglers everywhere.

"Dimitri has such nice things to say about you," Jill says, her words pulling my gaze back above her neckline.

I want to return the compliment, but what am I going to say? *Hey, Dimitri tells me your ass is like a juicy peach waiting to be bitten. Hey, my good buddy Dimitri always likes girls with big boobs, but you seem the nicest . . . personality-wise, that is . . . oh, and your breasts are nice, too.* I run through a few more options in my head until I decide it would be best just to smile.

Jill looks past me and blows her whistle. A shrill tweet pierces the air, and the two kids stop dead. "How many times do I have to tell you two little bastards? No running!" She stands up and walks toward the boys. Her ponytail, which is sticking out through the hole in the back of her cap, bounces against her neck. "You want to get kicked out? Want to sit in your stuffy apartments the rest of the day?"

Both kids shake their heads guiltily and begin to do that fast walk with stiff arms and legs that really is more like a run anyway.

Jill sits back down. "They can crack their heads open for all I care," she says. "Their parents use the pool like a damn babysitting service. But if my dad comes over and sees them running—forget a sling—my ass is going to be in a plaster cast. Insurance nearly doubled last year when Mrs. Vandenberg slipped on the ice and dislocated her shoulder."

Dimitri drops into the seat next to Jill. "Jill's dad is the complex manager," he says.

"And a real pain in the ass," Jill adds.

"Aren't they all?" I say.

"All condo complex managers are pains in the ass?" Jill asks. "How many condo complex managers do you know?"

"No, I mean dads," I say. "All dads are pains in the ass."

Dimitri lifts his hands to the sky. "Say it again, brother!"

"Hey, Caitlyn!" Jill calls out. The girl in the pink-and-green-striped swimsuit lifts her head. "Come over here."

The girl ties a sheer wrappy-thing around her hips, slips her feet into sparkly flip-flops, and walks over like she's on the runway for a Victoria's Secret fashion show. The pink and green together reminds me of watermelons.

I scowl at Dimitri, who just shrugs and smiles. I've been duped, totally suckered, but considering Caitlyn is the girl in the pink-and-green-striped bikini . . .

"This is Caitlyn," Jill says. Dimitri and I introduce ourselves to her, and we all exchange smiles and waves and more smiles. Caitlyn lowers herself into a recliner and stretches out. A sticker shaped like a Playboy bunny clings to her right hip. It peeks at me above her wrap.

"What's that thing?" Dimitri says, pointing to the sticker.

"It's a tanning decal," she says. "It's supposed to leave the shape of the bunny on me. You know, like untan or whatever."

"Does it work?" I say.

"I don't know." Caitlyn runs her fingers over the sticker. "I've never done one before. I just like bunnies."

For the first time in my life—and possibly the first time in recorded history—I'm wishing I had been born a bunny sticker. With my luck, though, rather than ending up on a hot girl's pelvis, I'd have ended up on some three-year-old's overalls because he went poopy on the potty.

"Caitlyn lives in the complex, too," Jill says. She points over her shoulder as if I might know the exact apartment. "Right down the row from me. We've been tight since, like, forever."

"We were baby buddies," Caitlyn adds.

Caitlyn pops in her earbuds and angles her face to the sun.

Dimitri pulls off his shirt and lies back on his chair. I can almost see the thin film of sweat set up shop on the dome of his belly.

"What're you listening to?" I ask Caitlyn.

She pulls out one earbud. "Huh?"

I point to her iPod. "What're you listening to?"

"Oh, just a mix I threw together last night."

"You make your own mixes?" I say.

"Just some old songs from my laptop. The computer does it, really. I just pick the songs and the order and the software takes care of everything else—transitions and all that."

"What program do you use?" As soon as I say it, I want to reel the words back in. So geeky, at least by Dimitri's definition. "I mean, what song is playing?"

"Katy Perry," she says. "'Hot N Cold.'"

No! That song makes me want to blow Technicolor chunks.

I nod as though I don't hate every song like this that's ever been recorded and shift in my seat, unsure of what to say next.

Should I lie down on the recliner next to her? Should I stay where I am? Should I get up and dance an Irish jig? I'm going to crucify Dimitri for springing this on me.

Caitlyn offers me an earbud, and I slide my chair next to hers. The scraping sound is loud enough to send ripples through the pool. I lean in to bring my head closer so that I can hear the music. She smells tropical, like bananas and coconuts. The beat of the music is fast, and, even with only one earbud in, the music seems to swirl around. Caitlyn lowers her sunglasses and peers at me over the top of them with huge chocolate brown eyes. My heart races, and I tell myself it's from the tempo of the dance music.

"What do you think?" she says.

"Cool." I'm sure I sound like an idiot, so I lie back to avoid saying anything else. Reluctantly, I pull off my shirt and toss it under my chair.

"Dude, those are deeper than I thought," Dimitri says, pointing to the scratches on my shoulder.

I glance down at them. I managed to hide them from him back at my house by keeping my shoulder turned away, but now they are out in the open for everyone to see. They don't hurt so much anymore, but they sure look ugly—four crimson lines across the ball of my shoulder.

"What have you been up to?" Jill says playfully.

My face gets hot. "It's from rosebushes," I say. "I was weeding in my backyard and the thorns . . ."

"Don't give me that," Jill says. "I don't have to be CSI to know claw marks when I see them. You must've been—"

"Seriously," Dimitri cuts in. "They're from sticker bushes. I was sitting right there on my lazy ass when he did it."

I turn to Caitlyn. "They're not—"

"I don't care if they're claw marks or not," she says.

"Well, they're not," I say again.

I hate the idea of making a bad first impression, but I like the thought of someone *not* knowing anything about me. I can be whoever I want without any of the old baggage of who I used to be. There's no one to bring up the time in third-grade gym class when I shot the winning basket for the other team. There's no one to bring up how my lip got caught in my soda can in fifth grade and I ran bleeding from the cafeteria to the nurse's office. There's no one to mention the time in eighth grade when I rushed out of the locker room and warmed up wearing my tighty whiteys over my soccer shorts. I wonder if this is what it's going to be like my first semester of college. Fresh start. No baggage.

"Hey," I say to Caitlyn. "You have any more of those tanning stickers?"

She digs through her tote bag and pulls out a big red heart. I peel it from the glossy backing and stick it on my left shoulder—right over my claw marks.

"How appropriate," Dimitri says. "A heart for the love doctor."

I shoot him a look.

"What'd he mean by that?" Jill asks me.

"No idea," I say. "Dimitri comes out with some weird things."

Caitlyn offers me her earbud again. "Want to listen some more?"

"Sure." I usually hate cheeseball pop music, but somehow—lying here next to Caitlyn with a big red heart on my left shoulder and her in her pink-and-green-striped bikini—cheeseball pop music doesn't sound so terrible.

EXCERPT FROM THE LOVE MANIFESTO ▶▶▎

Intro Music: "She Blinded Me with Science" by Thomas Dolby

Welcome back to The Love Manifesto. *That last tune was "She Blinded Me with Science." I read once that Thomas Dolby had no idea what that song was about as he was writing it, but I think I know.*

Everyone runs around talking about love. You see it in shows, read about it in books and poetry; you hear about it in music lyrics. But ask anyone what love really is, and the best you'll get is a shrug and some dopey comment like "I dunno, but I know it when I feel it."

Well, that's not good enough for me, so off I went to the library to find out.

In a nutshell, when you fall in love your brain churns out a whole bunch of chemicals and dumps them into your system. You heard me. Chemicals. The crazy thing is that it's a different chemical cocktail depending on what type of love we're talking about.

First let's talk about lust. You see someone, and something gets you going. It could be their eyes or their body or how they sing or how they play baseball. Whatever. Before you know it, you're lusting after them. The racing heart, sweaty palms, feelings of bliss, sleeplessness, focused attention, and all that other stuff are the result of this hormone called dopamine and this other stuff called norepinephrine.

According to scientists, when we feel lust, the part of the brain that is involved with addiction goes nuts. You heard me. I said addiction. And the crazy thing is that the body quickly builds up a tolerance to these chemicals, so people need more and more to get the same feeling.

Do you text a lot when you start dating someone? Me too. My ex and I texted hundreds of times every day when we were first together. I couldn't stop thinking about her. Day, night, whenever. My father freaked when he saw the bill, and sneaking away to the reference section to text is what got me fired from my job at the library.

After a while, those head-over-heels feelings change. They change to what scientists call attachment. Attachment involves a whole other set of chemicals. Oxytocin helps create an emotional bond with a partner. Endorphins are painkillers. Scientists believe this is what probably keeps us with our partner for the long haul . . . at least usually. Painkillers.

I remember that part, too. It's not like things changed

overnight, but after a while it was just comforting to be with her. It was like we were two puzzle pieces that fit together. When she wasn't around, something was missing.

With lust, when I wasn't with her it was like a gaping wound. With attachment, it was more like a feeling of not being whole.

I wonder if that is what's going on with my father. Years ago, he met my mother and the dopamine and norepinephrine dumped into his brain. He became a love addict, and they got married. Of course, the same thing happened with my mother since we can assume she lusted after him, too. Then they had sex at least once, as evidenced by me. As time wore on, vasopressin came on the scene and blocked the dopamine and norepinephrine. That's when the oxytocin and endorphins jumped in and did what they're supposed to do. They blocked the pain and caused them to stay attached to each other—at least for a while.

So what made my father stray with the tramp? Good question.

Another interesting thing I noticed during my research is that chocolate kept coming up. Turns out chocolate has a chemical in it called PEA. This PEA stuff is known as the "love chemical" since it releases dopamine into the brain and jacks up feelings of attraction, giddiness, excitement, and euphoria. Sound familiar? You think all those bored housewives are replacing real kisses with Hershey's Kisses? It might explain a lot.

Now I'm going to jam a Butterfinger in my mouth and

add a few more reasons to the ex list. Resistance is futile. You know you secretly love it. And by the way, I'm loving the theme songs you're sending in! I just got two more this morning, one from a guy named Tris McCall and another from a band called the Falling Motors, which makes a total of sixteen. Sixteen theme songs! I'll play the new ones for you in our next segment. They are awesome.

Reason number eighty-six is how she knew what I wanted without having to ask. I don't care if it was a VitaminWater or something dirtier, she just knew. And for those of you who don't know, I like the grape VitaminWater.

Anyhow, you're listening to The Love Manifesto. Check out this next song. This is "Hot N Cold" by Katy Perry. Let's see if it makes you as nauseous as it makes me.

Outro Music: "Hot N Cold" by Katy Perry

CHAPTER TWENTY ▶▶▍

"**W**hy in hell did you sell that club?" Mr. Motta swoops down on me the instant Mr. Howard leaves the pro shop with his new purchase tucked under his arm. "That lob wedge was clearly marked blue."

"At least it wasn't an indigo," I mutter.

"Don't sass me, Baumgartner. I specifically told you to sell reds and oranges."

Dimitri snickers and heads to the front to re-refold the shirts.

"It's . . ." I take a moment to choose my words as I glance through the window at Mr. Howard. He's sliding his new club into his bag, obviously bragging to his partners about his new TaylorMade. "It's the wedge he needs."

"Who are you to decide what wedge Mr. Howard needs?" Mr. Motta looks past me at him. "What makes you think you're any better at picking a wedge for him than he is? It's your job to put red and orange products into his hands. It's his job to buy them."

"Then why do we carry the yellows, greens, blues, and purples? Why don't we just carry the reds and oranges?"

"I don't expect you to understand," he says. "We need to create the illusion of variety, and we have to have a wide array of products in case people ask for a specific item. But even if someone comes in with something in mind, if you see it doesn't have a red or orange sticker on it, you've got to put a similar item in their hand that does."

I hoist myself onto the stool behind the counter. "Seems to me we'd get better customer loyalty by doing the right thing."

Mr. Motta softens. "Seth, m'boy, I'm not asking you to do anything wrong, but we have a captive audience here. No such thing as customer loyalty in a pro shop. People buy equipment here because they need something last minute or because they're too lazy to shop anywhere else. And these people have money to burn. All of our products are good, all name brands, all well reviewed, so we need to get the biggest bang for each sale."

"I agree that all our products are good," I say. "But not all our products are good for every customer. Take that wedge I just sold, for instance. It's got an offset head, which'll be good for him on account of Mr. Howard always having trouble with getting the ball up in the air."

Dimitri chuckles from the front of the shop. "This isn't going to turn into a Viagra joke, is it?"

"Butt out, Martell," Mr. Motta barks.

Dimitri ducks his head and goes back to folding.

"Not to mention," I go on, "Mr. Howard is always complaining about the arthritis in his hands. That TaylorMade has an oversized grip, which will make it easier for him to hold. It'll transmit less vibration. It's the right club for the guy."

Mr. Motta considers what I say, but I can tell he doesn't want to give up his beloved sticker system. "All I can say, Baumgartner, is that you'd better move some product here. Selling the lower-margin stuff is going to make your job harder. You'll have to move twice as much merchandise to make the same profit."

"But in the long run I think—"

"Keep it in your pants," Mr. Motta says. "I've heard enough." He grabs his iced coffee from the countertop, leaving a liquid ring on the glass. He disappears into his office and slams the door.

Dimitri, who was only making a show of folding shirts, hustles over to the counter. "Why do you bother?" he asks me. "Just sell the reds and oranges. It's no fur off your hamster's ass."

"Nah," I say. "These people take golf seriously. Why let them buy something that isn't going to help them? It's what I would want if I were shopping here."

"When you think about it, golf is sort of stupid in the first place," Dimitri says. "You're swatting a little white ball around a field with a metal stick until it falls into a four-inch hole someone's dug in some random spot."

"That's easy to say when you pull it apart like that,

but tell me you think that way when you're winning a two-dollar Nassau that's been pressed three times and are stepping up to the eighteenth tee box. Tell me you think about it that way when you're watching the final round of the U.S. Open and the two guys in the final pair are going stroke for stroke."

Dimitri shrugs.

"Anyhow, look who's talking," I say. "You've got a good chance of walking away with the tournament money this year. You take the game as seriously as anyone."

"I suppose, but it's still just a game."

"Sometimes it's better to just enjoy golf for what it is," I say, "to not pick it apart like that. And if I can help these people enjoy their game by putting the right equipment in their hands, then that's what I'm going to do."

Dimitri smirks. "So you're saying you like putting your equipment in people's hands?"

"Why do I even hang out with you?"

Dimitri grabs a fistful of golf tees from the jar on the counter and lets them tumble from his hand back into the jar. A few of them bounce out and clatter on the glass. "So, when am I coming over to the multimillion-dollar studio for my first appearance on *The Love Manifesto*?"

"I guess I can set up my old mike on the pool table," I say. "I've got something going on tonight. How's tomorrow after work?"

"I'm there," he says.

I perch on the stool and review today's schedule. It's pretty slow until around four o'clock. Then it gets busy through seven. Dimitri drags the tip of a golf tee across the circle of water left by Mr. Motta's iced coffee. He draws an arrow sticking off to the side, which makes the moisture ring look like the symbol for a male.

"Hey, don't you guys do any work around here?" The voice comes from behind me. It's Audrey. She's wearing her restaurant uniform and her hair is twisted up on top of her head, held in place by what looks like two red chopsticks. She is holding yet another chicken salad sandwich for me. For the past week or so, Audrey has been bringing me chicken salad sandwiches every day at lunchtime. After the first one, I haven't dared unwrap any of the others. We've also been sitting outside at the picnic tables after work. She plays her DS while we both talk about nothing important.

"Hey, thanks," I say. I place the sandwich next to the cash register.

"What are you guys talking about?" she asks.

"Just bullshitting," I say.

"Where's *my* sandwich?" Dimitri asks her.

"You must have left it at home."

"That's okay," Dimitri says. "Your sandwiches suck."

"No, they don't," I cut in. I don't want Audrey to feel bad. Anyhow, no matter how terrible they taste, it's nice that she thinks of me.

"Maybe you're used to eating triple-decker ass on a hard roll," Dimitri says, "but I'm not."

There is no good end to this conversation. I decide to change the subject. "So, what's going on?" I ask Audrey.

"Actually, I have to get back upstairs." She heads to the

front of the pro shop. "We're setting up for the Montgomery party. He won some local election. Assembly, school board, library board. Something like that."

"Sounds like a fun guy," I say.

"Yeah, pretty lame." Audrey stops in front of the neatly stacked polo shirts Dimitri had been working on. "They'll probably sit around all night eating cheese sandwiches with the crusts cut off."

Audrey eyeballs the shirts, and with a sweep of her arm she sends all four piles flying to the floor.

"What the hell?" Dimitri cries out. He dives at the shirts as if the three-second rule might apply.

"*Shh!*" Audrey flips a thumb toward the back room. "You might wake up Mr. Motta."

"What did you do that for?" Dimitri asks, picking up the shirts one by one.

"You insulted my chicken salad," she says. "Looks like you've got some work ahead of you, big brother." Audrey makes her way back to me. She kicks the toe of her black waitress sneaker at the carpet. "So, I won't be able to meet you after work at the picnic table." She jiggles her wrist, which has a hunter green rubber bracelet around it. "I forgot I promised Kevin I'd go to the movies with him."

"What's playing? *Save the Whales, Part Thirty-two*?" I say.

"Oh, that is hilarious." She glances at Dimitri, who is sorting shirts. Then back at me. Then down at the counter again. "Just wanted to let you know."

"Okay." I'm getting a weird vibe from Audrey, like she

wants to tell me something else, but before I have a chance to ask, my cell phone chirps. I get a roller-coaster feeling in my gut. I plunge my hand into my pocket and put my phone on vibrate.

Audrey starts toward the door and then turns back around. "So I guess I'll see you later."

"Cool," I say.

After she leaves, Dimitri swoops down on me like a vulture on the hunt for fresh eyeballs. "What's going on between you two?"

"Relax," I say. "We're only friends."

"Friends, my ass. Do you think I'm stupid? She's been bringing you sandwiches every day, and you guys meet outside to talk for hours on end—"

"First of all, her sandwiches are crap, and we don't talk for hours on end."

"If you put all the time you've spent together out there . . ." He points through the window toward the picnic tables. "It adds up to hours. Anyhow, just look how she looks at you."

"How does she look at me?"

"I don't know. Weird."

"Wow," I say. "I've never seen you so protective."

"Just stay away from her. I know how guys think, and I don't want you thinking that way about my sister. There are plenty of girls out there. You don't need to go after her."

"I'm not going after anyone," I say.

"Well, good." Dimitri holds up a yellow polo shirt.

"Hey, what does this logo remind you of?" he asks.

The logo shows a vertical golf club with two tiny white golf balls at its base. I don't take the bait. "Umm, a golf club and two golf balls? Why? What do you see?"

Dimitri shrugs as if I've disappointed him. "Nothing, I guess."

I arrange the sleeves of golf balls into a pyramid on the countertop. Then I take the basket of minipencils and sort the stubby, dull things so they're all pointing in the same direction. I'm wiping down the countertop with Windex when Dimitri breaks the silence.

"So, what's going on tonight?" he asks.

"Nothing."

"Bull," he says, an edge still in his voice. "Ten minutes ago you told me you have something going on. It's why we're doing the show tomorrow instead of tonight. 'Fess up."

"Okay, I'm 'fessing," I say. "I'm going out with Caitlyn."

"Caitlyn?"

"Yeah, you know. Caitlyn from the pool. Jill and Caitlyn."

"I know who Caitlyn is." He moves in closer and leans on my newly polished countertop. "Why didn't you tell me?"

"Because I knew you'd be on my case about it all day, telling me how you told me so and all that. Just like you're going to be on my case about this thing with Audrey, which isn't even a thing."

"I wouldn't have been on your case about it," Dimitri says. "But damn. I told you to get back in the saddle, not to start a freakin' stable."

"What's it matter?" I say. "Lust, love, attraction, they're all just because of chemicals dumping into our brains. It's all just a matter of input and output. None of it really matters."

Dimitri chuckles. "You said *input*."

"Seriously," I say. "We're practically robots programmed for breeding. Chemicals cause emotions. Emotions control your thoughts, your actions. It's a total joke."

"Okay, dude, you're starting to sound weird. You're like an antilove geek with some dork overtones and a few dashes of nerd for flavor. I know this crap with your dad, with Veronica, hit you hard, but you've got to come down off the ledge."

"I'm serious," I say. "Why should I put myself into the same position I was in with Veronica, or my mother got into with my father? I bought into all that love crap, and for what? My father is cheating on my mother. Veronica ditched me and went out with Shovel Face."

"Shovel Face?"

"Forget it," I say. "My point is that from this day forward I'm going to rise above all that emotional stuff and make sure love works for me, not the other way around."

"Seth, you're starting to sound creepy."

"It's not creepy. It's how it is."

Dimitri goes back to refolding.

"And look who's talking," I say. The words come

bubbling up before I have a chance to stop them. "Ever since you supposedly hooked up with what's-her-name mystery girl in the Starbucks bathroom freshman summer, you haven't gone out with anyone. You talk like you're some expert, but you don't know the first thing about girls."

Dimitri snaps a shirt hard before he turns in each sleeve. Then he flops the shirt over on itself, just like I taught him. He does it another dozen times until the tension is like static in the air. After a few minutes, he looks up. His face is bright red. I've never seen him look this way before. "What about Jill?"

"Jill will be just like every other girl you hang out with. You'll talk to her for a week or two, and that'll be it."

Dimitri drops another shirt on the stack and lines it up square with the others. "Do you think I like that?" He steps around the table and over to the counter. "Do you think I like that?" he says again.

"Maybe . . ."

"Well, I don't."

"I just thought maybe . . ."

Dimitri cuts me off. "I just think you're a jerk."

"You never said—"

"You never asked." Dimitri drops the shirt he was folding on the floor and heads to the door. "Tell Motta I'm going back to watercoolers and sand traps. I'd rather deal with the dozens of assholes out there than the big one in here."

Before I have a chance to say anything, the door slams shut and Dimitri is gone.

CHAPTER TWENTY-ONE ▶▶▎

When Caitlyn suggested we change plans and hang out at some party in the parking lot behind her apartment complex because some guy from the building next to hers scored a bottle of Alizé and some Coronas, I considered backing out.

My mind has been racing through my fight with Dimitri for hours, and it's put me in the foulest of foul moods. One on one with Caitlyn would have been tough enough, but playing it up for dozens of people I've never met is going to be next to impossible.

The parking lot is a large rectangle of cracked blacktop bordered on two sides by redbrick apartment buildings and on another by a cinder-block retaining wall and four Dumpsters. A few dozen kids are hanging out—sitting on the wall or on the hoods of cars and passing around bottles. Some kind of club music pulses out of a yellow

Honda Civic that boasts a bass tube in the trunk and an exhaust pipe the size of a coffee can.

As for me, I'm standing between Caitlyn and Jill with one hand stuffed in the pocket of my cargo shorts and the other holding an unsipped Corona, the lime still perched on the lip of the bottle. Caitlyn is wearing purple shorts with the word *Juicy* emblazoned across the back.

"None of the tenants say anything about us hanging out back here as long as we don't get too out of hand," Caitlyn says over the music. "Most of them can't hear us anyway. Their air conditioners are too loud."

"And they never change the batteries in their hearing aids," Jill adds. She takes a slug from a bottle and passes it on. "We don't bother them, and they don't bother us."

The music transitions into some dance song that everyone but me seems to recognize. Caitlyn squeals in delight. She leaps on the hood of my car and begins to shake her booty so the word *Juicy* starts doing a figure eight in the air. The others—guys and girls alike—gather around to cheer her on. They start pumping their fists and chanting along with the music. Jill pushes her way to the front of the group and starts chanting, too.

Caitlyn starts shaking it faster and really getting into it. With her short shorts and tight tank top, I wonder if she'd prefer a neon-lit stage and brass pole to the hood of my car. She spins around a few times, and I'm afraid she might stumble in her flip-flops, but Caitlyn twirls with confidence, like this isn't the first car hood she's danced on. Two other girls get up there to join her. I wonder what my mother would think if she knew her old Camry was being used as a stage right now.

I wonder what Dimitri would think, too. He'd probably say something along the lines of *Who would want to advertise that their ass is juicy? It would be like a girl wearing a hat that said* dented *on it or a bra that said* lopsided.

I stuff the lime down the neck of my beer with a pinkie and watch Caitlyn dance.

What am I doing here? Why did I agree to come to a party in the Schuyler Village parking lot? Why didn't I just suggest we catch a movie instead? None of these people know me. They just want to drink and see Caitlyn shake it on the hood of a car.

My chest feels filled with lead. I sit on the low part of the wall until Jill joins me.

"What's the matter?" she asks, bumping me with her shoulder.

"Nothing."

"Then why do you look like you're at a funeral?"

"Just taking it all in."

Jill glances at her cell phone, smiles, and keys in a message. "Is it about you and Dimitri?" she asks me.

"He told you?"

"Just that he was majorly pissed off. I pressed him for details, but he wouldn't budge. He was going to come down here tonight, but once he found out you might be coming he decided to stay home."

"Was that him texting you just now?"

"He wanted to know if you actually showed up."

I take a sip of beer. "I'm sure the two of us will iron everything out soon."

I watch Caitlyn some more, a fake smile pasted on my face, until Jill hands me a heavy green bottle. "Why don't you take a ride on the Night Train?" she says. "All aboard."

The burgundy label reads NIGHT TRAIN EXPRESS. A picture of a steam engine chugs across it. My guess is that the fortified wine makes your skull feel like it's been run over by that train. I make the mistake of taking a swig and manage to choke the stuff down without spraying it on the pavement. It tastes like juice if you made it from rotten fruit and floor wax, then let it ferment in a can of rusty nails.

"Sucks, huh?" Jill asks me, nodding to the bottle.

"You're not kidding."

"It's the best bang for your buck, though," she says. "Tyler over there has a fake ID. We all toss in a few dollars and he stocks up downtown. Whatever he can get. Quantity over quality, you know?"

I take another swig to make sure I won't forget how revolting the stuff is and then pass it to a kid walking by. Best to keep that bottle away from me. "Hey," I say to Jill. "Do you know a lady here in the complex named Luz? Luz Rivera?"

Jill shakes her head. "I don't think so. It's a big complex."

"She drives a green Integra? Long black hair?"

Jill almost chokes on the beer she's swigging. "You mean the *cougar*?" she says.

Caitlyn hops off my car and saunters over. Her face glows from all the dancing. She grabs my beer and sucks back a sip, then works her way between my knees and squeezes my legs with her hands. I can almost pinpoint the instant the dopamine and norepinephrine dump into my brain. My face flushes, my heart speeds up, and being here seems far more interesting than it did ten minutes ago.

"What's so funny?" Caitlyn asks Jill. "You hitting on my date?"

"Seth is asking about the cougar in eleven-oh-three."

"What, she's into younger guys?" I ask, thinking about how wrong they are. My father is definitely older than she is.

Caitlyn gives my thighs another squeeze. "She has some young soldier boyfriend who comes around to visit. Hey, maybe you're her type!" She closes her eyes and turns her face toward the halogen streetlamp. The pink light bathes her cheeks. She begins to sway to the music, oblivious to everything else around her.

Jill's phone chimes, and she glances at a text. She keys in something and hits Send. "So Dimitri tells me your podcasts are getting really good."

My stomach lurches. *He told her about that? The last thing I need is for Caitlyn and Jill to hunt me down online.*

"No, I still suck," I say.

"What's your show about?" Jill asks.

"Mostly music." I take a swig of beer.

"Yeah, but what do you talk about?" Caitlyn asks me.

"Whatever's on my mind."

"Oh," Jill says. She sits up again and begins watching the kids still clustered around my car. "Is it on iTunes or something?"

"Something like that." I try to stay vague and pray neither of them asks for the name of the show.

"What kind of music do you play?" Caitlyn asks. "Maybe I could pick out some songs for you." She bends toward me, and I can see major-league cleavage peeking at me. Pink bra.

"Sure," I say. "Hey, where's the bathroom?"

She points up the driveway. "Just find a bush up there someplace. Then hurry on back."

The driveway is steep, and the concrete sidewalk sparkles in the streetlights.

I so want to leave. I so want to start up my car and go, but everyone else is still partying. I don't want to seem like a drag. Maybe by the time I get back, Caitlyn will be bored and we can head down to Ben & Jerry's or something.

I wander the complex until I find a curb that looks inviting. It's cooler up here, and I lie back in the strip of grass, careful to avoid any doggie deposits. A few cars roll past, but I'm too busy looking at the stars to watch them.

I once heard that some stars are so far away, by the time the light from them reaches Earth, the star may have long since died. It's creepy, like a message from beyond the grave. But no matter how creepy, someone should appreciate it, someone should remember. Lying still in the strip of grass between the sidewalk and the road, I realize my head feels a little light. I spend a few minutes wondering which stars are alive and which ones are dead. Dimitri might know. If we were on speaking terms, I'd ask him.

The sound of flip-flops approaches, and I decide to tell Caitlyn that I just needed a minute to unwind. Then I'll suggest we take off in a few minutes.

"Hey there, redneck."

Luz Rivera smiles down at me.

My breath catches in my throat. I scramble away and look for her apartment. I know the condominium complex winds around, but I was sure I was nowhere near her place. "I— I—"

"I'm the one who should be apologizing," Luz says. "I didn't mean to—" She gestures to my shoulder. "After you took off, I realized you were probably looking for those kids who party down behind the complex, not stalking me."

"Yeah." I'm glad she came up with the explanation. I would never have thought of it myself.

"Anyway, I'm sorry." She claws the air like a cat. "Sometimes I forget how deadly acrylic tips can be."

I sit up and glance at my shoulder. "It's okay."

Luz sits down next to me, stretches out her legs alongside mine. Compared to hers, mine look paler than paste.

"My son would have loved hanging out down there if we lived here when he was in high school," she says. "Now he's in the service. Grew him up real fast."

Ah, that must be the infamous soldier who always visits. "How old is he?"

"Miguel is twenty-two." She smiles. "He's on leave right now, but he's being redeployed to Afghanistan soon. No wonder I've been on edge lately." She holds up a pack of cigarettes. "You mind?"

"Go right ahead."

Luz shakes the pack until a cigarette pokes out. She lifts it to her lips and lights it, takes a drag. The tip of her cigarette glows hot.

"You want one?"

"No, thanks," I say.

"Good." Luz puffs at her cigarette and blows the smoke toward the stars.

"Did I hurt you?" she asks.

I run my fingers over my shoulder.

"It was a total accident." She wiggles her fingers. "I grabbed your shoulder just as you hit the gas."

"It's fine," I say.

"Let me see, tough guy." Luz slides closer to me and rolls up my sleeve. I resist the urge to recoil under her touch. "What's this?"

I look down to see the heart-shaped tanning sticker Caitlyn gave me. I had forgotten all about it. It's peeling around the edges, and the point at the bottom of the heart is wrinkled and folded under. For the first time I notice it's sitting crooked on my shoulder.

"Oh, that's nothing," I say. "Just a tanning decal. I put it on as a goof."

Luz works her finger under the edge and slowly peels the sticker away. The glue tugs at my scabs. Pain shoots through my shoulder.

"It's never going to heal covered up like this. Haven't you ever heard of bandages? Surgical tape? Bacitracin? This wound has to breathe."

"I'll be fine."

Luz works the sticker away from my skin and gives my shoulder a good look. *"Ay, carajo,"* she mutters. "Those are some deep scrapes."

The music from the rear parking lot gets louder. I hear a few girls squeal. A bunch of guys laugh. Someone from one of the apartments calls out for them to knock it off and turn down the music.

Luz rolls my sleeve back over my shoulder. "Come on upstairs with me. I'll fix you up."

Into her apartment? "No, thanks," I say. "It'll be fine. Anyhow, my friends—"

"Nonsense," Luz says. She gets up and pulls me to my feet. "I hurt your arm, and I'm going to mend it. Come with me." She places her cigarette between her lips and extends her hand to shake. "I'm Luz Rivera."

"My name's Seth—" I almost tell her my last name but manage to shut my mouth before "Baumgartner" escapes.

Luz leads me to the concrete steps that lead to the landing that leads to the well lit stairs that lead to apartment 1103-D. That apartment is the last place in the world I want to go, but it might be the only way I'll find out anything else about her. I have to go in.

"Don't worry," she says. "My son is out for the night."

Although Luz obviously said it to put me at ease, knowing that no one else is in the apartment makes me freak out even more.

CHAPTER TWENTY-TWO ▶▶❙

The dim light from the kitchenette barely spills into the living room. It's probably for the best. Luz's place isn't shabby, but Martha Stewart would have a field day in here. A sofa and a recliner, unmatched but both in good shape, sit against one wall. A futon mattress is sprawled across the floor. A folded blanket and pillow are stacked neatly on top of it.

"I've only been here a few months," Luz says as she makes her way into the kitchen. "I haven't really had a chance to do anything with the place. Take off your shoes. Sit anywhere you like."

I take off my sneakers and place them neatly by the door. Then I loosen the laces so I can pop my feet in quickly in case I have to make a speedy getaway. I take a seat on the edge of the recliner. *Has my father sat in this very chair? Has he been on that futon?* It's probably where her son sleeps. My knee starts to bounce, and it gets the whole recliner rocking.

"What's your favorite color?" Luz asks me. I can hear her opening cabinets and rummaging through whatever is hiding in them.

"Blue, I guess."

"You guess or you're sure?"

What does it matter? "I'm sure," I say.

She leans back so she can see me through the pass-through to the kitchen. "I knew it. You give off a murky blue light."

"Huh?"

"Aura stuff. You're one sick puppy."

"Oh," I say, as if I have any clue what she's talking about. I double-check to make sure I know exactly which way my sneakers are pointing. I scope out the locks on the front door. An unlatched chain, an open deadbolt, and the twisty thing on the doorknob. Perfect for a quick exit. My leg bounces some more.

Luz finishes gathering things in the kitchen and makes her way to what I figure is the bathroom. She has a green plastic basin in her arms. It's filled with different objects I can't make out. She rummages around and finally comes back, her arms loaded with everything from gauze to tape to exotic-looking jars.

"Take off your shirt and lie back," she says.

"I don't think—"

"It's fine," she says. "I've done this a million times."

She's mended the wounds on her no-good cheating

boyfriends' sons' shoulders a million times? Somehow I doubt it.

, Luz is authoritative, almost clinical. Something about it makes me want to believe her. I lie back and let the footrest unfold under my legs. I peel off my shirt and look at my shoulder for the first time since I slapped that tanning sticker on it. The skin is bright pink, almost red. The scratch marks are oozing clear liquid and some blood from where the scab pulled off.

"Yeesh, you really are one sick puppy," Luz says. She lifts my arm and slides the basin under my elbow. "Put as much of your arm in there as you can. I'm going to have to clean this out. It's going to be a little messy, and it's not going to tickle."

"Umm—"

"Don't worry," she says. "I'm as steady as they come." She holds out her hand to show me she's not shaking. She unscrews a plastic bottle and dribbles some sort of disinfectant on my wounds. My shoulder stings, and the four scratch marks fizz up.

"It'll only hurt a second," she says as she dabs at it with a gauze pad. She rinses it with the fizzy stuff a few more times and then unscrews the lid from a jar. A pungent odor escapes. "It's an ancient herbal remedy."

"Is it FDA approved?"

She smiles. "It's homeopathic." Luz dips a cotton swab into the black paste and smears it across my shoulder. As far as I'm concerned, hygiene and the color black do not go together. I look away to get the thought out of my head that she might be using driveway sealer on my open wound.

I stare at a photo hanging on the wall of a guy who could only be Miguel, Luz's son. He's wearing a military uniform. Instead of dark eyes, though, he's got greenish hazel ones. Eyes that are not Luz's.

The paste stings and I jump a little.

"It only hurts for a second," she says.

"So, you said my aura is murky blue?"

"Actually, now that I've had a closer look, it is alternating bands of muddy green and blue with gray overtones. Not good."

"It's not indigo by any chance, is it? I could show my boss. . . ."

"No, this is more like murky blue. Like the sky before a summer thunderstorm. We'll take care of that after we patch up your shoulder."

How do you see an aura, let alone take care of one? Every word out of this woman's mouth convinces me more that her cheese is sliding off her cracker, but I figure the easiest way to get through this is to let her do her thing. I can wash off all the weird goop when I get home.

My shoulder starts to tingle more intensely as she applies a gauze pad and tapes it around the edges. She secures it further with a crisscross pattern. When she's finished, my shoulder looks like a tic-tac-toe board with an asterisk over it.

"Leave this gauze on for three days. Then change it every day after that." Luz puts some extra pads and a roll of surgical tape into a Ziploc bag and tosses it on top of my shirt, which is rumpled on her carpet.

"Sure thing," I say. "Is it supposed to tingle like this? It kind of hurts."

"That'll wear off, but the tingling means the salve is doing what it's supposed to do." Luz lights a white candle in a glass jar and places it on the end table next to me. "Lie back," she says. "I need to cleanse your aura. Your meridians are completely imbalanced."

"My aura? My meridians? I don't believe—"

She lifts a finger to her lips. "You don't have to believe. *Eso sí que es.*"

"Did you just spell *socks*?" I ask her.

Luz smiles reassuringly. "No, it's Spanish. I said *eso sí que es.*" She pronounces each word slowly and separately. "It means 'it is what it is.' It doesn't matter whether you believe in auras or not. Having a clean one results in better health just like having lower cholesterol results in better circulation. Just lie back and close your eyes. It won't hurt. I won't even touch you."

I do as she says, but I only close my eyes part of the way.

Luz stands over me and begins scooping at the air as though I'm buried in invisible snow and she's trying to gently uncover me. I don't care if she shakes chicken bones and starts doing a rain dance. I just want this to be over with. She scoops the air around my body some more and then flicks her fingers toward the floor like they are covered with some sort of filthy goop. Then she comes back, running her hands around my body but never touching. Scoop, scoop,

scoop. Flick, flick, flick. Scoop, scoop, scoop. Flick, flick, flick. Over and over again, she scoops and flicks, every once in a while standing back to inspect her handiwork.

Each time I think Luz is finished, she comes back for more, and before long, even though I struggle with my eyelids, I fall asleep.

EXCERPT FROM THE LOVE MANIFESTO ▶▶▍

Just an FYI: We hit a major benchmark the other day. More than two hundred fifty downloads after my last podcast. I must be doing something right. A special thanks to all my loyal listeners for getting the word out there. And, in other news, more theme songs are rolling in. We're up to twenty-two now. I think I'm going to start my own record label. I like the ukulele duet by Keiki and Robin and the theme song played entirely on Fisher-Price kids' instruments. You guys rock.

So, in the last segment I told you all about finding myself in the belly of the beast, in the lioness's den, in the coils of the serpent. It all came about because I was hanging out with this girl. Like I said before, this girl's got a kickin' bod. No, she's beyond that; she's slammin'. I saw her in a bathing suit last week, and I couldn't keep my eyes off her. The trouble is, all she talks about is club music. And if I change the subject, somehow she finds a way to bring it back to . . . you guessed it, club music. They say there's a perfect match for everyone, but I think this girl's perfect match would have to have an earbud jack on the side of his head and a USB port in his ass.

My buddy tells me to suck it up, to put up with her babble in order to get with her, and, believe me, it's a tempting thought.

I hate to admit it—I know it makes me seem shallow—but I want to keep it real here on The Love Manifesto. *Should I put up with her just to score, or should I hit the road because there's no connection? I mean, if love is just a chemical reaction, then why should it matter if I like her?*

Anyhow, back to meeting my father's mistress. Here's the crazy part. If I didn't know she was screwing around with my dad, I would've thought she was pretty cool. I mean, the hocus pocus stuff was weird, but aside from that. . . . Now I don't know what to think. It was so much easier hating this woman from the parking lot. Once I got to meet her, I found out she was sort of a nice lady with troubles of her own. It doesn't look like she's got a lot of money. Her kid's being redeployed to Afghanistan. . . .

Can my no-good cheating father really bring her happiness? And if he does . . .

I guess I'm not sure what to think.

Hey, I'd better crash. I've got a full day of work tomorrow, and I'm already whipped. As a consolation,

I've decided to post my full list of 156 Reasons I Love My Ex. Maybe loved *is the better word. Anyhow, I've been working on it for the past few weeks. I'll probably regret it tomorrow and delete the thing.*

You're listening to The Love Manifesto. *I hope you have a better day tomorrow than you had today. Ciao for now.*

Outro Music: "My Curse" by Killswitch Engage

CHAPTER TWENTY-THREE

"I've been working in catering for months and it just hit me a few weeks ago," Audrey says. "Instead of just serving, it would be far more interesting to be on the production side of things."

"You mean . . ."

"Making it."

We're lying on the hill that slopes down to the fourteenth green. It's the spot where all the workers meet on Wednesday nights. Dimitri, who hasn't said a word to me since he freaked out, is chipping a bucket of balls down the hill with a few of the other employees. A bunch of girls from catering, all of them still wearing their tuxedo shirts, sit in a cluster nearby. A radio pumps out some love song I've heard on my mom's show about a thousand times.

It's a clear, moonless night. The stars are so bright that I feel like I could reach up and pluck one from the sky.

The white smudge of the Milky Way stretches across the fairway from tree line to tree line.

I turn to see if she's joking, but blades of grass tickle my cheek. I look back to the sky. "What do you find interesting about it?" I ask her.

She doesn't answer right away. "All of it," she finally says. "I mean, you take a bunch of ingredients, most of which taste nasty on their own, and combine them so something delicious comes out. That's so cool." Audrey pulls her knees to her chest, and we look at the sky some more.

"Is that what you want to study in college?"

"Nah, just a hobby. You like my sandwiches, right?"

Doesn't she taste them herself? I want to tell her the truth, but I don't. "Sure," I say. "They're great."

Dimitri takes a swat at a golf ball. It pops up and trickles down to the green. The ball takes a few bounces and settles into a nice roll. It curves toward the hole and hits the flag, coming to a stop within six inches.

"Boo-yah!" he calls out, mostly toward me. He picks up his beer and takes a swig. "Now that's what I'm talking about."

A few of the other employees cheer Dimitri on.

Dimitri downs the rest of his drink. "Now that's the game I'm bringing to the tournament!"

The green is spotted with range balls, almost more so than the night sky is with stars. I am tempted to tell Dimitri that even blindfolded, if you throw enough darts, you're bound to hit the bull's-eye once in a while.

"Ignore him," Audrey says.

"Way ahead of you."

She crosses one leg over the other. "So, you're sure you like my sandwiches? I didn't follow the recipe exactly. I tried a few things of my own."

"No, seriously. Your sandwiches are excellent." I pluck a fistful of grass from the ground and roll the blades between my fingers. I want to tell her the truth, if only to save others from the trauma, but something in me tells me to stay quiet.

Audrey's cell rings, but she silences it without checking the number. "Probably just Kevin."

"You can answer it."

"I know," she says. "I'll call him later."

"How are things going with you guys?" I say.

Audrey pauses. "It's good."

"That doesn't sound so 'good.'"

"I mean, I don't want to complain because he's such a good guy. And I really admire that he cares about helping people. It's just that sometimes I wonder if we really connect on a deeper level, you know?"

"Yeah, I know what you mean. That's a tough one."

"A real tough one." Audrey plucks a handful of grass and starts tossing the blades into the air.

The song on the radio fades out, and my mother's voice comes on.

"Welcome back to *Gayle's Romantic Rendezvous*. I'm Gayle, and we have Roz from Schenectady on the line. How can I help you tonight, Roz?" My mom sounds so different on the radio than in real life. At least, I think she does.

"Hi, Gayle, I'd like to send a song out to my husband, Ralph."

"What's so special about Ralph?"

"Oh, Ralph is the man of my dreams. He works two jobs to support us and still finds time to spend with my kids. We only got together a few months ago, but he treats those kids like they're his own. We were just meant to be together."

"How do you know you were meant to be together?" my mother asks.

"I can just feel it in my bones," she says. "I know it in my heart."

"Well, I'm going to send a little Lionel Richie your way, Roz. I hope Ralph is listening. . . ."

"Who put on this channel in the first place?" Dimitri asks. "Shut this crap off."

One of the tuxedo-shirt girls picks up the radio and nestles it in her crossed legs. "It's my radio, and I'm leaving it on," she says.

"If you want to hear a *really* great show, you should check out *The Love Manifesto*," Dimitri says.

I want to go over there and hit him, throw his clubs in the stream, anything, before he says any more, but I don't.

"Go back to your lame golf career," one of the girls says.

Dimitri curls his body over his next shot. "I dunno," he says. "I just think a woman who talks on the radio about

216

love should have her own house in order first. I hear that lady—"

Audrey chucks a golf ball at him. "Shut up, Dimitri. Stop talking stupid."

Dimitri hits another ball. It barely reaches the front edge of the green. "I'm talking stupid? Why don't you ask Seth over there if I'm talking stupid?"

I start to get up, but Audrey grabs my arm.

"Don't go," she says.

"It's only going to get worse," I say. "Dimitri will keep pecking at me until I say something back. Then it's going to get ugly."

I get up and head toward the cart path, back toward the clubhouse.

"Come on, Seth," Dimitri calls after me. "Tell Audrey how stupid I'm talking!"

I don't turn around.

I hear light footsteps coming up behind me. It's Audrey. I notice her T-shirt. It reads:

> *To Kill a Mockingbird*
> *Get hammer*
> *Hold down mockingbird*
> *Hit it in the head*

It's exactly what I want to do to Dimitri.

"Drive me home?" Audrey asks.

"Sure."

We walk silently along the cart path.

Behind me, Dimitri's club slices through the grass much harder than it needs to for someone chipping. The golf ball punches through low-hanging branches on the far side of the green. It strikes a tree trunk with a loud *thwack* and bounces into the underbrush. There is no doubt that ball is lost for good.

CHAPTER TWENTY-FOUR ▶▶▎

As we turn onto Audrey's block, I catch sight of Kevin's Wrangler. Kevin is leaning over the side, messing around between his surfboard and the seat.

"Probably pulling out the drain plug," Audrey says. "He doesn't put the top up when it rains, and the thing fills up with water all the time."

"Doesn't that—?"

"Get my ass wet when I sit in the seat? Yeah, thanks for asking."

"Actually, I was going to ask if it made the floor rusty."

"Kevin is all about communing with nature," Audrey says. "Rain is part of nature, and he wants to get close to it. Something like that. All I can tell you is that my ass does not like communing with nature."

"Maybe I should drop you off and head out," I say.

"I don't want to cause any trouble with you guys."

"No trouble to cause." Audrey turns down the music. "Kevin won't care."

I pull up to the house, and Audrey hops out. Kevin is right there to hug her. He's wearing what I'm learning is his standard uniform: surf shorts, flip-flops, and a tattered tee.

"Hey," he says.

Audrey smiles and scrunches up her shoulders.

"What's up, man?" he says to me.

We bump fists.

"I was just giving Audrey a ride home from work," I say. I feel like I need to explain. After all, Audrey is his girlfriend. "A bunch of us were hanging out and . . ."

"Yeah, that's cool," Kevin says. He grins at me, his head bobbing. He pushes his hair from his eyes.

"You weren't waiting long, were you?" she says to him.

"Nah, just a few minutes." He looks at me and then down at Audrey. Then he pulls a purple rubber wristband from his pocket. "There's a sleepover in the park to raise awareness for the homeless."

Audrey shoots me a look but slips the bracelet on her wrist.

"Hey," Kevin says to me. "You want to come along?"

I point back to my car. The last thing I'd want to do is hang out with the two of them in the park, slapping tambourines all night. "Actually, I've got a thing later on." My excuse sounds lame, so I try to add to it so it won't sound like a blowoff. "I'm meeting a few of the guys from . . . you know, this thing I do."

Audrey laughs. "Yeah, well, have fun doing that thing you do."

I start back to my car when a white SUV turns the corner, deep bass pumping from the speakers. The truck stops in front of the house, sandwiching my car between itself and Kevin's. Dimitri stumbles out. He looks us over and chuckles. "Hey, all the players are present and accounted for," he says.

Kevin's smile melts just a little. "Yo!" he calls over to Dimitri. "I burned that CD for you. I'll bring it over sometime tomorrow."

"Cool," Dimitri says. He taps the hood of the white SUV, and it drives off. Then he heads up the walk to the house. "By tomorrow, though, I'm not sure you'll be coming around all that often. Tonight might be serious talk night."

Audrey walks up to Kevin's car and flings open the door, accidentally bumping her head on Kevin's surfboard. She climbs into the passenger seat and jumps a little, probably from the wet upholstery. Then, she slams the door and flips Dimitri the bird. "You're such an asswipe," she hollers to him as she and Kevin pull away from the curb.

Dimitri looks to me with a satisfied smirk and disappears into his house.

CHAPTER TWENTY-FIVE

"You've got to shorten that backswing," my father says, scooping grass seed onto the strip of dirt I cut into the turf after my lame drive. "You're trying to kill the thing."

Funny he should say that, considering I was picturing his face on the ball as I drew back my club. I snooped through my father's briefcase last night and discovered a whole bunch of receipts from the flower shop. It turns out my father is no stranger to that place. Over the past month, he's gone there a few times. First it was a huge summer arrangement, then he went to roses. The time I saw him with Luz, he ordered a bouquet of blue and white irises with red tulips.

Delivery date: "To Be Determined."

I lay awake trying to figure that one out. To Be Determined? Why would he do that? I can't remember the last time flowers crossed the threshold of our own house.

It's like my mother doesn't exist anymore.

The only reason I'm playing this round is because my father spent a hundred bucks to hire me from the pro shop to be his caddy. I practically passed out when I found out he left the office to play in the middle of the work day. Mr Motta thought it was strange, too, but a hundred bucks is a hundred bucks. Pure profit for the shop.

I toss my broken tee into the bushes. Tugging my golf cap low over my eyes, I plod back to the cart and slide my driver into my bag. I sit in the driver's seat waiting for my father to scrape the face of his club with his wire brush before returning it to its place in his meticulously organized bag.

"The tournament isn't far off," he says.

"I know." I try to seem enthusiastic, but my words come out sounding defensive.

"Have you been practicing?"

I don't answer.

"Look, Seth," my father says, scraping extrahard at his club. He blows on it, then scrapes some more. "You've got to get out here on your own. Hit buckets at the range. Play a few holes before work. Stay late. Whatever it takes. You've got the time."

"I've been busy lately."

"With all that computer stuff in the basement?" My father slides into the seat next to me, and I stomp on the pedal. The cart lurches forward, and we make our way along the path to my ball. It's easy to spot, sitting up on the short cut of rough to the right of the fairway. "This tournament is more important than that. There's a ten-thousand-dollar scholarship riding on it, not to mention bragging rights."

"But the podcasting—"

"Are you going to make ten grand podcasting? It's a dead end."

I get out of the cart. I pull out my four-iron and my five-iron, not sure which one I'll need. The yard marker says the center of the green is a hundred and sixty yards away, but the pin is positioned near the front edge, and the green is at least ten feet below us. I opt for the five-iron and line up. I draw back and give a few light practice swings, knowing I have more than enough club to get there.

I clear my mind and hit the ball. My right elbow stays glued against my side, and the power comes through my hips. My ball pops into the air with a sharp *thwap*. It lands on the down slope of the hill and takes a great bounce. My ball trickles onto the front of the green and curls to the left. It hooks around to within five feet of the hole.

"And we have a shot," my father says. "That swing of yours is finally waking up."

I trot back to the cart, where my father has already slid into the driver's seat. He hates when I'm behind the wheel. As we wind down the path to his ball, nearly fifty yards farther than my drive was, he says, "We came in third last year, and both kids who beat us are off at college now. We've got a chance if you can find a way to play like that last shot of yours."

"Dimitri's in the tournament this year," I say. "He's as

good as I am, maybe better. I hear his dad is good, too. He plays over at the municipal course. He's in a league on Thursday nights, and he hits another eighteen on Sundays. Sometimes twenty-seven. Dimitri says his dad's short game is wicked."

"Has Dimitri's father ever played here at the club?" he asks.

I shrug. "Not that I know of."

"Then he's got no chance. You know how tough our greens are. They're the hardest in the Capital District. You've got to play them to understand them."

"Dimitri plays them all the time," I say. "He'll be like a caddy for his father."

My father hits up, and his ball lands in the center of the green. It's got so much backspin that it rolls off the front edge into a shallow rut. "Crap on a crostini!" He thrusts his club back into his bag and eyeballs me. While he was swinging, I slid back into the driver's seat. I smile at him innocently, and he stomps around to the passenger side.

I head up the left side of the fairway toward the back of the green. "Plus Dimitri—"

"Enough about Dimitri," my father says. "You sound like you want him to win."

"Nah, he and I are on the outs. I'm just saying—"

"What happened?" he asks.

"Oh, nothing. I'm just saying that we shouldn't discount those guys as serious competition."

"That's one of the great things about golf," my father says. He pushes back his hair and resets his cap on his head.

"The competition is really against ourselves. As long as we do well, there's nothing they can do to stop us. If you focus on your game and I focus on mine, we'll win. Ten grand in our pockets and our names on the brass plaque in the clubhouse."

"No problem," I say. I pull the cart up to the green and hop out. Before I have a chance to slide out my putter, I hear the hum of another golf cart coming up the fairway.

It's the snack cart.

Audrey.

My father grabs his wedge and putter and makes his way toward his ball. "No food for me." Then he reconsiders. "Maybe I'll take a bottle of water."

Audrey pulls up alongside me. She's wearing a white polo shirt and khaki shorts. I prefer her "To Kill a Mockingbird" tee.

"Nice outfit," I say.

"New policy. The board thinks some of us cart girls have been dressing too provocatively to get better tips." Audrey pulls out a black cap and puts it on her head. In bold white letters it reads I ♥ MIDGET PORN across the front. "Nothing in the dress code bans this, though."

"Have you ever seen midget porn?"

"Nope," she says. "I just liked the hat. It made me wonder if it's midgets who like midget porn or if it's some kind of regular-sized-person fetish."

"I'm sure someone has the data on that one," I say.

"You think?"

"Sure. It would determine whether the midget porn

goes on the high shelf or the low shelf at the porn shop."

"Would you guys mind quieting down?" my father says. "I'm trying to hit over here."

Audrey slips out of her cart and stands alongside me. All I want to do is ask what happened after I left last night, but I'm guessing now is neither the time nor the place.

"I hate playing middlewoman," she whispers, "but Dimitri wants me to tell you to shove an umbrella up your ass and press the Open button."

"He told you to tell me that?"

My father glares up at me.

"He told you to tell me that?" I whisper.

"You don't think I made that up, do you? That's a Dimitri-ism if I ever heard one." She places a wrapped sandwich, likely her famous-for-being-terrible chicken salad, on the dashboard of my cart. "You need anything else?" she asks. "I've got to run a cheesesteak up to Assemblyman Wright on the fifteenth."

"No, I'm good."

Audrey hops into her cart and hits the pedal just as my father swings. His ball pops up, barely touches the fringe of the green, and rolls back down the hill.

"Sorry, Mr. Baumgartner!" she calls over her shoulder as her cart winds up the path to the next hole.

Before my father has a chance to shout obscenities, I tell him to take a do-over. His next shot brings him within a few feet of the pin. We both putt out, and I beat him back to the cart so I can drive to the next tee box. As we make our way up the path, my father unwraps Audrey's sandwich.

"You mind?" he asks me.

"Knock yourself out."

He takes a bite, and his face twists up. He gags twice and spits out the half-chewed wad of nastiness. "What the—?" He looks between the slices of wheat bread and tosses the rest of the sandwich into the weeds as though being near it might traumatize him more. "What the hell kind of sandwich is that?"

"It's supposed to be chicken salad," I say.

"More like chicken *shit* salad. Did she remember to pluck the chicken before cutting it up? There might be some beak in there."

I stifle another laugh and keep my eyes forward.

"Where's my water? I've got to wash my mouth out."

"Crap," I say. "I forgot to get one for you."

That's when the curse words start to fly. As I roll up to the next tee box, my father leaps out of the cart and holds his face under the spout of the watercooler. He rinses his mouth a whole bunch of times and spits over and over again into the bushes. I can't help but think karma played a hand in my temporary amnesia. What goes around comes around. It was an honest mistake, forgetting to get his water from Audrey, but one that will probably put a smile on my face for all time.

CHAPTER TWENTY-SIX

"Let's get a move on," my mother says, racing ahead of me. "The mall closes in half an hour."

The golf tournament is in two days, and my mother insists I have a new outfit for each of the three days of competition. My standard golf uniform, a navy polo and khaki cargo shorts, would be fine by me, but once Mom gets an idea in her head, it's hard to shake her from it. And her idea tonight is to make me "stand out among all the other guys in the tournament."

It doesn't matter if you win or lose, she said to me as she weaved her Lexus through traffic. *It's whether, at the end of the day, people remember who you are.*

We've already been to Macy's, J.Crew, Dick's Sporting Goods, and the Gap, and we're still empty-handed. Now we're headed over to Abercrombie, which is the last place I want to be with my mom. Likelihood of being seen by someone I know: high.

"Let's go, Seth!" She barks at me like she's the drill sergeant and I'm dragging ass on a basic-training march.

I trail behind with my head down and my hands stuffed into my pockets. I stay far enough away that people might not suspect we're together but close enough that she won't spin around and start leading me by the arm.

As I follow her into the store, the pulsing music drowns out the click of my mother's heels on the tile floor. The stench of Fierce punches me in the face so hard my eyes tear up. Why does this place have to pump so much cologne into the air? It's like pollution. We walk past a clerk, his head buried in the racks, and make our way to the tables piled high with polos.

"This orange one is nice," my mother calls to me, too loud even for the music. She picks up one of the neatly folded shirts. After all the folding I've been doing at the pro shop these past few weeks, I sympathize with the employees here. By the time my mother is done riffling through the inventory, they'll have a few hours of extra work ahead of them. "And the stripes . . . Doesn't Tiger Woods wear stripes?"

"You're thinking of real tigers," I say. "Anyhow, who cares what Tiger Woods wears? He cheated on his wife with, like, twenty women."

Mom shrugs. "Who doesn't these days?"

I glance at my mother but she doesn't look up. *Does she know about my father and what he's been up to? I so want to say something. I so want to say something. I so want to say something!*

But all that comes out is, "Tiger Woods wears red. His mother thinks it's his power color."

My mother slings the orange shirt over her shoulder and starts pawing through the others. "Well, orange is *your* power color. You'll wear this one on Sunday."

She moves to a table arranged with shorts and grabs a pair of pale pink ones covered in tiny blue embroidered moose.

"No way," I say.

She holds the shorts at arm's length. "I think they're cute."

"Maybe I'll wear them with the orange shirt," I say. "I'll look like a toucan that flew through a wood chipper."

"Don't be silly," she says, scoffing. "We could find a neutral shirt to pair them with. Navy or white."

I lean against one of the clothing racks and shake my head. Clueless as my mother is, I know she means well. "Put the shorts down," I say to her. "I'd rather play in those ratty old Grinch boxers I have."

She reluctantly nods and drops the piglet-colored moose shorts on the table. "Why don't you check on what they have in the back of the store? We should divide and conquer."

My mother doesn't have to say it twice. It's not the conquer part that interests me; it's the dividing. I weave my way through the tables to the rearmost section. More of the same. Clothes stacked high on tables and shelves. Dramatic overhead lighting and loud music. The only difference is the stench of cologne might be stenchier back here. Probably

231

less ventilation. I feel a headache coming on but decide to wait it out, stay invisible, until my mother wants to leave. I search out the discount rack and sort through the polos.

I'm not sure if I see the hand first or feel the slap across my face.

"What the hell?" Caitlyn growls, her eyes drilling into me.

Anger swells in me, but it's quickly overcome by confusion. My face tingles, stings. It feels sort of prickly. My fingers make their way to my cheek and move across the spot where her hand made contact. It's the first time anyone's ever slapped me, and I'm not quite sure how to react.

"What's the matter?"

"You know damn well what's the matter," Caitlyn hisses. She pulls her walkie-talkie from her belt and announces to her coworkers that she's on break. I had no idea she worked here. I never even thought to ask if she had a job. "That podcast of yours?" she goes on. "*The Love Manifesto*? I listened to the whole thing—every episode from the beginning. Sure, you altered your voice, kicked up the bass, threw in some echo, but I can tell it's you. You make me sound like, like . . . What did I ever do to you?"

My mind scrambles to figure out how Caitlyn might have found my show, who might have told her. Then my mind scrambles to remember exactly what I said about her in my podcasts. Something in my chest plunges into my belly. I said I'd rather shove ice picks in my ears than hear her talk about club music. I said her perfect boyfriend would have an earbud jack in his head and a USB port in his ass. At the time I thought it was funny, but now that I look back I know I deserved the slap.

"*I'm* boring?" she says, advancing on me. "Why don't you take a good long look at yourself, Seth Baumgartner? Do you have any idea how boring you are? You barely even talk. Hanging out with you is like work. Hell, it's worse than work."

"Who told you about my podcast?" I say.

Caitlyn plants her fists on her hips. "Now you think I'm too dumb to find your stupid show on my own? I have a brain, you know. You just never took the time to figure that out. You were too busy staring at my tits."

Of course, her mentioning her chest and gesturing toward it—along with all the angry bouncing she's doing—causes my gaze to drop. She slaps me again.

"Jeez, Caitlyn, I—"

"You nothing," she says. "You messed with the wrong girl. If I ever catch your lame, pencil-dick, womanizing ass anywhere near me again, I'll make sure you aren't just rebounding from your last girlfriend; I'll make sure your face is rebounding off the sidewalk."

I want to make things right with Caitlyn—to apologize—but every time I try to say anything, she jumps in and tears me into smaller pieces. I want to tell her it's only a podcasting personality, that none of it is real. I want to tell her how I exaggerate everything, play things up for the drama of it.

"Caitlyn, let me explain."

"Don't even say my name, you pathetic player wannabe. You make me want to puke." She pokes me in the chest with a stiff finger. "You talk about anonymity on the podcast, but it was clear to everyone who you were talking about."

"You're right," I say.

"Damn straight, I'm right!"

"What's going on over here?" A woman wearing a black sleeveless turtleneck and tight jeans is standing on the opposite side of the table from us. She's wearing a lanyard around her neck that holds a bunch of keys and a name tag that says YVONNE: STORE MANAGER. "Is there a problem, Caitlyn?"

"No problem," she says. "Just taking care of a little business. I'll be done in a minute."

"You'll be done now. Like, right now." She leans over the table toward Caitlyn so she doesn't have to raise her voice over the music. "The only business you should be doing when you're here is A&F business. Take care of your personal affairs on your own time."

"I'm on break," she says.

"You're still wearing your lanyard. You're still in the store."

Caitlyn folds her arms and nods.

"Seth? Is everything okay?" My mother comes up alongside me, one arm loaded with shirts and shorts. Her free hand runs up my back to my shoulder.

Caitlyn's eyes alternate between me, my mother, and Yvonne. She goes back and forth a few times as though she is weighing her options. One side of her face curls up into

234

a devious smile and she extends her hand to shake. "You must be Seth's mother," she says cheerily. "It's so nice to meet you."

My mother awkwardly shifts the clothes to her other arm and shakes Caitlyn's hand. "Why, thank you," she says. "Are you one of Seth's friends from school?"

Caitlyn lets her hang for a few seconds too long—until I jump in.

"Did you find any good shirts up front, Mom?"

Caitlyn nudges me aside with her hip and faces my mom. "Have I got something to tell you, Mrs. Baumgartner. I was listening to Seth's podcast the other day. Have you listened to it? It's really funny. . . ." Caitlyn seems to be enjoying herself, relishing every moment.

I glance at my mother's face. She's smiling, expecting to hear something nice about her precious son. The fact that it's about podcasting, something I do because of her, swells her up even more. Little does she know the bomb that's about to drop.

I step in. "Caitlyn, I don't think—"

She spins on me. "That's right, Seth. You *don't* think." She turns back to my mother and goes on. "Seth was podcasting the other day, and he was talking about—"

That's when instinct takes over. I grab Caitlyn by a shoulder, scoop her head in my hands, and kiss her. I kiss her long and hard. I don't want to come up for air.

"Oh!" my mother gasps. She steps back, unsure of how to react.

I want to keep kissing Caitlyn—to keep her lips locked—

until my mother is ushered from the store at closing time and they drop those metal gates. I want to keep kissing her until there is enough space between Caitlyn and my mom that her angry words won't destroy my family.

The knee to the balls cuts things short.

If the slap was a tingle, this is a full-on electrocution. For an instant, my vision goes white and my bottom half short-circuits. I crumple to the floor. Then the slow locomotive of pain starts rumbling through my pelvis. I always thought getting nutmegged would feel like a speed bag getting punched by a boxer—something external with lots of rattling around of the chandelier—but the pain of Caitlyn's knee strikes deeper. It weaves somewhere deep between my hips, around my spine, and then takes hold of my whole body from my chest to my knees. Heat flashes through me, then come the chills. I curl into a fetal position, but it does no good.

From under the table, I hear Yvonne bellow the words at Caitlyn that have become so familiar to me: "You're fired!" she yells. "Get the hell out of here!"

"You should have raised your son to be a gentleman!" Caitlyn yells at my mother.

"Get out!" Yvonne booms.

The last thing I see before my eyes clench shut are Caitlyn's feet weaving between the tables toward the front of the store.

EXCERPT FROM THE LOVE MANIFESTO ▶▶|

Intro Music: "Addicted" by Saving Abel

This is going to sound weird, but does it seem like I'm always nursing a wound when I do this podcast? A few weeks back I had those scratches across my shoulder. Now I have an icepack on my crotch.

All I can say is if having a baby is one-tenth as bad as getting kicked in the cashews, I vote for mandatory epidurals for every pregnant woman. Mandatory. Shouldn't even be an option.

Does anyone out there find that no matter how much you want to hold things together, sometimes they just seem to fall apart? Almost like the more you try, the worse things unravel? Well, how come my summer seems to be turning out that way?

I start off getting dumped by my girlfriend and seeing

my father out to lunch with his mistress. I get fired from my job and end up with a snoozefest of a position working for a guy who thinks it's more important to make money than it is to serve the customer. Then, my best friend in the world decides to freak out and hate me.

I've been podcasting about things in my life, trying to figure out what love is all about. Sure, I've been cynical about everything, but who wouldn't be, after the cascade of crap that's come down on me? This is my parents' marriage we're talking about. They've been together for nearly twenty years, and I know something that could wreck it all. Do any of you out there know what that feels like? Well, let me tell you . . . it sucks big-time.

And when it's all said and done, how much closer am I to figuring out anything about love?

<long pause>

I have no clue. . . .

I've got to get some sleep. I have that big golf tournament coming up, so I need to practice before work. I'm guessing my natural swing will be severely hampered by bruised balls. So, later, gators. Oh, and you know the routine. Feel free to leave me a voice mail or send me an email. Tell your friends about the program. All that stuff. I'm out of here.

Outro Music: "Rehab" by Rihanna

CHAPTER TWENTY-SEVEN

Veronica's fingers comb through Mr. Peepers's short fur. He rolls onto his back and stretches out. Tiny grunts escape the little traitor's throat. "Don't you think Mr. Peepers is a weird name for a Chihuahua?" she asks me.

"I think calling anything that small *mister* is weird."

Veronica goes back to scratching Mr. Peepers's belly. Her hand on my dog seems foul. I don't want Veronica bonding with the family pet. I want to scoop him away and kick Veronica out. After freaking out on her on the front porch two weeks ago, I didn't expect to see her anywhere near my house ever again, let alone sitting on the floor of the TV room.

But here she is. She showed up all hugs and smiles. My mother ushered her inside before I had a chance to protest, even before coming to get me.

"I can't believe the tournament is tomorrow," Veronica says.

Small talk.

"I know," I say.

"Been practicing much?" Mr. Peepers shifts to his other side. Veronica scratches him faster and his leg starts pumping.

"Not as much as I should."

"Seth," my mother calls from the kitchen, "can you let little Peepy out? He probably has to go wee-wee. It's been a few hours."

"In a minute," I call back.

"Please do it now," she says, this time more firmly.

Little Peepy? Veronica mouths.

I shrug.

Veronica lifts up Mr. Peepers like he's an infant and kisses him on the nose. "Oh, let the poor guy out. His bladder's probably smaller than a grape."

I plod across the family room and heave open the sliding door. When I drop back onto the sofa, Veronica still has Mr. Peepers cradled in her arms. Strangely, she's sitting a few feet closer to my spot on the couch.

"What's the weather supposed to be like tomorrow?" she says.

More small talk. Weather—the worst kind.

I want to tell her that it's supposed to be hot, like, fire-and-brimstone hot, that Mr. Mackie, the oldest living club member, is probably going to keel over from the heat, but small talk only goes so far when your ex-girlfriend who cheated on you and then dumped you in the middle of Applebee's shows up unannounced and is sitting in the middle of your family room petting the family dog.

"Why did you come here, Veronica?"

"I don't know. I just wanted to wish you luck, to see what's going on. It's been a few weeks and—"

"Stop," I say.

She stops.

"We both know you didn't come down here to check on the weather. And I've known you long enough that I can tell when you're lying."

"No, you can't."

"Sure, I can," I say. "You lower your head and look at me through your hair with your eyes turned upward."

Veronica brushes her hair aside. She glances toward the kitchen, where my mother is drinking her coffee over the newspaper. It's through a door and around a corner, so there is no line of sight. Veronica slides even closer. "I've been thinking about it for the past few weeks," she says softly. She sets Mr. Peepers down, and he waddles off toward the kitchen, his nails *scritch, scritch, scritch*ing on the hardwood. As he passes the open sliding door he peers out into the sunshine. He growls someplace deep in his chest for a few seconds, then continues into the kitchen. "I think maybe we should get back together," Veronica says.

"What?" I say.

She smiles. "I've been thinking about it, and I think we should give things another try."

I can't believe she's finally saying the words out loud I've been fantasizing about for weeks. The tough skin I had worked so hard to grow melts away. I want to say yes. Something about it feels like it would erase all the other terrible things that have happened over the past month. Like pushing a reset button.

I want to lean in to kiss her.

I know I could.

The electricity between us tells me she'd kiss me back.

Veronica shifts to her knees and leans on my thigh. I can smell her perfume. It reminds me of fumbling around with her in the dark of the basement. "What do you say?" she barely breathes.

Every cell in me is screaming yes, screaming for me to get nearer to her. It would be so easy.

"What about Anders?" I say.

She sighs. "I just don't see myself with him. I see myself with you."

Veronica leans toward me. She leans in close, her lips inches from my ear. Her breath tickles the hairs on my neck. "Maybe we could, you know, go downstairs or something," she whispers.

My hand slides to her hip.

She presses her body against my thigh.

I want to kiss her so badly.

While I'm taking my time thinking about it, Veronica makes the decision for me. Her lips touch the line of my jaw and kiss it softly. I turn toward her. Our lips meet and anything that was left of my resolve drops away. She feels so familiar, like an old glove. Soft, warm, comfortable. I know it's not the right thing to do. She cheated on me. She hooked up with Anders before breaking things off. My mind says no, but my body screams, "Hell, yes!"

We kiss for a while longer, long enough for me to be aware of *scritch, scritch, scritch*ing across the tile as Mr. Peepers heads outside. Then I hear grunting and the tearing of paper. More grunting. Then a loud hack. And another.

I push Veronica off me and head over to the sliding door.

"What's the matter?" she says.

I poke my head out into the blinding sun. Mr. Peepers is digging through wax paper and gnawing on a sandwich that lies half eaten on the ground. It's chicken salad. His face is covered with it. Mr. Peepers shakes his tiny head violently and starts hacking some more, coughing like he's trying to vomit up his whole digestive system. I pick up the sandwich. I wrap it back up in what's left of the wax paper and set it on the patio table.

What's one of Audrey's sandwiches doing on the deck?

I look past the rusty swing set, past the privacy fence, into the neighbor's yard. Our gate swings in the breeze. That thing is always closed. My father checks it every night before bed and every morning before he leaves for work.

I head through the gate and check the side of the

house. Nothing. I walk through the Beattys' yard and the Connors' yard. I check Mr. Venter's yard, even though he calls the cops when kids set foot on his sod. Still nothing.

I call out Audrey's name a few times.

No answer.

I head back inside. Veronica is still kneeling by the couch.

"You've got to go," I say.

"Why?" she asks.

"I've got a lot to do. The tournament's tomorrow. I've got to go to the range and hit a few buckets, practice my flops."

"What about . . . ?" She motions to the spot where I was just sitting.

I shake my head. "It's not a good idea."

"But what about your hundred and fifty-six reasons?"

My breath catches somewhere deep in my chest. "Where'd you hear about that?"

She sits back on her heels. "Everyone knows, Seth. It's everywhere—someone posted it on Facebook last night."

Probably Caitlyn. I guess a kick in the nuts wasn't enough punishment. This will be worse. Much worse. Did I say anything on the show that might have insulted anyone else? Anyone at school? What's going to happen when classes start back up in September? It's one thing to be a faceless personality on a podcast; it's another for everyone to know it's me.

"I had no idea that was how you felt about me," she

says. "You never told me any of it. If I had known . . . well, things might have been different." She grabs my forearm, pulls me toward her. "Maybe they still can be."

I pull away. "Look, Veronica, I don't think we should—"

"Of course we should."

"No," I say. "We shouldn't. We're done."

Veronica stares at me. Her lips press together, but she doesn't make a sound. She grabs her purse and walks out through the sliding door. She passes through the same gate Audrey went through not five minutes earlier.

"What's going on?" my mother says, coming up behind me. She takes a sip of her coffee and runs her hand up my back. "Is Veronica okay?"

"You should be more worried about Mr. Peepers," I say. "He's choking."

My mother looks down at him. He's walking in circles around the deck and shaking his head. His tongue is sticking out of the side of his mouth like he'd rather have it surgically removed than suffer one more second of Audrey's chicken salad.

"What'd he eat?" my mother asks me.

"Hell between two slices of bread. A little lettuce. Some tomato."

She watches him a moment longer. "He'll be fine."

"So will Veronica," I say.

We watch her cross the Connors' yard and head toward the side street that leads to her house. "She looks upset," my mother says. "Are you sure she's all right?"

"Sometimes you can't see things clearly until you've taken a big bite of the worst chicken salad sandwich in the world."

My mother smiles. It's a puzzled sort of smile, but it's the biggest one I've seen on her in a long time. It takes a decade off her face. "Seth Eugene Baumgartner, have you been listening to my radio program?"

"Nah," I say. "I've got one of my own."

CHAPTER TWENTY-EIGHT ▶▶|

Preparing for a golf tournament is nothing like cramming for a test. It's not like you can stay up late the night before with a golf ball in one hand and a nine-iron in the other and somehow figure out the secret to hitting well. Golf has to do with timing and feel and something my old golf instructor called "muscle memory." I have no idea what that is, but I'm pretty sure my muscles don't have it. Aside from the few rounds I played with my father and the one time I played with Dimitri a few weeks back, I haven't practiced at all. My muscles probably have amnesia.

The greenkeepers have been setting the pin locations and placing the tee markers since before dawn, but I was the first player to arrive. I was staring at my bedroom ceiling all night anyway. I figured I could putt for a while to see how the greens are running and hit a few buckets at the range, but instead I decided to hang out in the locker room. There is something relaxing about being in here. It's quieter than a coffin, and the polished oak lockers, huge leather armchairs, and thick red carpeting make me think of royalty. Although my father, like each of the other members, has a double locker with an engraved brass plaque toward the front, I prefer an unmarked one in the back.

Some kind of smooth jazz saxophone music floats down from the speakers. It reminds me of the day in Applebee's when I first saw my father with Luz. The day Veronica dumped me. Is Kenny G stalking me?

I wonder what Luz has been up to. I haven't seen her in over a week, not since she re-dressed my wound and scooped away all my bad energy. I'll have to admit that my wound has been healing quickly, but I'm not sure if it's from what Luz did or just because she took off the heart-shaped tanning sticker. I haven't seen much of my dad this past week, either. Must be nice to be able to blow off your family and hang out with your mistress in her love nest across town.

I twist the wrench, tightening the last rubber spike to the sole of my shoe. My dad knows I haven't been practicing, and he is making sure I won't be able to blame it on any sort of equipment failure. A brand-new box of spikes was waiting for me on the kitchen table next to my car keys.

I can hear his voice in my head. *Power comes from your hips, and your hips can't transmit power unless your feet have a firm grip on the earth. You need a solid foundation.*

I give each spike an extra quarter turn to make sure

they all stay tight and then I lean forward to put on my golf shoes.

"I had a feeling I'd find you back here."

At first I'm startled. Then I'm just plain surprised Dimitri came so early. He's a late riser.

"I couldn't sleep, either." He is bare chested, wearing only purple shorts, his black golf shoes, and a ridiculous attempt at a mustache that trails down in a swoop and attaches to his sideburns. He's holding a cardboard tray with two Styrofoam coffee cups in it. He drops his duffel bag from his shoulder and sits across from my bench on a leather wingback. He hands me one of the cups. Hot chocolate.

"So, what's with the . . . ?" I gesture to his face.

"The mustache?"

"If that's what you want to call it."

He strokes the fuzz with his thumb and forefingers. "Not enough guys do the mustache thing."

"You make a good argument for why."

"Come on, if guys stop growing mustaches, we'll see the disappearance of the best word in the English language."

"And that would be?"

"*Mustachioed.*"

Ignoring his mustache and any further conversation about mustaches is the best course of action here. "So, tournaments make you nervous, too?"

"Nah, I've got nothing to prove here. It's not my club."

"What about the ten grand? The scholarship?"

"What about it?"

"Don't you feel pressure to win? Isn't your father on your back about it?"

"It's found money," Dimitri says with a shrug. "If it weren't for me working here, I wouldn't have a shot at it in the first place. Anyhow, by the time I get out of school I'm going to be so buried in loans that ten thousand dollars isn't going to make much of a dent."

"How come you had trouble sleeping, then?"

Dimitri lifts a foot and inspects his spikes. They're old, caked with grass and dirt. "Just stuff, you know?" He picks at some of the grass and tosses it to the carpet. "Stuff between me and you, I guess."

"Look," I say, "I've been thinking about what happened and—"

He lifts a hand to stop me. "No worries."

"What do you mean, no worries?"

"I mean, don't sweat it. It's water under the bridge. Ancient history. Let bygones be bygones. That poop's been scooped."

"That poop's been scooped?" I ask.

"There's always room in the lexicon for a new figure of speech."

I hate to admit it, but I've really missed the bastard. I want to forget all the bad stuff between Dimitri and me, to let things go back to the way they were before he stormed out of the pro shop, but that's exactly what I was thinking when Veronica came to the house yesterday. What good would it do to ignore things? I'm still not quite sure what set Dimitri off. How could I ever be sure I won't say something else that will bother him?

"No, Dimitri." My face swells with heat. "We need to talk this out."

"What's to talk out?" he says. He fidgets with the lid of his hot chocolate. The white plastic flap snaps off. "Just let sleeping dogs lie."

"Enough with the clichés," I say. "They're not going to stop me. What's going on?"

"Nothing." Dimitri scratches the plastic flap against his thigh and slouches low in the armchair. "It's going to sound stupid."

"It can't be more stupid than me being hung up on Veronica for the past month. I've been so wrapped up in my own problems that I didn't stop to think you might be having some of your own. What's going on?"

I'm not used to seeing Dimitri at a loss for words, but now that I think about it we haven't had many conversations in the past few months deeper than which girls in our school he'd like to have sex with.

Dimitri places his cup on the bench I'm sitting on. He crosses his arms over his chest. "You've been talking all summer about Veronica, wanting to get back with her. You've been podcasting about love. You went out with Caitlyn. . . . Sorry to hear about you getting shucked in the oysters, by the way."

"You listened to the podcast?"

He nods. "You're going to have to fill me in on all the gory details."

"Gory they are."

"Anyhow, you had a girlfriend for months," Dimitri says. "You split up with her and bounce right into all this other stuff. Things happen for you, Seth. Nothing ever happens for me."

"That's not true."

"Yes, it is."

"Maybe it's just that I make things happen."

"Yeah, right," he scoffs. "Aside from me, you barely talk to anyone. Now my sister is interested in you, and it freaking pisses me off."

"Audrey?"

"Come on," Dimitri says. "Don't act like you haven't noticed."

"We're just friends."

"What about all the sandwiches?" Dimitri says. "It's practically like a cat leaving dead mice on the doorstep."

"That's the problem," I say. "The sandwiches *taste* like dead mice."

"That makes no difference. She's putting in the effort. She's never done that for anyone. Not Kevin. Not anyone. Audrey is hot for you. No matter how much it disgusts me, she likes you." Dimitri looks up at the high windows. The sun is just starting to peek in. "And I've got no one."

"What about Jill?" I offer.

"She blew me off. No explanation. Just a total blow-off."

"That sucks."

Dimitri shrugs.

"What about all the other girls you talk to?" I say. "Every few days you're boasting about someone else, about the phone number she's scribbled on your hand."

"It never pans out," Dimitri says. He flicks the plastic tab from his hot chocolate lid into the corner.

I feel like a full-blown therapist now, at least like the ones I've seen on television. "Why do you think that is?"

"I don't know."

I let time pass, let him think about my question some more.

His jaw muscles clench a few times. He looks down at the carpet and finally goes on. "Have you ever heard the saying about fat chicks and scooters?"

"What saying?"

"You know. How fat chicks are like scooters . . ."

I shake my head.

"Come on, you've heard it. They're fun to ride, but you don't want your friends to see you on one?"

"I don't see your point," I say.

"I'm like that in reverse. I'm the scooter. The trouble is that girls don't like riding scooters, not even if no one sees them." He's starting to sound tense, and I begin to regret pushing this conversation so far right before the tournament. "Girls want to be my friend, but none of them want to be my *girl*friend."

"That's not true—"

"Come on, Seth. It's totally true. Look at me." He stands up and slaps his bare belly. Everything from his neck to his legs jiggles. "I'm gross. You said it yourself. I have man-boobs. What girl would want to be with me?"

"You talk to girls all the time."

"And every single one gives me the same line: *Let's just be friends.* Everyone says it's about personality, but it has nothing to do with personality. It has everything to do with looks. And looks are something I've got in short supply."

He punches a locker. The sound shakes the walls.

Now that I've opened this can of worms, I feel like it's my responsibility to close it back up. The trouble is that I'm afraid anything I say will sound like something my mom would tell someone on her radio program.

Finally, I say the first thing that pops into my head that is nothing like that.

"Dude, you should see Caitlyn dance on the hood of a car."

Dimitri turns to me. "You saw Caitlyn dance on the hood of a car?"

"She danced on the hood of the Red Scare," I say.

"You've got to be kidding. Tell me everything."

I tell Dimitri every detail I can remember about the parking lot party. I tell him everything that happened afterward in Luz's apartment. I tell him how my father and Mr. Peepers both choked on Audrey's sandwich and how Veronica came to my house to see if I'd get back with her. I tell him every detail, and I don't leave out a single thing.

Slowly, the smile I'm used to seeing on Dimitri's face finds its way back there. He doesn't interrupt me, doesn't say a word. He just smiles, nods, and takes it all in. And when I'm done, he asks me only one question: "Was it all worth getting iceboxed in the plums over?"

I think on that one a while. Finally, I nod. "Absolutely."

Dimitri pulls a polo shirt from his duffel bag. It's neon green with large white polka dots. Beside it, he lays a purple-and-green plaid beret. "Oh, and you have my blessing," he says, pulling the shirt over his head.

"Your blessing to do what?"

"To date my sister. That Kevin was a total tool. I hate to say it, but you're less of a jerk than any of the guys she's gone out with." I don't know what to say to that. Part of me wants to deny liking Audrey. Part of me wants to tell him I'll date whoever I want, with or without his blessing. Another part of me wants to give him a hug. He goes on. "But if I find out you're jerking her around, I'm going to do worse than kick you in the balls."

"I don't think you could—"

"Believe me, I could," he says. "Oh, and one more thing."

"What's that?"

"Audrey can be a raging bitch, and I'm not getting involved to patch things up." Dimitri pulls his shirt over his head and stands in front of the full-length mirror at the end of the row of lockers.

"Dude," I say, "where'd you get clothes like that?"

He turns from side to side, admiring himself. Then he puts the cap on his head. He looks like someone ate a clown, digested it for a while, and then threw it back up.

"It's amazing what you can find on eBay."

"I'm going to have to object to that outfit."

"Overruled," Dimitri says. "This is perfect. Totally Jack Nicholson Joker. Wait until you see what I'm wearing on Sunday."

CHAPTER TWENTY-NINE

Kyle Sanders and his father, last year's tournament winners, sit at the head table along with several of the board members and their families. Just like at the Masters, the reigning champion gets to choose the menu. Kyle picked lasagna as the entrée, which is fine by me. It beats the borscht that Alex Grosheva chose a few years back.

After the cursory words from the sponsors and organizers, Kyle got up and told everyone how golf helped him better his life and how his scholarship helped pay for his first semester at Duke. He talked about playing on the team down there and how they're ranked in the top twenty-five nationwide. After the smattering of applause, they reviewed the day's standings. Neither Dimitri and his father nor me and mine are in the lead, but both our pairings are within striking distance. We're both in the lead pack.

The air under the heavy blue catering tent is stifling,

made nearly unbearable by the hundred or so sweaty people and twenty or thirty flaming Sternos crammed under here. My dad and I are sitting with Dimitri at one of the smaller tables. My mom had to host her radio program tonight, and Dimitri's parents both had to work late shifts. Audrey is working the banquet. She hasn't stopped scurrying around all evening.

"Interesting wardrobe selection, Dimitri," my father says.

"Thanks, Mr. B. Purple-and-green tartan is traditional wear on the island of Skye as well as in Orkney. This tartan, though"—Dimitri tips his cap to my father—"is from the Cooper clan. The Cooper clan—"

"What clan wears green shirts with white polka dots?" my father cuts in.

Dimitri looks down at his shirt. It's already streaked with lasagna stains. "I believe that's the clan of the Loch Ness monster."

My father takes a sip of his wine and turns his attention to his plate.

Audrey carries in a fresh tray of lasagna and heads to the buffet table. She lifts it up and sets it onto the silver rack over the small blue flames. She's wearing the required tuxedo shirt and bow tie, the black skirt and hose. She's even wearing a proper name tag, one with her own name on it. Is she starting to take her job seriously? Then I notice her shoes. Black sneakers with black skulls and crossbones all over them. Subtle, but very Audrey.

Audrey checks the other trays to see which ones need

replacing. Then she straightens up the beverage area. I notice she's wearing a red rubber wristband with a white stripe on it. I've never seen one like it before. I wonder what cause it supports.

She wipes her cheek on her shoulder and looks up at me. She smiles. It's an icy smile with tight lips. She looks back down at what she's doing.

I want to go help her, to see if there are any more trays that need carrying.

I want to grab her by the hand and talk to her, to take her out to our picnic table or that spot on the hill next to the fourteenth green and explain that no matter what she saw through the sliding door at my house, Veronica means nothing to me.

Audrey turns and walks back to the kitchen.

Dimitri nudges me under the table. He mouths, *She's pissed*.

When Audrey comes to clear our table, she doesn't look at me. When she leans across to take my plate, I see her wristband. Stamped in block letters along the length of the red-and-white rubber bracelet, it says: No DICKHEADS.

"Audrey," I hear myself say.

She looks at me, then turns away.

I catch up to her near the edge of the tent. Although her arms are loaded down with stacks of plates, she stops and looks up at me. Her face is flushed, tears welling in her eyes.

"Is everything all right?" I say.

"I'm fine." Audrey tries to get by, but I get in her way.

"I'm going to drop these plates, Seth. Let me past."

I step toward her, place a hand on her arm. "Did something happen between you and Kevin?"

She looks at me for a long while, a puzzled expression on her face like she's trying to do long division in her head. "You really are that stupid, aren't you?"

Audrey pushes past me and I'm left looking at Dimitri, who is leaning against a tent pole. His head shakes from side to side and he says, "I've been telling you that for years, but you never believed me."

EXCERPT FROM THE LOVE MANIFESTO ▶▶|

Intro Music: "Cupid's Chokehold" by Gym Class Heroes

Hi there. Welcome to The Love Manifesto. *I'd like to lay things right out for you today. There's lots to tell and something of a sad ending. But it's for the best. At least, I think it's for the best.*

Over the past few weeks, I've really screwed things up. Sure, I was handed a raw deal with my girlfriend dumping me and finding out my father is cheating on my mother and getting fired from my fourth job this year and all sorts of other crap, but none of those things are reason enough for me to do what I've been doing. I've been rude. I've disrespected people. I've trampled on people's feelings. And I shouldn't have done any of it.

Yesterday, my ex-girlfriend came back into my life, and although it was tempting, I decided getting back with her is not the right move. Don't get me wrong. Things might be different for you. I'm not saying you can't get back with an ex. I'm just saying that it's not right for me right now. I know there has been a lot of buzz around the "156 reasons" I posted, and I hope somehow it helps someone, but no matter how many reasons I had when I wrote it, I'm just not feeling it anymore.

To the girl I met at the pool, I don't want to say your name for fear of another knee in the balls, but you know who you are. All I can say is I'm sorry. You're right. You were nothing but nice to me, and all I did was disrespect you. I never took you seriously. I hope you can forgive what I did and how you lost your job. If it's any consolation, I went down and had a talk with the store manager. She seemed understanding. Not sure if she'll offer you your job back, but I did what I could.

I still don't know what to make of my father and his mistress. That one is going to have to simmer on the back burner. Sorry to leave everyone hanging.

Now, before I sign off for a final time . . . yeah, you heard me right . . . this is the final episode of The Love Manifesto *. . . I think I should talk a little about what I've figured out about love.*

All I can say is, what good are 156 reasons if all of them put together don't add up to both people being happy? It's easy to become addicted to someone, it's easy to get those chemicals dumping into your brain, but the hard part is getting them to dump for the right reasons.

You can break love down into smaller and smaller parts,

talk about hormones and mating rituals and biological responses. You can poke fun at all the stupid things people do for love. Little piece by little piece, it all looks ridiculous. Like golf is just hitting a white ball around a field. That is, until you allow yourself to stand back and enjoy the game for what it is.

You can't dissect love, you can't explain it, because once you do you prevent yourself from being able to experience it. You pull yourself out of the enjoyment of it, the excitement of it, the meaning, no . . . the importance of it.

And that's what it's all about, isn't it?

Love is important.

There's someone else I want to reach out to before I sign off. And all I want to say is that I'm sorry you had to see what you did when you came to my house yesterday. Just know I was confused.

I was confused then, but I'm not confused now.

But you didn't have to try to assassinate my mom's dog with a chicken salad sandwich. That was downright cruel.

I'm going to miss you, my loyal listeners, but I better quit now before I mess things up more than they already are. So on that note, make sure your day is a good one, make sure your life is a good one, and make sure everyone you love in your life knows it.

Outro Music: "I'm Yours" by Jason Mraz

CHAPTER THIRTY ▶▶▶

"Nice putt," my father says as I tap in a four-footer that, as far as I can tell, ties us for the lead. "Almost lipped it out, though."

"How about just 'nice putt' and we'll leave it at that?"

It's the first time I've snapped back at him in three days. I've been on good behavior, not a single slip of the tongue, not a single nasty comeback, but each time my father pecks at me about something, I inch closer to wrapping a club around his neck.

We hop in the cart, and he steers us toward the next tee box. Drizzle spots the windshield. It's been hot and sunny all weekend, but these summer storms can come quickly. The sky is streaked with alternating bands of muddy green and blue with gray overtones—murky blue, just like Luz described my aura.

The tournament is going better—and worse—than I

imagined. It's Sunday afternoon, and my father and I are in the final pairing. The trouble is that the other team is not Dimitri and his dad.

It's Anders and his father.

Yes, *that* Anders.

Dimitri and his father were ahead of everyone until they three-stroked out of a trap yesterday. After that, the wheels came off and they dropped to fifth place. I'm not sure how they did today—there's no scoreboard like in the tournaments on television—but when I spoke to Dimitri last night he was not optimistic. *Six strokes back is insurmountable,* he said. *At least I've got an outfit that'll wow them.*

He wouldn't say a word about his wardrobe plans, but if it's any more bizarre than Friday's Joker outfit or Saturday's one—bright yellow polo, bright red pants, and a bright blue Kangol (he called it a tribute to primary colors)—he might get tossed in a padded room for the rest of the summer.

As for me, ever since I teed off on Friday morning, something about my game has been different. Good different. My swing has had more conviction than ever and my ball seems to have a mind of its own. Some people might argue that my muscles have a memory, after all. I think it's more likely that my father is getting on my nerves. Just being near him tightens up my shoulders and straightens my back. Now that Anders is around, my game rocks even more.

But Anders and his dad have been golfing well, too.

We're approaching the eighteenth tee box and we're tied at +19. That might seem lame if you watch professional golf, but actually it's pretty amazing, considering we're all amateurs. It's the total of almost three full rounds, and the flags have been placed in some diabolical spots.

The format of the tournament is what they call "foursome," which means my father and I alternate hitting the same ball from the tee to the hole. It's supposed to be about teamwork, family unity, partnership, all that. I just can't wait until it's over. The past three days have been hell.

"The Terrys are having trouble with par fives today," my father whispers to me. I stare at his hand clutching the sleeve of my orange striped shirt until he lets go.

In another attempt at teamwork, family unity, partnership, and all that, my mother bought my dad and me matching outfits and demanded we wear them together. "Team Baumgartner" she called us. As if.

My father goes on. "Neither one of those guys is strong off the tee. They'll have to lay up to make that dogleg on the eighteenth."

"Super," I say.

"Stop rolling your eyes at me."

"I did not roll my eyes."

"Look, Seth," my father says, "we have a shot at the ten thousand here. Our names on the bronze plaque in the clubhouse. Let's not let some squabble with your girlfriend or some feud with your fashion-challenged friend get in the way."

I nod.

"See? Right there," he says. "You rolled your eyes."

"I didn't roll my eyes."

"You just did it again! Get your head in the game, Seth. We can beat these guys."

I wait in the cart as my father unsheathes his driver, tees up his ball, and launches it down the fairway with a loud *ping*! It sails straight and low with a little fade. Easily a two-hundred-seventy-yard drive, which will put our ball in perfect position to see the green on the next shot.

"Nice drive," Mr. Terry says to my father as he tees up his own ball.

My father winks at me.

I turn away. My eyes land on Anders, who is sitting in his cart, grinning at me. It's the first we've acknowledged each other all day, aside from the cursory handshake at the first tee. While my father is watching Mr. Terry and Mr. Terry is eyeing his shot, Anders raises a fist next to his face and starts jabbing the side of it toward his mouth, simultaneously poking his tongue at the inside of his opposite cheek, the universal blowjob taunt. Thunder rumbles in the distance, and Anders turns a nervous eye to the sky.

I go back to watching Mr. Terry. Thunder usually means a tournament will be delayed, but since we're on the last hole they might let us finish up. It depends how far off the storm is. We keep playing unless we hear the air horns blow.

As Dad predicted, Mr. Terry's shot is short. They will have to lay up on this hole, which means Anders will have to hit to where the fairway bends in order to see the green.

My father and I will have a major advantage.

We drive along the cart path to the Terrys' ball. Anders grabs his seven-iron and takes a few practice swings. He swats at the ball, and it pops into the air. It bounces just as the fairway starts to dip to the right and picks up an extra fifty yards of roll. I'd pay him a compliment if he wasn't such an ass cheek.

My father pulls up alongside my ball. "You're using the three-wood, right?"

"I was thinking about using my five," I say. "Play the hill to the edge of the green. Let you chip up."

My father clicks his tongue. "With your five, you're guaranteed to be short. Why don't you go for the green instead of leaving all the work for me?"

"Either way it's still two strokes, right?"

"Do whatever you want," my father says dismissively.

Now I'm faced with a decision. But it's not over which club is the better one to use. It's about what will happen if I hit well or poorly with each of the clubs in question. Here's how it shakes out: If I hit well with either club, I'll get a pat on the back and a "Nice one" from my dad. If I hit poorly with the three-wood, the club he suggested, he'll say something like "Must've caught the turf a little funny with that swing" or "You didn't keep your head down." However, if I hit poorly with the five-wood, I'll never hear the end of it. He'll be bitching for years about how I blew the tournament, how I let ten grand slip through our fingers, and how I never have the family's best interests in mind.

It pisses me off to think I'm making this decision based

on fear of my father's criticism, but that's what I do. I pull the three-wood and approach my ball.

I gaze down the last two hundred forty yards of fairway. The late-afternoon light coupled with the storm in the distance makes for some weird shadows across the green. For the first seventy-one holes, for the better part of three days, there was no one in sight. No officials. No spectators. No media. All scoring is left to the honor system. That and knowing your opponent is probably counting your strokes even closer than you are. The final hole, however, is mobbed. Every last member of the board of directors sits on a small covered grandstand around an easel that holds an oversized novelty check written out for ten thousand dollars. The families of the participants—easily more than a hundred people—stand clustered around the small kidney-shaped green. The blue-and-white striped tent from Friday night still stands on the patio next to the clubhouse. I can smell the grills from here, cooking hot dogs, hamburgers, sausage, peppers, and onions.

I've played this shot a thousand times, and it's probably a twenty percent chance I can land it on the green. I take a few practice swings as I stare down the fairway. The snack truck sits on the cart path to the right of the green. I think I can make out Audrey sitting behind the wheel. I pat the large pocket of my cargo shorts to make sure the bundle I put in there this morning is still safe.

I line up alongside my ball, waggle my club head a few times, and swing.

If I thought I was playing well all weekend, that's

nothing compared to how well I connect with this shot. Barely grazing the turf beneath it, my club face hits the ball like a hammer coming down on an anvil. I can practically see sparks. The ball sizzles through the air, climbing higher and higher as it soars. Sounds of cheering make their way up the hill as that baby continues to rise. When it starts to descend, the cheering gets louder. And when my ball takes its first bounce and practically sticks to the green as if it's glued there, the cheering turns to a roar.

I can hardly believe it myself. It's tough to tell from here, but it looks as if I'm within eight feet of the flag.

"Son of a bitch," Anders mutters.

I turn to him and poke my tongue into my cheek a few times. He stomps on the pedal and steers his cart down the hill to his ball.

My father claps me on the back. "Nice one," he says.

Both his hand on me and his compliment feel rank. Even the shot feels tainted. It might sound crazy, but I'd rather have hit a crap shot with my five-wood than sink it in the hole with the club he suggested.

We drive down the cart path until we're even with the Terrys' ball, my father whispering the whole time about how we've got the championship in the bag, how we're a stroke ahead, all that. I ignore him and scan the crowd looking for Dimitri. For Audrey. For my mom. Even for Mr. Motta. Anyone to remind me that I'm a normal high-school kid with a normal life who knows and likes—no, is known and liked by—normal people.

Mr. Terry swings. His ball hangs in the air and goes

long. Even with backspin, he left Anders a twenty-foot putt. The crowd give a feeble cheer. Golf claps all around.

"Yessssss," my father whispers, pumping his fist slightly below the level of the cart window so no one sees.

Anders tosses his arms in the air in frustration. "Oh, super," he says. "Way to go, Dad."

Mr. Terry shrugs, then smiles at my father. "You win some, you lose some, huh?"

"You ain't kidding, Bill. Bad break."

We head to the green and check out the situation. It's Anders's twenty-foot putt to my father's eight. But we picked up a stroke on the fairway. Even if both teams two-putt, my father and I will be a stroke ahead. Short of a Tiger Woods miracle, Anders won't make his shot. It turns out the Fates aren't smiling on him. The drizzle seems to have slowed down the greens, and his ball rolls short. It curls even farther away with the slope of the green. Anders's father has still got a four-footer, not a gimmee by any stretch.

My dad kneels to line up his shot. I should be standing right behind him to offer advice, but instead I scan the crowd some more. I can't help but notice the board members fumbling with the oversized check. One of them is already printing my name on the recipient line. My mother, her purse clutched in her hands, stands alone at the foot of the grandstand. She gives me a smile, and I return it. Veronica is standing on the other side of the green next to a woman I don't recognize. When I see her square face and how intently she's watching the match, I figure she must be Anders's mother. Typical. Veronica came to my house three days ago

271

to hook up with me but didn't break up with Anders yet. She's like a monkey swinging in the jungle, never letting go of one vine until she's grabbed the next. Dimitri and Audrey are nowhere in sight.

My father rises and stands over the ball. The crowd goes silent.

It starts to rain a little harder, but no one moves.

In the distance, a car door slams. I look over the heads of the spectators to the parking lot. A green Acura Integra sits diagonally in the fire lane. Luz walks to the fence. She's holding a sheet of paper and nervously shifting from side to side. When she spots me, her eyes bulge and her jaw drops. I'm not kidding. It's like a cartoon. I'm probably doing the same. I glance at my mom, who has already followed my gaze.

The crowd comes alive, which tells me my father has taken his shot. I watch our ball roll directly at the cup and then come to a stop just short. Inches short. A mere tap-in. I mark the ball and wipe it on my shirt. Even though we're a stroke ahead and sure to win, it's customary to let the winner take the last stroke of the tournament.

I step back to let Mr. Terry hit. My mother's head is shaking from side to side, her face red. Everything in me wants to run to her, but I have to wait until the tournament is over. I want to find Dimitri or Audrey. The snack cart is empty. *Where could they be?*

I glance back up at Luz. She is clutching the paper more tightly than before, almost strangling it. Her eyes dart between my father and me.

Mr. Terry's putt rolls true. His ball arcs slightly to the left and drops into the hole. People clap.

It's time for my tap-in.

I return my ball to its marked position and grab my Odyssey 2-Ball putter, the one I got from my folks for my birthday last year. I squeeze the grip and look down. Two inches from the cup. Two inches from glory. Two inches from my name engraved on a brass plaque, immortalized for all time next to my father's behind the glass of the clubhouse trophy case.

I squeeze the grip harder and look at my father. He's giving me encouraging nods, a grin ready to spring onto his face, his arms ready to pump into the air in victory. When his gaze locks on mine, I look up at Luz. She's already in her car, the engine growling to life. I will my father to look at her, too. When he does, his face pales. He takes a small step toward me but not in time to stop what I'm going to do. I spin around, line up toward the parking lot and draw back my putter like I'm going for a five-hundred-yard drive. What should be a tiny tap comes as a colossal swing. I strike the ball with all the strength I have—with all the anger and frustration that have been building up. If I thought my podcast was a good stress reliever, this feels infinitely better. My club carves a foot-long divot in the velvety green, and my ball launches like a rocket over the fence.

It's the best shot of my life and possibly the farthest anyone has ever hit with a putter. My ball takes two bounces on the concrete walkway, one bounce on the blacktop, and disappears into the brush alongside the driveway.

A collective gasp rises from the crowd, and then a whole bunch of things happen at once. A ruckus breaks out among the spectators, and a handful of board members rush down the steps of the grandstand. My father starts toward me, but my mother calls him over before he has a chance to kill me. Anders and his father start jumping around, high-fiving each other and chest bumping like they've just won the Super Bowl. Veronica runs across the green and throws her arms around Anders's neck, and Mrs. Terry hops in glee. One of the board members screams something at my father about paying for the damages and about how I made a mockery of the tournament. Another starts crossing out my name on the oversized check.

My mother's words echo in my head: "It doesn't matter if you win or lose, it's whether at the end of the day people remember who you are." Somehow, I doubt this is what she was getting at, but I'm pretty sure everyone here will remember me.

"Everything all right, Baumgartner?" It's Mr. Motta. After what I've just done, he's the only one who came to talk to me.

"Actually, it can't get much worse."

He places a hand on my shoulder. "You know you're going to get a ration of shit over this, don'tcha?"

"I suppose so."

"And you know I have to fire you, right?"

"Pretty much figured that. Who're you going to get to replace me?"

"Not many youngsters can fold a shirt like you, Seth,

274

but I think that boy will do fine." Mr. Motta points to the grandstand, where Dimitri, wearing a green sleeveless sweater and knickers, argyle socks pulled to his knees, and a matching argyle scally cap, is receiving the ten-thousand-dollar check from the board. He looks like something straight off an old-fashioned golf trophy. "What taste in clothing that boy's got. I'll start him back up tomorrow. You can be his first sale." Mr. Motta points at my putter. The shaft is bent a few inches above the club head. "I'll still honor your employee discount."

I hold it up. "Is this a red or an orange?"

"Neither," he says. "The Odyssey Two-Ball is an indigo."

"What happened?" I point to Anders and his father, who are arguing with Mr. Haversham. They are holding several scorecards between them and bickering over the numbers. "Don't the Terrys win?"

"Nope. Dimitri and his father were the bee's knees today. Came in at two under par. Amazing. You'd have been even with them for the three days cumulative if you had tapped in. Would've gone to a tiebreaker, but this stunt of yours ended things early." Mr. Motta squints at the darkening clouds. "Good thing, too," he says. "Looks like it's about to piss down."

Mr. Motta and Dimitri are going to get along just fine without me.

I poke my toe at the divot I made in the green. The edges are clean, smooth, like someone used an ice-cream scooper instead of a golf club. I look over at my parents

275

arguing. A few of the board members are speaking with them. One of them is gesturing toward me.

"You ain't kidding," I say to Mr. Motta. "It's gonna piss down awfully hard."

Audrey appears out of nowhere. "Jeez, Seth, I like bucking the system and all, but this is ridiculous. Where'd that shot come from?"

"I was thinking about the worst chicken salad sandwich in the history of mankind." I reach into my pocket and pull out the wax-paper bundle. It unfolds in my hand to reveal the sandwich I took away from Mr. Peepers. After sitting in my pocket for an entire round of golf, it looks more like a soggy mass of dirty socks.

I hold it up. "Down the hatch," I say.

Audrey steps forward. "No, Seth, don't."

But I step away and take my first big bite. The taste is excruciating, like touching your tongue to a nine-volt battery. I chew and swallow. I take another bite.

"Seth," she says. "My sandwiches—"

"Your sandwiches suck," I say. "They are the worst thing I've ever allowed near my mouth."

"Then why . . . ?"

I take another bite, and her words trail off. My shoulders hunch and I fight off the convulsions, the wretching, that want to consume me. "Because that's what you do when you care about someone."

She smiles up at me.

"You mind if I spit this out?" I manage to say.

"Feel free, but you might want to get out of Dodge

first," she says. "You're going to have to answer to some real hotheads soon."

I make my way off the green and head up the hill to the parking lot. Audrey trails behind me.

The paper Luz had been holding lies folded in thirds on the ground next to the fence. Raindrops splatter on it, soaking in. I bend down and pick it up, stuff it into my pocket.

"What is that?" Audrey asks.

I step closer. "It's not important right now." I take Audrey by the shoulders and kiss her. She recoils, probably from the taste of her chicken salad in my mouth, but she tilts her head back to meet me. It crosses my mind that the last time I kissed a girl I kicked her out of my house. The time before that, I got kicked in the nuts.

It's only a brief thought.

Audrey breaks away and looks me in the eyes. "Is this Seth kissing me or Mr. Love Manifesto?"

"You know about that, too?"

"What can I say? My brother's got a big mouth."

"It's all Seth," I answer. I kiss her again. "It's all me. So you have to tell me. What's the deal with the sandwiches?"

"It's a long story." She glances over my shoulder. My father, mother, and several board members are walking toward us. "I don't think we have time."

Good old instinct tells me to run, but something stronger tells me to stay. "I might be tied to the back of a cart and beaten to death with golf clubs in a few minutes. I have to know."

Audrey looks up at me. "My grandmother tells me that the way to a guy's heart is through his stomach. She feeds my grandfather like there won't be food for sale at the supermarket tomorrow. I think you can tell more about a guy by making him bad food. It might have taken you a while, but you told me the truth, Seth. That's hot."

"I'll eat more of it if you want."

"Hell, no." Audrey snatches what's left of the sandwich from my hand and hurls it into the woods. She grabs me around the waist, presses her body against mine, and kisses me. Hands down, it's the best kiss I've ever shared with anyone. We kiss as the rain falls down around us. We kiss until we both have to gasp for air through our noses. We kiss until my father spins me around by the shoulder and breaks us apart.

With an index finger in my face, he hollers, "You've got a hell of a lot of explaining to do, young man!"

CHAPTER THIRTY-ONE ▶▶|

"They've already decided we're disqualified," my father says. Before any of the board members could get a hand on me, he ushered me into his car. Now we're driving the streets of Albany. "One stroke away, and you had to blow it."

I gaze out the window. The clouds have blackened and are pressing down on us. The sky feels thick, heavier than before. It hasn't started raining past a drizzle, not yet at least, but the streets are wet, slick. Even with the Beemer's skid control, my father takes the turn a little too fast. I grip the door handle tight.

"They're calling a special board meeting on Tuesday to decide if there will be any additional repercussions. There's no doubt you'll have to pay for the repairs to the green, but who knows what else they'll do? Seth, what were you thinking?"

I gaze out the window. I want to will myself out of this

car. I want to be anywhere but sitting next to my father right now. I see a parked Prius and I try to will myself into the backseat. I see a McDonald's with an indoor playground and I try to will myself into the tube slide. I see a dentist's office and I try to will myself into the chair with a rusty drill poised over my mouth.

"Look, Seth, this isn't going away by ignoring it, and this isn't one of those situations where you can take a mulligan."

"I'll pay for the stupid green."

"It's not the green I'm concerned about. A golf club is a place of tradition. They don't take unsportsmanlike conduct lightly. They hold their parties and their tournaments in high regard, and you just spat in their faces. You just told them to shove their scholarship up their asses."

My father saw her, yet he's trying to turn this around, to make it about the tournament. "Who is she, Dad?"

"Who's who?"

"I know you saw her," I say.

I look at my father. He shifts his eyes back to the road. His hands go to ten o'clock and two o'clock on the steering wheel. I wonder if he is willing himself to be anywhere other than with me right now.

I toss the folded-up piece of paper Luz dropped in the golf club parking lot into his lap. It's soggy and stuck together, but he manages to unfold it with one hand as he drives. He reads it.

"Jesus." My father takes a hard left turn and fishtails into Washington Park. He barely slows at the yield sign.

"How did you find out?"

"What difference does it make?" I say. "Who is she, Dad?" It feels good to be on this side of an argument. The side that feels right. I let the silence lengthen. Every second that passes feels like a tiny victory.

Finally, my father lets out a breath I didn't realize he had been holding in. "Luz was my girlfriend before I met your mother. We dated when I was in college."

"And what?" I say. "You never stopped? You've been running around behind Mom's back with some other woman for twenty years? How could you expect—"

"Don't be ridiculous," my father says.

"I'm not. You take her out to lunch, bring her to the flower shop. Who knows what else?"

"She's the mother of my other son."

He could have fired a cannonball at my stomach and it would have stunned me less. *The mother of his other son?*

I let the words jump around in my head until they start to make sense. I think back to the evening I sat in Luz's apartment, to the photo on the wall of the young soldier—of his greenish hazel eyes. They looked nothing like Luz's wide brown eyes. They're my father's eyes. I flip down the sun visor and stare in the mirror. My eyes.

"His name is Miguel," he says. "He's in the service, and he's going to be redeployed to—"

"Afghanistan," I cut in. "I know."

"Been doing your homework, huh?"

"The early worm catches the bird."

"It looks like he's going back next week. A month

early." He tosses the paper into my lap. It's a letter from the United States Army.

My father shakes his head. "When Luz had Miguel, I was still in undergrad. I was working two jobs to support the baby on top of a full course load. It was tough. No health insurance, no scholarship, nothing. Your grandparents didn't speak to me for two years."

With the coming storm, there aren't many cars on the street. My father weaves through the winding roads of Washington Park. He hits the lights perfectly to get across State and Central.

"I wanted to marry Luz," he says. "I used to joke about how I wanted to make an honest woman out of her, but she didn't want any part of that. She enjoys her freedom. She likes making all the choices, coming and going when she pleases. She had no interest in getting hitched."

I think about that word: *hitched*. Like a horse to a fence post. Like a boat trailer to a car. Either way, it's something to stop you, something to slow you down.

"We played that game for a while," my father goes on. "Me living in the dorms. Her in her apartment. She was doing telemarketing back then, working insane hours. She ended up with carpal tunnel syndrome in her wrist. I know it sounds stupid, carpal tunnel syndrome having anything to do with this, but she was terrified of the surgery, anesthesia and all that. She went to some Reiki healer and got better in a few weeks.

"She was amazed by that, and the next thing I knew she was packed up and headed west. She went to some alternative healing school in Sedona. Arizona. She relocated, took the baby with her. Gone. Off to learn aura cleansing or something. It tore me up. I can't tell you how many times I tried to get out there, but something always got in the way: school, family, whatever. Then your mom came into the picture. . . ."

I wait for him to go on.

"The minute I met her, everything changed. I fell hard for your mother. We shared the same goals. We wanted the same things."

"When were you planning to tell me about this?" I say.

"That's the trouble. Your mother and Luz never got along. Always snipping at each other every chance they got. After a while, they just started ignoring each other's existence. Your mom was living here with me and Luz was on the other side of the country. I helped support Miguel. I paid child support. . . ."

My father tries to beat the light on Clinton Avenue, but it turns too quickly. He stomps on the brake and we jerk to a stop. "We decided not to tell you when you were young. You know, so you wouldn't be confused. We wanted you to have a traditional family."

"Dad, I'm seventeen now."

"As you got older . . . I don't know. It just became harder and harder." The light turns green and we continue on Henry Johnson Boulevard. "Maybe it just became easier and easier *not* to tell you."

It might seem like the same thing, "harder and harder to tell someone something" compared to "easier and easier not to tell someone something," but to me it makes perfect sense. I think about Veronica and how I never told her anything that was going on in my head. I think about Audrey and the kiss we just shared. I did lots of things wrong when it came to Veronica; I promise myself not to make the same mistakes with Audrey.

My father fidgets with the buttons on his armrest. "It used to be so important, you know, for people to have a traditional family. One mom, one dad, all that. It wasn't so long ago, but back then it seemed important. Maybe it's because I was younger. Luz only got back to town a few months ago. She wanted to be on the East Coast so it would be more convenient for Miguel when he came home on leave."

"And you just figured you'd pick up where you left off?"

"What are you talking about?"

"Come on," I say. "I saw the two of you at Applebee's. I wasn't born last week, Dad. She was all over you. The way you reached over. The way you touched her."

"I'm sorry you had to see that. Luz and I never got married, but I still have feelings for her. She still has feelings for me. It's hard to explain."

I want to say "give it a shot," but instead I try to let the silence work for me again.

"Your mother and I . . . with her working nights, me working days . . ." The light turns green. We continue on through the Arbor Hill neighborhood. "Sometimes it just feels good to have someone lavish attention on you for a change. You know what I mean?"

"Marriage is about loyalty," I say. "It's about love."

I want everything to be black-and-white, no gray. The trouble with gray is that there are so many shades of it that it becomes impossible to draw a line. Black-and-white is simple. I want the world to have defined colors like Roy G. Biv, but there are infinite colors between red and orange, between orange and yellow. There are colors between those colors too. And colors that come before red and after violet that we can't even see.

My father slouches deeper in his seat. He's still talking. ". . . someone who likes you not because you're the breadwinner, not because you live under the same roof, not because you owe each other anything. I don't expect you to understand any of this."

The strange thing is that I do understand. Veronica and I are in the same classes. We were study buddies. We live close to each other, and I have a car. It was a relationship that made sense. It was comfortable, convenient. But did I really love her?

My father sits back up. "Nothing is happening between Luz and me. I promise."

I stare out the window and let the buildings slide by. Each one houses one or more families with their own shades of gray, their own definitions of love, no two exactly alike. The buildings blur past.

"I swear on my life," he says.

I either have to believe the man sitting next to me or not. Mom will be able to verify everything anyway. No doubt she'll want to sit me down and explain as soon as I get home.

A few more blocks pass before he goes on. "Miguel is twenty-two. When he was nineteen, he joined the service. He wasn't supposed to be redeployed until September." He motions toward the soggy paper still lying in my lap.

I don't even know the guy and I feel bad for him. For Luz. For my dad.

My father slams the steering wheel with an open palm. "He should never have enlisted! He should have stayed in school like I told him."

"Dad," I say, "he's twenty-two."

He nods. "We're going to have to move up the going-away party."

I think about the flowers he ordered, the receipts I found in his briefcase. He changed the summer arrangement to blue and white irises with red tulips. Red tulips. White and blue irises. Red, white, and blue. Delivery date: To Be Determined. Because no one knew exactly when he'd be going back. All the details I used to convince myself my father was a complete and utter scumbag really start to make better sense now that I know his side of things.

I hadn't given any thought as to why we might be driving through this part of town, but when my dad steps down on the emergency brake—when that clicking sound grinds through the silence that has built up—it all becomes clear. We are sitting in the guest parking spot in front of Luz's building. The bank of mailboxes sits off to the side. Luz's Acura is parked to my right, FOR SALE sign in the window, moon roof open. Half of the red taillight is missing, the white lightbulb and silver reflector visible underneath.

Luz sits on her front steps, her face in her hands. Her shoulders heave. She's crying. A guy in his early twenties with short, dark hair stands over her. He looks up at us. My dad might not be cheating on my mom, but he's got a son. A son in the army—a son getting redeployed—with a life of his own and a mother who raised him without having a father around. Everything is different than I imagined, and I don't know what to make of it.

That's when I open the door and throw up. The worst chicken salad in the world is even worse going out through the in door.

"I'm not ready for this yet, Dad," I say.

"Okay." He pats my back. "Okay. Just let me go over and make sure Luz is all right."

CHAPTER THIRTY-TWO ▶▶|

The Red Scare idles in front of Luz's apartment building. Cracked concrete steps and a closed door loom above me. My hands curl around the steering wheel. They don't want to let go. The sun beats down on the car, makes it feel like an oven in here. If it gets any hotter, I'm packing up and driving north until I drop into the Arctic Ocean.

My father and I only spent a few minutes at Luz's apartment building, long enough for her to calm down and for the three of them to talk for a few minutes. I stayed in the car, looking at my muddy golf shoes on my father's clean car mats. When we got home, my mom was waiting for us. When I saw the anguish in her face, I just walked over and hugged her tight. Then we went inside and talked for hours, the three of us. Ever since, it's been like a fog has lifted from our house, like the diseased layers of an onion have been peeled back to reveal the good parts underneath.

I paid the club for the damage I did to the green and decided to steer clear of the place for a while on account of the nasty looks I was getting from the old codgers in the locker room. But it's a small price to pay for immortality. Sure, I didn't get my name on any brass plaques, but people will be talking about what I did at that tournament for decades. It may rival Man-Boob Mickelson birdying five of the last seven holes in the 2004 Masters to beat Ernie Els by one stroke.

Audrey squeezes my leg. "You sure you want to do this?" she asks.

"Miguel has to be back at the base soon," I say. "I'd rather do it this way than meet him for the first time at his going-away party tomorrow. There'll be too many people around."

Dimitri taps my headrest from the backseat. "Yeah, but wouldn't it be easier to do it like that instead of this one-on-one stuff?"

"No way," Audrey says. "Seth's got to meet him without everyone else around."

Dimitri slouches in his seat. "Then why'd he ask us to tag along in the first place?"

Audrey turns around. "Haven't you ever heard of moral support?"

"Give *this* moral support." Dimitri hooks his flip-flopped foot around Audrey's face. She smacks it away.

Two kids—the same two who were running around the pool when Dimitri and I were here—dart past my car. Both are laughing. The taller of the two takes a bottle of sunscreen from the other. He squirts the word *fart* on the concrete with the white lotion and both boys continue on, giggling even harder than before.

A whistle pierces the air that cuts through the music playing from my speakers. It's Jill. "Get back here with my sunscreen, you little bastards! If I have to tell you one more time, I'm going to beat you with a pillowcase filled with nectarines!"

Jill sees my car and slows to a trot.

"Uh-oh," I say. "Ex-girlfriend alert."

"Jill is hardly an ex-girlfriend," Dimitri says.

Jill comes up to my window. Her white crewneck covers her much better than the tank top she was wearing last time I saw her working. "Hey, what's up?" she says. "Going up to see the cougar?"

"Something like that," I say.

"Seriously?" She looks up at Luz's window. "I was just kidding."

"No," I say. "I was just headed up there now."

"Well, be sure to give me a full report." Jill pokes her head into my window and surveys the backseat. "Hey, Dimitri," she says. "You hiding from me back there?"

"Just chillin' out," he says.

Jill pokes my arm. "Might want to keep a lookout for Caitlyn," she says. "I hear her left knee is worse than her right."

"I figure if I stay in the car she can't do too much damage."

"How's the podcasting going?" she says. "I saw you

290

pulled down all the old episodes."

"It wasn't right to leave them up," I say. "Too much personal stuff. I did just apply for an internship at Haywire 98FM, though."

"Cool," she says. "Well, keep keeping it real, guys. I've got to unleash a whole load of freeze-dried ass-whoopin'. That was a brand-new bottle those kids swiped from me." She leans farther into my car and looks Dimitri over. "You still have my number?"

He holds up his left hand to reveal a black smudge. "I was keeping it wrapped in a plastic bag when I showered, but it looks like I sweated it off playing golf."

Jill snatches the felt tip from my cup holder. "Come here," she tells Dimitri.

Dimitri leans forward and she writes her phone number backward across his forehead. "Now you'll remember to call every time you look in the mirror."

"You really think Dimitri looks in the mirror?" Audrey says.

Jill laughs. "Call me," she says to Dimitri. Then she darts after the boys, following the trail of sunscreen.

"What does she see in you?" Audrey says after Jill rounds the corner of the building.

"That I rock?" Dimitri says.

And it's true. Dimitri does rock.

"What about that girl from Oregon?" I say.

"Yeah," Audrey adds. "What about Starbucks Girl?"

"Her?" I can see Dimitri's grin without looking. "I totally made her up."

"I knew it!" Audrey cries out, laughing. "You're such a freakin' liar!"

My hand finds its way to the door handle. "I guess I've sat here long enough," I say. "Time to do my thing."

Audrey grabs my leg, this time more firmly. "You sure you don't want me to come up with you?"

"I'll be fine," I say. "Once I push the doorbell, everything's out of my hands. It's just a matter of saying hi, right?"

Audrey leans across and kisses my cheek. A trickle of perspiration makes its way down her neck and over her collarbone. I want to get her alone and follow where it went, but I'm distracted by Dimitri patting me reassuringly on the shoulder.

I get out. The sun beats down on me.

It's strange. I spoke to him on the phone a few times, but meeting Miguel face-to-face still seems bizarre. After all, he's my half brother, a half brother I've never met. I didn't even know he existed until last week. He could have stepped on a land mine in Afghanistan and I would never have had a chance to meet him in the first place. I might never have found out about him at all.

This is important. Majorly important.

I cross the sidewalk and prepare to climb the apartment steps when a car pulls up next to mine. It is a silver Subaru, almost as beat-up as the Red Scare. The windows are down, and music is blasting. A skinny guy with a ratty beard and a rattier bandanna tied around his head gets out and pulls a bouquet from the backseat. Blue and white irises with red tulips. The flower arrangement my father ordered for Miguel all those weeks ago.

I walk over and tip the guy five dollars.

"I'm only supposed to give the flowers to the person living at the address." He looks down at the card. "Eleven-oh-three-D."

"It's fine," I say. "I'm going inside now."

"You sure? I could lose my job—"

"I'm positive."

The man nods and hands over the arrangement. "I'm way behind on my deliveries anyway. Thanks, man." He stuffs the tip into his pocket and drives off.

I glance up the stairs, then back to my car. Audrey is smiling at me from the front seat. Dimitri is watching from the back. They both give me a thumbs-up. The flowers tickle my nose, so I shift the basket to my side. I gaze up at the apartment and climb the stairs.

When I get to the top, I take a deep breath and press the doorbell.

ACKNOWLEDGMENTS ▶▶|

Although in large part books are written in solitude, none are produced in a vacuum. If they were, it would get awfully crowded in the dust bag.

I'd like to thank my editor, Alessandra Balzer, and all the great people at Balzer + Bray. You let me do some unorthodox things in this book and I appreciate you humoring my wacky ideas. Thanks also to my agent, Linda Pratt, for connecting me with all the right people and introducing me to the lounge at the Algonquin.

The concept of podcasting would never have been familiar to me if not for my good friend and pioneer of all things technological, Mark Furnish. And Caleb Bacon, you picked up where Mark left off.

Thank you to self-proclaimed "bitzes" Maria Cruz and Maria D'Andrea for pointing me toward the right music. And thanks to Keiki and Robin Cabanos for working on the first *Love Manifesto* theme song. You made me feel like a rock star.

Eternal gratitude to my team of incredibly excellent readers and critiquers: Laura Bowers, Loree Griffin Burns, Nancy Castaldo, Debbi Michiko Florence, Rose Kent, Liza Martz, Kate Messner, Coleen Paratore, and Leonora Scotti. All of you *are* rock stars.

Special thanks to Brian and Lisa Payne for lending me their wickedly awesome lake house for a long weekend, where I had nothing to do but stare at mounted animal heads and finish this book. And also to Eric Weinstein, the closest thing to a patron of the arts a writer could hope for.

And, of course, all my appreciation and love to my power plant, Elaine, and my two little wind turbines, Ethan and Lily. You three are the best renewable resources I can imagine.